Indivisible

By

Aurea C. Franklin

Aurea Press

WOODBRIDGE, VIRGINIA

Print ISBN: 978-1-7375086-4-9

ebook ISBN: 978-1-7375086-5-6

DEDICATION

To my children who continually inspire me:
Cliff II, Jodie, & Evan; Christopher John, Patrick Henry, their loved
ones and their friends.
To my family and friends in the Philippines, Hawaii, Canada,
India, and around the world.
To my editor Barbara D. Arnold for her brilliant mind and creativity.
To Kat for connecting me with my editor.
To Gerard for his advocacy.
To Mr. Black Hawk of Pennsylvania for his strategic insight. To
Dominic in the U.S. Navy for his insight about submarines. To Kris,
Army Airborne Vet for his insight about helicopters.
To the Veterans and the valiant men and women in uniform
who continually help preserve our cherished freedom.
To those who helped in making this book into reality.

I Salute you!

Thank you!

FOREWORD

Indivisible is a refreshing story during a time of so much division in the world. Recent events have challenged values, strained, and even destroyed long-term relationships between countries, friends, family, and lovers alike. Our differences have been exploited while our freedom and commonalities have been overlooked.

This novel of a bond based upon commonality between people especially during a state of chaos can remind us all of what is really important.

In this novel, Rowe and Antonette have lived the values, Duty, Honor, Country. They have embraced these values during their military service and a motivating force in working for the greater good.

Faith, Love, Hope. For Antonette and Rowe, these are the values that calm the storms of life. They also believe the price of Freedom is eternal vigilance.

Rowe and Antonette are long-lost soul mates who found each other but were separated by life's challenges and war. In wishing to pursue their patriotic duties, Rowe and Antonette joined the military at a young age. Their paths intersect at Fort Jackson, South Carolina, and both knew there was something special and sacred about their destined meeting. Their souls were attracted to each other like magnets; it was a much deeper bond than either had ever known.

After years of separation, they finally reunited in Richmond, Virginia. The embers of true love that had smoldered in their hearts for more than a decade still burned. The physical chemistry of their new union brings them closer together as loyal partners. But chaos threatens the Nation, and the two patriots must face their deepest fear, the risk of losing each other again, as they join together with faith and hope to fight for their country.

Rowe and Antonette's journey is a thrilling romantic adventure written for patriotic fans who enjoy fantasy and science fiction. *Indivisible* is a Silent Freedom Novel and the first in a series. This fiction novel follows the release of Aurea Franklin's acclaimed debut publication and military autobiography: Silent Freedom: A Memoir of Service with the 101st Airborne Division (Air Assault) in Iraq.

Praise for the Indivisible
by Aurea C. Franklin:

"Aurea's range of words and assortment of characters in the storyline keeps you intrigued throughout the book."

Noah Wilson (Journalist)

"If you are looking for an appealing plot embellished with realistic characters and a beautiful romantic entanglement tinged with just the right amount of mystery, this book is spot-on for you."

Olivia Miller (Strategist)

"This is Aurea's finest depiction of her work of fiction. Remarkable!"

Abraham Anderson (Social Activist)

"Hats off to the writer for coming up with such a brilliant collection of ideas."

Olivia Williams (Financial Manager)

"The way the characters grow and entangle into each other's lives is one of the author's many talents."

Hannah Smith (Teacher)

"The book will make you laugh, cry, smile and blush all at the same time."

Alex Carlson (Writer)

"A roller coaster of delicate emotions!"

Sarah Jones (Architect)

"I loved Antonette and Rowe's vulnerable moments and when they opened up and shared as well. I especially loved the struggle each had to do to get closer to each other."

Sophia Robert (Research Analyst)

"The best part is each side character is precious in this book and worthy enough to have a story of their own."

Ava Young (Student)

CONTENTS

CHAPTER 1

One Nation under God, Indivisible, with Liberty, and Justice for all. Rowe had pledged allegiance since the day he was born. His father, a well-decorated Vietnam War Veteran, was proud to announce his birth and had declared that Rowe would protect the nation where freedom lives and a government of the people, by the people, for the people. And his grandparents said, "Roman, he is just born. He cannot even hear you yet." But in his dad's eyes, Rowe was born a hero, a guardian of his nation. He would protect their freedom, and under Almighty God, he would unite the people with unwavering hope and resolve. With Liberty and Justice, indivisible Rowe would protect the country against all enemies, foreign and domestic. And God would help Rowe. His father kissed Rowe's tiny forehead and was filled with hope and enthusiasm for his newly born hero. He gently put the baby back in his loving mother's arms. Rowe's mother adored her son's thick dark hair, deep blue eyes and shared his father's dreams. His grandparents had also repeated the dream while he was growing up, until their last breath. The pledge of allegiance was generationally carved into Rowe's heart, which was draped with heroism. He was committed to fighting the enemy and protecting the people, his country, and their freedom.

It was no surprise when at 24, Rowe had opted into the special forces selection, aced the Q-course, and having been promoted to Sergeant, he then joined the Special Forces. Rowe, in the best shape of his life, with a 6'2 muscular frame, easily commanded the respect of his peers. By then, his deep blue eyes had turned to a captivating steel blue that his fellow soldiers had grown to trust. If Rowe looked them in the eyes and told them the mission would succeed, they believed him.

The eyes are the window to the soul, and this is how Antonette fell in love with Rowe. Rowe had found Antonette, the lady who shared his dreams, through the military. They had met for the first time during a training program in Fort Jackson, South Carolina. Rowe and Antonette were in the same class. Antonette was 5'7" tall and strikingly beautiful, even with no makeup. He found her dark silky hair and wide brown eyes incredibly attractive, but it was her gentle heart and soul that captivated him. Rowe and Antonette were both married, so, they did not consider any sort of relationship, yet both knew that there was something special about their connection. But as classmates, they made amazing leaders together and complemented each other so well, and it was as if they had known each other a long time. Even their voices seemed familiar to each other; when Antonette spoke, it soothed Rowe's soul like a gentle hand washing over his heart. When Antonette looked into Rowe's eyes, she could see the depth of his beautiful soul, and she silently loved him. But they were separated again and again by life's challenges, war, and the military life that brought them together had also kept them apart.

When Antonette was assigned to Fort Benning, GA, she saw Rowe for the second time; she remembered their teamwork in the training program in Fort Jackson, SC. She saw Rowe briefly at the Readiness Center, Fort Benning, GA, as he waited for his flight to Iraq with his comrades-in-arms. She had actually forgotten his name, but she would never forget his face. Antonette was still married at the time. Rowe saw her and reminded her of his name.

"Rowe, from our training in Fort Jackson, SC? Do you remember me?" And he showed her his name tape on his right breast pocket. They both laughed and had a good but brief conversation as Rowe had to leave with the others so they wouldn't miss the military aircraft leaving for Iraq. Antonette was happy to see him; although it was a brief meeting, it was sad because they parted ways again. She noticed that her heart felt lighter when he was near and understood the depth of their soul connection. Antonette was humbled that he had remembered her and kept it to her silent freedom that she secretly loved him. Rowe knew that something special was there, but he did not yet understand.

They saw each other for the third time in a chapel in Camp Slayer, Baghdad. This was the most difficult time to part ways. By then, the two had realized that their deep love for each other was sacred.

He believed that he would find her again, or she would find him. It was uncertain, but they shared the same faith and hoped that the universe was conspiring to bring them back together. And they had finally united again for the fourth time in Richmond, Virginia, after 12 years.

The Dreams

On the third night that Antonette and Rowe spent together, Antonette expressed the verities of her vivid dreams to Rowe, and he reminded her that everything would be alright. "It's just a dream," he promised.

On that night, Antonette's worst nightmare came back. In this recurring dream, the enemy fired rockets with an explosive warhead from a rocket-propelled grenade (RPG) launcher and landed a direct hit to Rowe's helicopter. She woke up crying and screaming, "No! No! No!" Her screams and wracking sobs woke Rowe from a deep sleep. She was drenched in sweat, and her heart pounded out of her chest. He cuddled and gently soothed her back to sleep, assured her that everything would be alright, and he wasn't going anywhere. Nothing terrible would happen to him, he persuaded. Antonette hugged him tightly and tried to release her fear and agitation from the night terror. She finally calmed down and relaxed.

Antonette quipped, "Maybe I need to drink more water to get up to go to the bathroom often and stop having these nightmares."

Rowe couldn't suppress himself but chuckle after Antonette had recovered. He knew she was feeling fine, as she cracked a joke about drinking more water and going to the bathroom more often. She was always cracking jokes, and he loved her positivity. Rowe gave Antonette a glass of cool water, and the intimate gesture of care touched her. She finally calmed down and nuzzled into his strong shoulder. As she closed her eyes, she said a silent prayer asking God to protect Rowe, and drifted back to sleep. He felt satisfied after listening to Antonette's light snore and raised her pillow so she could sleep better. The ceiling clock projector showed 0033 hours. Five more hours, and he would be up, getting ready for the day.

Two hours later, Antonette had another vivid dream. This time she dreamed that the Central Intelligence Agency (CIA) was briefing the President. The National Security Advisor (NSA) presented HG Hawk, the CIA director, to brief the President, his

Chief of Staff (COS), the Secretary of State, the Commanding General in the Pentagon, and his deputy.

HG Hawk was named Helene Grace by her mother but always hated the name because she thought men would consider her weak or a princess. Helene grew up a tomboy and much preferred to go by HG Hawk. Most of her peers referred to her as Hawk, a nickname she earned with her sharp mind and tough demeanor. Hawk was an impressive 5'9" tall, with pale blue eyes, pouting lips, and a lithe figure. Her shoulder-length strawberry blonde hair was always styled in a twisted bun. HG was divorced three times, and it was well known that she was not interested in trying for a fourth at this point in her life or her career.

The vivid dream started as HG Hawk, wearing her standard dark business suit and white collared shirt, briefing the President as calmly as she could muster.

"Mr. President, I urge you to make a public announcement now and tell the people to stay at home and don't attempt to go outside until the streets are safe." The room was silent. She continued, "My intel has reported an enemy infiltration, called KAKO. My sources revealed that KAKO hails from Kakogryztan, located within the borders of Iraq, Pakistan, and Afghanistan. They have misled people from those countries and are responsible for killing our troops in Iraq and Afghanistan. There have been massive terrorist efforts detected; suicide bombers, and their improvised explosive devices (IEDs)." Hawk urged, "There is an immediate threat to seize our land, strip us of our freedom, and an evil ambition to eliminate us all at once. We are at war in our very own country!" Hawk added emphatically, looking the President dead in the eyes with a glare of conviction that said she meant it. "I trust the Commanding General (CG) has heard of the incidents this morning and has activated the troops?" She asked rhetorically.

HG Hawk then launched into acknowledging the mysterious heroes that had appeared and couldn't be ignored. "I have seen two indivisible superpowers since this unimaginable crisis began.

First, a miraculous Lady Savior rescued you, Mr. President. She protected you from being killed by the KAKO that infiltrated Camp David. She delivered you and your Secret Service agents unscathed from the horrible explosion that decimated the Camp. Second, we saw another male superpower, The Guardian, who saved our troops from the killer KAKO. This ruthless terrorist group has been known to cut the throats of our armed forces and use suicide bombers and IEDs." She said with gravity, her voice filled with a wave of simmering anger. "Next are innumerable rescue operations of our people by these dual indivisible superpowers without using the help of any single troop from our armed forces. Our heroes have saved the people from these radio-controlled or mobile phone-controlled weapons, which were turned into magnetic IEDs. This is a more difficult device to control because they chase vehicles, stick underneath the cars, and kill with a high success rate."

"We are surrounded by the KAKO," Hawk continued. "How did we miss it? How could this happen under our noses?" She said, her voice starting to rise steadily. "They are on our ground, they are in our waters, they are in the air, and they have pillaged communities all over our nation as well as in Canada, Germany, and the United Kingdom. Who is financing this operation? Is it the Russians again, Iran, or the Chinese? To date, we are on a deep dive to discover who is providing them money, weapons, and a multitude of support. These dogs strip our people of their cherished freedom and democracy. Our analysts believe in having narrowed it down to Russia or China, and our teams are working feverishly to determine the source of the funding. Follow the money, find the evil. More updates to follow, Mr. President." HG Hawk finally sat down, feeling satisfied that she had conveyed the threat level appropriately.

It was the President's turn to speak.

"Thank you, Director, for your report. After the incident at Camp David, and based on all your reports this morning, the CIA is right in saying there are two indivisible superpowers." The President continued, "I have personally encountered Lady Savior, and I have seen the pictures of the enemy delivered by The Guardian and a large number of troops he has saved from the hands of the enemy. We have to keep the faith and, above all, pray that our people will continue to be safe. We must strengthen and intensely arm our troops with heavy, immediate, and necessary tools and protect our submarines and aircraft from enemy attacks. Ultimately, may our Guardian Angels be always on our side." As the President was about to close his speech, a glowing force spread across the room.

He spoke like thunder; the President and everyone else around him only remembered his simple and direct final words.

"Tell the Nation, Stay inside! Stay inside! Stay inside!"

Antonette awoke sharply at those words and sat straight up in bed. Rowe found her breathing rapidly, flushed, and sweaty, staring blankly at the wall.

"Antonette, Antonette, are you awake? Wake up!" Rowe shook her and looked at the clock, which now showed 0333 hours.

"You were thrashing around like a ninja in your sleep, crying and mumbling something I couldn't understand," Rowe said. Antonette was sweaty, trembling, and asked for water. Rowe lovingly obliged and returned with a new glass of cool water from the fridge.

Rowe said, "Are you okay, Mi Amor? Based on what I researched a long time ago, crying in your dreams is considered auspicious or represents pent-up emotions. Rowe wiped Antonette's forehead and gave her his dry shirt to wear. Even her pillows were wet with her tears.

Antonette finally realized what happened and said, "What a nightmare. We were in a total state of chaos, a dark dystopian land. Was I really thrashing like a ninja?" She added with a little smile.

"Yes, you kicked me in the shin twice," Rowe said and kissed her on the forehead. "Go to sleep, my little ninja."

Antonette laughed and tried to go back to sleep at least for another two hours but found it very challenging. Her eyes were widely open despite feeling safe in Rowe's loving arms. She remembered the first time she came to Richmond, and her thoughts drifted back to that time in her life.

It had rained for three days, but nothing would stop Antonette from looking for an apartment near her new worksite. She felt so excited moving to a new place and couldn't wait until she started her new job as the Director of a Contracting Division of the Government. The acceptance letter she had received from her new employer said that it would be temporarily virtual due to COVID-19 (Coronavirus Disease). Her swirling thoughts then turned to the pandemic.

The pandemic had affected everyone all over the world, and she thanked God for the continuous inventions of science towards a cure or prevention. Innovations in the research revealed new ways to thwart the killer virus. Most workers have been teleworking since March 2020 based on guidance from the government. The COVID-19 had taken a toll on so many lives. There were over half a million who passed away due to the virus, including Antonette's fellow employee and her friend Danny.

Antonette had worked with Danny; they were partners on the night shift. Her friend, who was energetic for 75 years of age, worked in the Pentagon and was her "go-to" guy. He was incredibly sharp, and whenever she had questions related to work, he was always available to help her. She took it especially hard when she found out that he passed away due to COVID-19. One day she had called another co-employee to discuss a work issue. When she asked how her friend was doing, Antonette was shocked to learn that he had passed away due to COVID four months prior. She didn't believe it at first and thought it had to be a bad joke, as they all teased each other to break the ice. But her co-worker kept saying that they heard about his demise a month after it happened and were also shocked and saddened to learn about the bad news. They never saw him sick at work, and he was very healthy all throughout the season despite his age. Antonette thought maybe if the COVID-19 vaccinations or other cures had been recognized or come a little earlier, he might still be here. She couldn't believe he was gone and searched for someone or something to blame. Antonette had hung up the phone that afternoon and stared at the sky for answers. She had a strong faith in God, yet, searching for an answer to the unanswerable question, "why?" She knew that death was inevitable, and it could visit at any time. There were no words that could express the depth of shock and grief at the loss of her good friend. Even though Antonette was intellectually aware that Danny was not invincible, it did not make it any easier when she found out that he had passed away due to the surging virus. She tried very hard to accept it and focused on the great things she had learned from her friend. When she finally got a grip on her emotions, she researched the obituary. It disturbed her that she didn't find anything about him; she needed the closure of reading about his life to helping with the acceptance that he was gone. Antonette knew exactly what needed to be done. She offered God her prayers and asked Him to open his doors for her friend because he was a believer and did good during his life on earth. In God's hands, she humbly entrusted her friend's soul and asked that he be delivered now from every evil and bid her friend eternal rest.

One night, her friend appeared in her dreams as if telling her that he was happy where he is now. That seemed to comfort her to know that his soul had accepted his fate and was elevated into a better place. That night, as she did every night, Antonette prayed the Holy Rosary. She believed that Rosary was a holy intermediary between the living and the dead. She prayed for all souls, especially the friend she had just lost and believed that the departed souls prayed for the living too.

At the time of Antonette's relocation to Richmond, some restrictions had been lifted, and gradually small and large businesses were finally back to in-person business. Initially, taking temperatures were required before using a facility such as a barbershop, and reservations were implemented to enforce social distancing. The Catholic church she attended was not exempt from the restrictions. They opened up the places of worship to the public with new and revised schedules to sanitize in between masses and practiced social distancing. As fully vaccinated people increased, more facilities opened up, and the restrictions eased. The restaurants had opened their doors for diners; people who had been fully vaccinated did not have to wear masks in public and could mingle with their family and others. The beach opened to the public, airports were opened, beauty salons began to receive customers, and a slow return to some form of normalcy began to emerge. Most people were allowed to telework for precautions and had been gradually returning to their worksites, adjusting to the new normal life. Just as everyone thought that our country had turned the corner, the Center for Disease Control (CDC) shared a pivotal discovery on COVID-19. The Delta variant was causing breakthrough infections in fully vaccinated individuals and was spreading more quickly among those unvaccinated. This led back to more restrictions and a heated battle for the new Administration about mandating the vaccine at workplaces. The country was in a state of division over opposing views on masks, vaccines, and possible cures. It was a dark time for the country, and Antonette knew that prayer was always part of the light that would shine in the dark.

Swirling thoughts about moving to Richmond, her friend Danny, her dreams, and the ongoing pandemic kept Antonette awake for another hour before she finally drifted back to sleep.

CHAPTER 2

"Your soul greeted mine like a long lost friend, and we loved as though we'd never known anything else."

(Green, Alicia N.)

Before Antonette moved to Virginia; her research showed that Richmond, Virginia had many things to offer. First, it was the State Capital. Secondly, it was one of the historical and original 13 colonies of the United States. It was bordered by Maryland to the northeast, the Atlantic Ocean to the southeast, North Carolina and Tennessee to the south, Kentucky to the west, and West Virginia to the northwest. Third, it was the state for lovers. Antonette wondered how "Virginia is a state for lovers" came about. One of her friends told her that the 1968 design of the slogan was a response to the 1967 court ruling in Loving v. Virginia. It legalized interracial marriage in the United States after an interracial couple was issued jail sentences for marrying in violation of Virginia law. The logo "Virginia is for Lovers" was created more than 50 years ago and has become one of the most beloved and iconic slogans in the world. People have different reactions to the logo, and while it has meant a lot of different things to them, one thing remains the same: LOVE. Love unites us all. It is the core of the human soul and transcends time and place.

Antonette accepted the new job in Virginia primarily because she hoped it might reconnect her with Rowe. She had heard from another friend that he worked in Richmond. Their souls had called out to each other, and she knew that she must follow the silent pulling of her heart towards his.

Antonette had jumped into her new position as Director of a Contracting Division with both feet. For the first six months, she had buried herself in work with vague thoughts of seeing Rowe still glimmering in the recesses of her mind. During the seldom quiet moments, her heart ached to see him, but she knew that divine timing couldn't be rushed and trusted her silent faith. She was distracting herself by staying busy but had finally decided to award herself a break by requesting a Friday off to enjoy a long weekend to rest and decompress after six months of hard work.

That Thursday afternoon, Antonnette was browsing through the PX on Fort Lee. She had finally decided to get in line and pay for her purchases. She thought she saw a familiar face off to her right. The same face she had seen at the chapel in VBC, Baghdad. She couldn't believe it; her heart raced. There he was! Standing with arms crossed and talking to someone in front of the customer service desk in the PX. Could it be him, or was it just someone else who looked like him? There was no mistaking his chiseled jaw, but she wanted to make sure her eyes were not deceiving her. There was only one way to make sure this was not a dream. Despite being skittishly nervous that he might just be Rowe's dead ringer, she approached closer and without hesitation, said,

"Excuse me, sir, Rowe?"

He stopped talking, paused at hearing her voice, and said, "Yes, are you talking to me?" Rowe was about to resume talking to the other individual, but he couldn't help to look at the attractive lady that just disrupted his conversation. And then he couldn't believe his eyes when he figured it was a familiar beauty and voice. "Wait, Ma'am… Antonette, is that you?"

Antonette, almost in tears, said, "Yes, yes, it is me, Rowe. It's been a long time, oh God! I've missed you so much."

She knew it sounded like the movies and waited for his reaction. When he recovered from the surprise, Rowe finally hugged her so tightly then actually picked her up off of her feet. Their hearts were beating wildly together; Rowe took a deep breath and let it out slowly. When he finally put her down, he gently swept the hair from the side of her face. She remembered that same hug before he had flown out of Baghdad and tore her heart apart. She had never felt such emotional pain, and her soul ached at the loss of him. She hurt to her bones, an ineffable sense of loss in the weeks after his departure. Now they had finally found each other again, and the fear of losing him crept slowly across her consciousness. She was crying, but they were both laughing at the same time. Would this be the last time? Rowe seemed to have read her mind and said that he would never lose her again. It sounded like a fairy tale, but she saw in his steel-blue gaze that he was telling the truth, and she believed him.

They hugged again, and Rowe said it first, "I love you!" he whispered in her ear.

He kissed her cheek softly, and she leaned in and kissed his neck, gently repeating the vow.

"I love you..." she whispered back.

Every cell in their bodies lit up with the energy of their souls reuniting and reconnecting; they would not lose each other again.

Finally, Rowe realized that Dexter was waiting for him. Rowe introduced her to Dexter, the man he was talking to before Antonette interrupted their conversation.

"Dexter, this is Antonette, a long-lost friend for 12 years." He almost said, 'a long-lost love', and looked at Antonette, who offered to shake Dexter's hand. She sensed immediately that Dexter was a close friend of Rowe. Dexter already knew at first glance that Rowe and Antonette were deeply in love, and there was much more than friendship to their connection. Everyone else in the PX watched Rowe and Antonette's excitement, embraces, tears, and joy of finally getting reunited. They overheard the conversation, and one woman emphatically said, "It must have been a painful separation after the war. Twelve years was a long, long, long time." Everyone applauded and cheered for Antonette and Rowe, who had given up on being reserved in public and kissed each other passionately. It was like the best tearjerker romantic movie they had ever watched. Most of the people in the PX had experienced war and deeply understood the feeling of loss and grief at being separated from friends, lovers, and family. To bear witness to the reunion and be in the presence of true love—something changed in their hearts that day.

Rowe was simply intoxicated to see Antonette again, as it took a mixture of nostalgia and fantasy combined to recreate their long-lost romance. He felt an intense urge to kiss her again and again but realized they were inside the PX, and Dexter was watching. He ignored the stares and passionately kissed her one more time. Antonette circled her arms around his neck, crying, and laughing simultaneously. They finally finished their welcoming embraces, and Antonette laid out her purchases and pay.

"It's been paid for," the cashier said. Antonette was left to guess which kind stranger had paid for her purchases. Rowe said, "C'mon, I want to show you something." They thanked the cheering crowd, who was fixated on their delightful drama, and exited the PX.

One of the women in the waiting line said, "Oh, what a story! It's great to know they found each other again after the war. It's a rare opportunity to witness romances such as this. I can't wait to read their story and find their pictures in the magazines as newlyweds… happily ever after."

Rowe, delirious with excitement, came back inside the PX without Antonette and yelled,

"If you all want to get invited to the wedding, you may give your name, phone number, and address to Dexter, the PX General Manager, and I will make sure you all receive an invitation!"

The lady gasped and said, "What a gentleman. Let me be the first to give my information to Dexter!"

Everyone in line for the cashier was excited, signed up, and was eager to receive an invitation. It was about 200 customers and 50 staff members after Dexter had finally finished the Visitor's Log for Rowe and Antonette's wedding.

Dexter was smiling and asked himself silently, "Did he even propose yet?" and chuckled.

Dexter and Rowe were both Special Forces warriors back in time and were assigned to 5th Special Forces Group Airborne (A), 101st Airborne Division Air Assault in Fort Campbell, Kentucky. They were green berets, and they shared multiple special operations such as the Persian Gulf war, Southwest Asia, Somalia, Horn of Africa, Iraq, Afghanistan, and many other repetitive missions in the middle east. They were like true brothers who protected each other from any harm.

Rowe felt that there would be a lot going on for him and Antonette in the next few days as they attempted to renew their feelings for the fourth time. "The fourth time, 12 years," he thought as he drove the winding country road to his place. It had started to storm, and she followed him carefully on the rain-slicked roads. Antonette parked her White Mercedes-Benz SUV GLC 300 4matic in the garage next to Rowe's black Jeep Wrangler. The sun was fading, but she could see that he had a huge garage with three other vehicles and a beautiful mansion. Once parked, she noticed that he also had a black Chevy Suburban with tinted windows, a fancy electric sports car she didn't recognize, and a Cadillac CT5. The black Chevy Suburban looked familiar and looked like the vehicles used in an official government motorcade, high-security convoys organized and manned by the U.S. Secret Service. She thought that it must have been a company car. However, the license plate showed 'Rowe.'

Antonette wondered why he needed such a large house but was in awe at its grandeur, nonetheless. Rowe grabbed her left hand, led her into the kitchen, and rendered her weak in the knees with another passionate kiss just as a bolt of lightning lit up the sky outside. Both their hearts were racing again, and this time, they were free to do whatever it took to stay together. Their long-lost love was still there, and the embers had never gone out after all those years apart. Both of them knew it was real love, and once that pink rose of their hearts had blossomed, it would never disappear. At that instance, both felt deeply in their hearts that they would be staying together. After finding each other for the fourth time in this lifetime, there would be no more separation to endure. They were happy to meet again in a peaceful land and not in a war zone this time. A sharp crack of thunder reminded them both of explosions they had witnessed.

At least nobody was shooting at them or launching an RPG. No grenade explosions disintegrating people and things apart. It was just the two of them this time, and they could do whatever they wanted without the fear of detecting an enemy lurking in the corners nor driving over a magnetic killer IED outside the wire.

Rowe apologized and remembered that he had promised to cook Antonette a fabulous dinner back at the PX. He had asked if she had eaten, and she said no, not yet. She was starving, but they were both still dazed and lost in the excitement of being together.

He had kicked off his black Tom Ford brogues right before they entered the kitchen, and Antonette followed suit, delicately sliding out of her brown leather Tod's driving shoes. Rowe glanced at her red toenail polish and recalled how he had always secretly adored her little feet. He wanted to give her the best dinner and celebrate their long-lost love. There was plenty of time to cook, unlike when they were in VBC, where they had depended on the mess hall. This time, he was free to prove his culinary skills to his long-lost love from war.

"Are you in a hurry?" He asked as he pulled a copper pan down from an oval pot rack directly above the antique brown granite island.

"No, I have no plans this evening or tomorrow," she hinted, taking in the chef-inspired kitchen.

Bravely he suggested with a glint in his eye, "It's raining cats and dogs. Do you want to stay over?"

She smiled knowingly, and her heart raced as she said, "Yes" again and again. Antonette marveled at her good luck to have taken Friday off and silently thanked divine timing. Luckily, Antonette also had her gym bag in the car with some clothes and a few makeup items.

They stared at each other; he set the copper pan down, they entwined and passionately kissed, again. It had been such a long time, almost 12 years since they'd seen each other in Baghdad airport. Then she reminded him about the promised dinner; Antonette had started to feel lightheaded. He was still enamored by her kisses, but slowly disengaged himself, removed his tie, rolled up his sleeves, and started cooking. He was wearing a dark navy suit and tie, and Antonette found this wildly attractive and said he looked very executive. He took some steaks from the fridge and asked if she would like to chop the onion.

She said, "Sure, the onions will prove that I really missed you to tears."

He cracked a good laugh and said that he missed her quirky sense of humor since they had last seen each other in Baghdad. Rowe really wanted to form a lasting relationship, and as they cooked, he started talking about his children and their families. Antonette begged him to continue. She was eager to learn what she had missed over the last 12 years. Rowe pulled two bottles of imported beer from the fridge and began to share the details of his family.

He had three grown children: Zenaida, "Zed," who was 33 years old, and the principal of an elementary school. She was married to John, a banker. Rowe did not yet want to disclose that John played a major role in his multi-billion-dollar industry. Not yet anyway; he would reveal that tidbit when the time was right. Zed and John were both the same age and had three children, namely, John Jr., who goes by JR, 10 years old; Mark, 7, and Isabella, 4 years old.

Rowe said, "They want to have a dozen kids!"

Antonette exclaimed, "How exciting!" and wondered how they could afford to raise 12 children. Rowe's second child was Emy, a 31-year-old real estate attorney. She chose to be married to a fellow attorney, Armando, who was 33 years old. They were partners in a real estate business running a title company and had two boys, Jeff and Elon. They also owned a catering business which was very successful and popular. Rowe continued his story as they sipped the cold beer and cooked up a stir fry with steak, peppers, onions, and rice. He said that his youngest child's name was William, 29 years old, and he was married to Rosgil, 28. William was a bank manager, and Rosgil was a chemical engineer. They met in Thailand when William was on a summer vacation. They had been married for five years and were expecting their first child.

Rowe continued, "The children's mother passed away five years ago from breast cancer."

Antonette already knew this. When she had learned from a friend that Rowe was single again, she had a mixture of feelings. She felt a pang of sadness at the thought of him losing his wife, the mother of his children, juxtaposed against a stirring hope that they might spend time together in the future. She did not want him to suffer for the sake of their union. Yet she knew deep in her heart that they were always meant to be together.

Rowe had not been dating since then, and his children had kept him occupied. His children and grandchildren often slept over on the weekends, which filled his heart. Rowe had sold his old house and bought a newly constructed home on 25 acres of land with the help of his real estate daughter, Emy, and her husband. His house had seven bedrooms and 10 bathrooms. Rowe skipped explaining why he had such a large acre of land and continued to tell himself silently, 'Not yet, the right time will come.' Rowe told Antonette that his children had urged him, ganged up on him in fact, to buy the house, so they could all come over. Antonette thought it was funny that they had made him do it, and they both laughed at the persuasive abilities of children. She could tell how successful Rowe had become since they were in the same classroom for training in Fort Jackson, South Carolina.

"You have done very well for yourself!" she said with pride. Rowe just smiled and said it was all hard work and saving every penny.

Antonette said, "You could give up working the government contract and just continue to build your industry."

Rowe acknowledged that was true but replied, "Never, I love my work!" She was surprised to hear that Rowe had saved every penny and did not expect that he was frugal. He was just the opposite when she first met him in Fort Jackson. Rowe had never shown frugality during their training, and he had even bought lunch for everyone at one time. She vividly remembered when he took everyone to Pizza Hut one weekend and offered to pay for everyone in the group. Antonette did not know that Rowe had set aside his millions in the bank and inherited large investment assets from his parents, which was passed on by their grandparents.

"This is a big house, but you don't look like a millionaire," Antonette said. Rowe humbly kept to himself that he had amassed great wealth from investing in an innovative technology, which had received a wide acceptance from both the federal government agencies and the commercial contracting industry. Rowe laughed hard at Antonette's description of not looking like a millionaire (because he was actually a multi-billionaire).

He offered her another bottle of beer as they finished dinner, telling her that she might as well have more since she was not going anywhere tonight. They gazed at each other again, a deep longing gaze that had traveled through centuries, as if they had known each other in previous lifetimes. Antonette said she felt secure staying as Rowe demonstrated his authentic hospitality with a fabulous dinner. They laughed and bear-hugged like best friends and kissed again.

Rowe lifted her up and carried her to his massive master bedroom. He undressed her in haste and couldn't believe he was finally holding her in his arms without violating any military order. They slowly ran their hands over each other's bodies, discovering the scars. Antonette had a scar on her right arm from her first deployment to Iraq. It happened from an explosion when their Ammunition Point center was on fire by the Life Support Area. Rowe had a scar on his left arm from when he was deployed to Somalia. They were like mirrors of each other. Finally, together again, they are free to make love now. They were not in Baghdad. They were not at war, and there were no more forbidden intimacies. This was their first intimacy outside the wire, after only having shared a passionate kiss the last time Rowe had disappeared. Their sensual whispers, smoldering gazes, and intimate touches couldn't have been any more seductive. Rowe's touch was like electricity on Antonette's skin, and his sensuous arousing words flowed like water over her parched soul. They were both mad with desire as Rowe's lips trailed across Antonette's neck, sending tingles down her spine. Their inhibitions and reservations disappeared like a fog lifting. Rowe and Antonette were finally free and madly in love with each other all night, not caring anything about the world. Tangled in the covers and completely spent, Rowe and Antonette slept more deeply than either one of them had in years.

CHAPTER 3

The next day, Zed, Rowe's oldest daughter, and John came by to drop off their three children. It had become a tradition that grandchildren stayed in their grandpa's house on the weekends. Zed rang the doorbell, and Rowe opened the door.

"Grandpa!" yelled his grandchildren in unison.

"Come in," said Rowe, "I would like you to meet someone!"

Zed and John looked at their dad wide-eyed and asked together, "Who?"

Rowe had never introduced them to another woman after his wife had passed away; they were curious. Rowe led them into the kitchen, where Antonette was sitting. She stood up and greeted them. Rowe introduced Zed, John, and their kids to Antonette.

"Hello," Antonette said shyly.

Zed answered, "Oh, hello. How are you? I am so sorry; I didn't know that my dad had a guest and didn't mean to interrupt anything. We could come another day."

John simply said "hello" and shook hands with Antonette.

Rowe said, "It's okay, no harm done. There will be no skipping of weekends with the grandkids!" And with that, they all laughed.

Instantly, Zed felt close to Antonette, and Antonette felt the same. Zed did not feel betrayed. She understood and welcomed her father's renewed interest to have a relationship and felt that it was about time. It had been five years since their mother had passed away due to cancer, and her dad had almost given up on life at one point. He felt beaten up by the trauma, and the emotional defeat was inescapable at times. Besides, her dad and

Antonette seemed to have wholesome love, a love that Zed guessed had been rekindled from long ago. She suspected that they must have known each other for a while by their easy banter. If her suspicion was right, she welcomed Antonette wholeheartedly.

Rowe had filed a leave of absence for months after his wife had passed away. It was hard on all of them, but Zed knew deep in her heart that her mom would have wanted her dad to move on eventually. There was so much in life to enjoy, but it's often easier said than done, especially when the children had lost their dear mother, which challenged all of their mental strength and emotional stability as a family unit.

There were other things Rowe could have done to combat the urge to go down the dark road of negativity. But he lost hope and chose to binge drinking alcohol to block his pain until he got sick. The doctor had prescribed him not to drink, or it would cost his life. Rowe was starting to elicit signs of kidney disease and became very ill for a long time. He almost lost his life to the darkness of alcoholism, which he welcomed. He wanted to die. Rowe finally listened to his children and his doctor's advice and went through a quick recovery. Because he was so physically fit before the drinking, his body regained health when he agreed not to drink for six months straight. He prayed and asked for God's help. Rowe did not want to see a single bottle of alcohol or beer once the haze of heavy drinking had subsided, and he realized that he had so much to live for in his children and grandchildren. Rowe loved them with all his heart, and it saddened him to think that he had wished a slow death on himself while feeling depressed. He now had five grandkids, three from his oldest daughter and two from his second daughter. His youngest son's wife was expecting their first child, and Rowe was looking forward to a more expanded family. Eventually, Rowe had allowed himself to drink on special occasions, but only in moderation.

Zed thought Antonette seemed to be a nice lady, and she hoped it would truly work out for them. She seemed to really like

Antonette for her father and hoped that it would renew his faith in love. When a soul loses hope and faith through disappointment, it should always draw closer to God instead of pulling away. Zed silently prayed for her father to receive faith through the eyes of unconditional true love that she saw when Antonette looked at him.

To clear her suspicion, Zed asked how they had met each other, and Rowe had the answer in the palm of his hand. For the next hour, he told them a tale of a long-lost friend, separated by life's challenges and war. He had last seen Antonette about 12 years ago in a war-torn country called Iraq, where love can be torn apart by grenades and surface-to-surface missiles and where intimacy was forbidden. Rowe paused and finished his coffee and the last bite of his cinnamon raisin toast. He told them the story of when and how they had first met in Army training and sang cadences during their physical training exercise in formation and in their platoon runs. Zed and John were fascinated by the story and wanted to hear some more. Rowe continued that they had formed a group training, and Antonette was his right arm. They demonstrated their leadership together and helped motivate soldiers to excel in mandatory written as well as physical training tests. It turned out to be the best group in class!

This made Antonette smile, reminiscing on their teamwork and looking to the future as if trying to visualize the two of them as a team, helping people. She was already feeling a camaraderie in the family.

Rowe's story was interrupted by Emy, the second child, her husband Armand, their two boys Jeff and Elon, and their Labrador named Denver and a Chihuahua named Chichi. Rowe excused himself to get everyone situated and promised that he would continue their 'super-sweet love story' of how they had survived multiple separations caused by challenges in life and brutal war. It was like a family reunion. They were all there, except Rowe's youngest child, William, and his wife, Rosgil.

Like the oldest daughter, Emy also felt close to Antonette once she was introduced and learned how they had met a long time ago.

She said, "Wow. Thank you for showing up in Dad's life just now. We really need you." There was no hesitation or embarrassment in what she said, and she did not apologize for it.

Rowe knew that his kids were being honest, and he did not mind them sharing it with Antonette. She empathized with Rowe and his children and was almost in tears. She didn't have any idea what Rowe had been through. Antonette caught herself and silently thought that Rowe did not have any idea of what she had been through either in war or after her divorce. She herself had almost surrendered by going down to the universe of negativity, to the extent of contemplating hurting herself and ending everything in her world. It was a rough road for her, surviving on her own. She wanted to escape her life, but instead, she held onto her faith. Divine timing, God's plan for her life was beautiful and worth the wait. Antonette knew this, but in the grips of despair, it was hard to keep holding on to hope. There were days that her soul hurt, and she would say, "It's too hard."

"Walk by faith, and not by sight" had been her mantra as she survived the rigors of life and war. She held onto her most cherished silent freedom, which eased the symptoms of post-traumatic stress disorder (PTSD). She rose from the ashes of depression, reversed her negativity to positivity, and found a rewarding choice. Her positive thinking and optimism were the key to her good health and survival from love, loss, and even from the atrocities of war. She was also able to help her own children in many productive ways by keeping a positive outlook.

Rowe and Antonette's lives had mirrored each other's at times. Antonette liked to think that her own strength, the light that was in her heart and soul, had somehow helped Rowe energetically when he had faced the darkest of times. She had risen from the ashes like the phoenix, and so had Rowe while they were separated from each other. They had often prayed for one another without the other knowing and without knowing each other's suffering.

There was nothing like the bond between a grandparent and his grandchildren, as exemplified by JR, who suddenly showed up by the kitchen door holding a basketball and challenged his grandpa, his brothers, and cousins.

"C'mon, grandpa, I am the man! Let's play ball!" And he ran out the garage door to the basketball court, followed by the dogs who were dancing around and barking with excitement. Rowe was not about to be embarrassed on his first date with Antonette at his home.

"Here we go. Watch out, kiddo! I hope you practiced more bank shots," Rowe said as he chased JR out the door. Rowe picked Antonette as his teammate, but JR laid down his own rule and protested that no two big people could be on the same team.

"I choose Antonette to join me on my team," JR demanded. Antonette executed a curtsey to mock Rowe, and everyone laughed. Elon said he was going to team up with Rowe, and they named their team "Shaq Diesel."

Jeff restrained his dogs and kept them busy with a tennis ball and out of the basketball court. Mark joined JR's team, and the game was on!

"That's a difficult team name to remember, but whatever!" JR said, trying to instigate already. "Our team will be called, 'The A team' easier to remember."

"OK. Let's play ball," said Rowe.

JR dribbled the ball and passed it to Antonette, who dribbled it and gave it back to JR. JR made a fluid, explosive upward leap and, at the apex of the jump, followed through by shooting the ball but missed. He almost cried. Rowe got the ball, passed it to Elon, and Elon passed it back to Rowe. Without strenuous effort, Rowe dribbled the ball, passed it between his legs as if in the middle of a show, dribbled twice, jumped, and made a long bank shot. The ball hit the backboard with a thud before heading into the net. Rowe winked at Antonette.

"Not fair!" she mouthed to him with silent lip movements and squinted her eyes at him in mock anger. She wasn't going to let

Rowe have all the fun, "Wait until he sees my skills," she thought with a giggle.

Rowe let JR pick up the ball, and he passed it to Antonette. This time, Antonette dribbled the ball, ran, and jumped in the air, controlled the ball above the horizontal plane of the rim, and scored by putting the ball directly through the basket with two hands touching the rim.

JR screamed with delight, "Alright! Yeah! Wow! Way to go, Antonette! The Score is even! Nanna was tougher than you thought." And he smirked in triumph at Rowe, who was surprised that the kids were calling her Nanna already.

Rowe, his two daughters, and sons-in-law were awed by Antonette's skill. Docile as she appeared to be, they never thought she could play basketball. Not just about playing basketball, but it seemed she could dominate a game if she wanted to. Rowe was not intimidated by his newfound competition. He grabbed the ball, dribbled it, and executed a successful hook shot. Everyone applauded, including Isabella, Rowe's number one fan in basketball. She jumped around and cheered for her idol grandpa and his team. JR grabbed the ball and dribbled away from the court, passed it to Antonette, who passed it back to him, passed it to Mark, who passed it to Antonette, and Antonette executed a long shot without any hesitation. It seemed to be effortless, and Rowe gazed with awe.

Everyone was amazed again and kept saying, "Wow! That's amazing! How did she do that?"

Finally, Rowe said that they would continue the game tomorrow. The kids groaned, "But Grand…" Antonette was quick to console Rowe's grandchildren and quipped, "Are you camping out tonight?" The grandkids stopped groaning and answered almost in unison, "What? Yes, we want to!" Antonette said, "And so you will!" Everyone applauded, and Rowe wondered how Antonette was going to pull off a camp out that night. Antonette just looked at him and said, "I got this." Rowe looked back at her as if to say, "I missed you," repeating what he had said last night and again early this morning.

Then he added quizzically, "Oh, by the way, where did you learn to play basketball?"

Antonette replied so that everyone could hear. "I have four brothers and three sisters, and I am the youngest. When I was about Isabella's age, my brothers and sisters played basketball in front of our house; they handed me the ball and brought me up to the basket so I could slam dunk. I had good practice growing up playing with my siblings. In fact, my brothers and sisters went to college under a scholarship. Two of my brothers had a basketball scholarship, and my other two brothers played football to go to college. And when they allowed women to play basketball, my older sister and I applied, and we were both accepted! She changed her mind later and got married before graduating college, but I stayed and enjoyed it thoroughly. My two other sisters preferred to join the band, and both became majorettes. Their performance as baton twirlers was often accompanied by dance, movement, or gymnastics. They loved it and were primarily associated with marching bands during parades. Mind you; they can also spin knives, fire knives, flags, light-up batons, fire batons, maces, and rifles!! They were great at what they did and were always invited to fiestas!"

Zed, John, and Rowe were highly impressed while Antonette talked about her family and how she had played basketball in college. She inspired the grandkids with her speed when she fluidly dunked the ball during the game, and they admired her energy.

Antonette broke their silence and reminded the grandkids to get ready while the sun was still up and that they were going to shop for camping gear. She asked if Rowe wanted to change his clothes to be more comfortable. Rowe vaguely understood Antonette's plan for the night, but he followed her suggestion and changed into a sports shirt and tricot track pants. Rowe and Antonette served the crew a light late lunch of soup and sandwiches. Rowe's daughters and their husbands left after eating lunch and told their kids to behave well.

They also told Antonette that they had really enjoyed the brief basketball entertainment and her story about the college scholarship. It inspired them as they were hoping to send JR to college on scholarship. He adored playing basketball with his grandpa and at school. Although they could well afford it, sending JR to college on a scholarship would help build his character, mold his personality, and he would become more disciplined. On scholarship, he would be held to higher standards and would be expected to lead by example. Before getting in their cars, they told their kids they would come by and pick them up later in the week and reminded them one last time to be good for Grandpa.

"We will! Bye!" the kids all said in unison, including Isabella.

Rowe picked up Isabella with the four little boys in tow. They all fit into Rowe's large black Chevy Suburban and proceeded to the PX on Fort Lee. Antonette drove separately and stopped by her apartment on the way to the PX to collect some more clothes and a few food items. They met at the PX, and Antonette led the way and made sure the grandkids picked great outdoor tents and also helped them find their favorite colors. Dexter saw them coming and offered to pitch in, looking for camping gear. Antonette was grateful, and out of the corner of her eye, she saw Rowe and Dexter do the special hand sign they had initiated when they served together. They all watched, fascinated by the kids' obsession to go camping later that night in Rowe's very own backyard. Rowe said he had several large tarps that were perfect for ground cover. They sampled the first tent and, when they had all agreed to it, bought a couple more. Dexter then led them to the camping accessories, where they found pillows, sleeping bags, blankets, and lanterns. Rowe and Antonette discussed whether or not they needed lanterns, and they agreed to buy four. Antonette finally laid out her plans for the placement of the tents, and Rowe's eyes became large as he widely accepted her grand idea. Rowe said he thought the lanterns would make it really exciting, and they agreed to give a safety briefing to the grandkids so they could have an unforgettable outdoor experience. Antonette asked Rowe if he had marshmallows at home.

Rowe said, "Of course not. What would I do with…"

Antonette hushed him before he could finish. "No worries," she said. "We'll stop by the commissary to pick up some marshmallows, graham crackers, and chocolate for s'mores."

Antonette led everyone to the cashier in the PX and laid out their purchases. Dexter was about to say something when Rowe interrupted.

"We got it, bud. No worries."

"I've got this one," Antonette stepped in front of Rowe and paid for all of the items. Rowe tried to stop her, grabbing at her credit card.

Antonette said, "It's okay. Please let me treat the kids. You can pay next time." Rowe whispered to her, "You are amazing. I truly missed you." Antonette just smiled, looked deeply into his eyes, and returned the compliment, "I really missed you too, Rowe." And Rowe knew it was a genuine compliment because he could read her mind without her knowing it yet. It was his secret for now, and he didn't want to let her in on it.

Isabella, who was perched on Rowe's hip, snapped him out of his thoughts when she tugged his ear. They all left the PX after giving thanks and saying goodbye to Dexter, headed to the Suburban to drop off their camping paraphernalia, and then headed for the Commissary. The Commissary at Ft. Lee had many isles. JR was the first to find the Kraft Jet Puffed Marshmallows. Then Antonette said they needed to look for marshmallow roasting sticks.

Mark, the second grandson, found them first, held the sticks up in the air.

"Yeah! I found it. I am the man!" Mark yelled.

Everyone laughed, and Rowe disclosed to Antonette that the grandkids had heard him say that mantra in a victorious half marathon race he had won. The kids had copied such an attitude, including "I am the man" since then. The oldest grandson was dancing around the aisle, saying, "I am the man! I found marshmallows first!" while JR tried to grab them away from Mark.

Rowe said, "Cease fire!" He got in the middle of the bickering boys then said, "Hey guys, we need to hurry up if you want to be camping tonight."

And the two boys stopped at once. They didn't want to spoil their shopping and camping tonight by upsetting their grandpa. With that, Antonette asked what else they needed. Rowe told her they have a raised cast iron wood burning fire pit at home. Antonette smiled, told him it sounded perfect and asked if they had food at home for camping. Rowe said no but thought about hot dogs and buns, so they picked up several packs of buns and bought three packs of hot dogs.

"Better to have extra than to run short," said Rowe.

Antonette agreed; having come from a large family, it was always better to have extra. They had condiments such as mayo, ketchup, and yellow mustard at home, and Antonette mentioned they needed to get some relish and red onions. Rowe said he was beginning to get hungry, and Antonette laughed. Antonette volunteered to pay for everything again, with Rowe protesting.

"Please, allow me to treat the kids." She said that she loved to do it and repeated that she'd allow him to pay next time.

They left the commissary, saw a popcorn stand in the concessionaire, and Rowe bought some for everyone. The granddaughter liked the sweet popcorn, and Rowe usually indulged his cherished granddaughter, Isabella. JR, Mark, Jeff, and Elon also chose sweet popcorn.

They had finally completed shopping for camping gear. Antonette and Rowe agreed that the grandchildren would be camping safely and comfortably that night.

As they both pulled into the driveway, Antonette admired Rowe's estate once again, and she was glad to have accepted Rowe's invitation to sleepover. Rowe told her that initially, he wished for a small place to live, but his children convinced him to buy a big house. His children were all grown and married; the number of grandchildren seemed to be expanding. Rowe's kids had convinced him that having a large place where they could all gather would provide unique opportunities to bond as a family. Rowe agreed, provided that he would have a hand in designing the layout. Emy sought Armand's help and invited their friend, owner of an Architect and Engineering firm in Hampton, Virginia, to help with the layout and the exterior. The newly built house sat on a 25-acre lot and was convenient to the military base and Rowe's worksite. It had a secret bunker, a cave in a basement just like the Batman house.

Rowe had explained to Antonette, "It is an energy-efficient house. The first time I saw an energy-efficient house was in San Antonio, Texas, and I fell in love with the concept. I wanted to live there, but all my family was here, so I decided to build my dream house in Virginia. I wanted to be close to my children, especially now that I am getting younger and needed company."

Antonette smiled at Rowe's statement of getting younger and said, "It was the right thing to do. It's a brilliant design, and having your family close brings you so much joy." Rowe added that he employed a maid once a week to clean and maintain the neatness of the house.

"Even if you lived here with me, I wouldn't want you to be working hard in cleaning the house. We would be both busy working, to say the least, and should be exploring places on the weekend with the grandchildren."

Antonette nodded, "That's a good idea." She loved the large house, but maintaining it seemed daunting along with her work.

At a glance, Rowe's house looked like a normal two-story building. It was filled with energy-saving home features like additional insulation, energy-efficient appliances, a radiant floor heating system, the rainwater was used for irrigation, and it had PV solar panels. However, the secret bunker was a grand creation in his basement that had remained unknown to anyone. Even if the grandkids had nowhere left to run around the house, he swore that he would never unlock the secret spy bunker. With a secret entrance behind a large built-in bookshelf, it was more than a sanctuary; it was a special place for a special mission and off-limits to anyone. It also had a full-sized bathroom and full kitchen.

In the main house, the master suite was the largest bedroom with a huge marble bathroom and a direct entrance to the indoor swimming pool. The second, third, fourth, fifth, sixth, and seventh bedrooms each had a full bathroom, one in the library, one bathroom in the hallway, and one in the basement. The pantry was in one room, and the shelves were always well-stocked. There was a temperature-controlled wine cellar in the basement under the stairs with a glass door. Rowe had made the windows quad panes with automatic blinds for privacy and energy purposes. The blinds were all programmed to go up and down throughout the day. Everything was on voice command and could be controlled through his phone or his watch. Rowe had told Antonette earlier that morning while they laid in bed, he greatly enjoyed the features of his smart house and would like to continue working on it with her help. Antonette stared at the ceiling and asked if he planned to install a smart TV on the ceiling.

Rowe's eyes became larger as if a light bulb hit him in the head and said, "What? Where did you get that idea?"

"I saw it in many places, including my own millennial son's house."

Rowe embraced her and said again, "I really missed you!"

The grandchildren dismounted the Suburban after Rowe had parked outside the garage so they could unload the camping haul. They all started to rush into the house, but Rowe reminded them about helping hands.

"Hey, hey kids. We need some helping hands here if you want to camp tonight."

JR grabbed the basketball that was lying on the ground between the garage and Rowe's Suburban and tried to shoot one more time but missed. Rowe gently said that he'd help him with his game the next day. Meantime, he redirected JR's energy and told him that he needed to help unload their purchases first.

Rowe knew how to teach his grandchildren about work ethic by letting them earn their rewards. He tried not to spoil his own children while they were growing up and always advised them to earn their reward by working hard or lending a hand. However, when it came to school, he had helped them develop a sound moral compass. They learned to sort behaviors, impulses, and feelings into appropriate and inappropriate. And be able to justify judgments about their choices for the sake of good decisions without using a reward. His children had groaned as expected, but they learned to live with their father's military discipline.

Rowe had always handed down the discipline, but sometimes it was hard not to spoil his grandchildren, especially Isabella, his first granddaughter. Rowe spoiled his precious Isabella with wonderful barbie dolls, pink and purple clothes, sparkly shoes, and toys. He did it as naturally as breathing. Rowe felt an instant heart tug, the deep love and pride, and the sheer wonder that settled in when he held his first granddaughter. His reasoning came in handy when Antonette asked, and Rowe professed that perhaps it's because with age comes wisdom. He appreciated how quickly time speeds by, how rapidly those little minds and bodies grow, and how they must savor each moment before they grow up. His immediate response when he saw the dangers in a sin-filled world was to protect and love, and he couldn't help himself but add more spoiling.

He loved all of his grandchildren, but Isabella was special because she was the first girl, and he wanted her to feel like a princess. His grandsons were a bit jealous of her, and Rowe had to explain why he indulged Isabella. Rowe had also taught them how to protect Isabella from the boys and made sure she was always safe. The grandsons acknowledged that they understood their grandpa and, since then, had protected Isabella from other kids, especially from the boys. Isabella was only four years old, but one could already notice her budding beauty, just like her mom.

The grandkids loved to play around Rowe's house and were hesitant to leave when their parents arrived to collect them. But Rowe had told them that he was not going anywhere, and his home was theirs too; hence, they could come by anytime. However, the one rule he maintained was that they needed to have good grades first before they were allowed to visit.

And the kids said, "We are the brightest in class!" "We have all A's grandpa, don't worry!"

That was enough for Rowe to spoil them on the weekends. He was glad they were all good students. If not for the grandkids, he would have been content staying in a one-bedroom house. His children were all so happy that he had chosen to build a place large enough for everyone to visit.

Rowe and Antonette unpacked the groceries in the kitchen. He paused for a moment and stole a kiss, then tossed the bag of marshmallows at her. Antonette snagged them out of the air, laughed, and got back to the idea of camping. Rowe then helped the grandkids with setting up their tents. Denver and Chichi were on his heels, leaping with excitement and a new adventure and wagging their tails. Antonette suggested that they could camp on the patio and use the bathrooms inside the house. Antonette and Rowe decided to 'camp out' in the living room so they would be close by. It was a good plan, and everybody felt comfortable with it.

Rowe thought that it would be fun to invite his children next time too, and looked forward to more camping with the whole family. Everyone would enjoy the break, and they could all bring various food dishes for each other to enjoy. Antonette dreamed of inviting her own kids to join the group for the next camping adventure.

The group had a blissful evening full of laughs and happy memories. The grandchildren all enjoyed catching fireflies and roasting hotdogs and marshmallows over the bonfire. After securing all of the kids in their tents, Antonette and Rowe were exhausted and finally fell sound asleep. Thankfully, during the camp night, the grandkids had only used the bathroom once and slept through the night otherwise. Around 0200 am, Isabella had opened the glass doors quietly so she could use the bathroom in the hallway. Mark helped his sister, and he used the other bathroom. JR, Jeff, and Elon were sound asleep.

Antonette prepared breakfast the next morning by cooking a simple omelet for the grandkids calling only for cheese and bacon chips, and made the omelets to their tastes. Rowe took breakfast sausages from the deli section of the fridge. Antonette tried to get it from his hands, but Rowe didn't let it go until Antonette looked at him and raised her eyebrows, and they both laughed.

JR woke up first, at 0800 am, and sat on the barstool, which kept turning in circles until Rowe told him to take it easy. Rowe never lost his temper with his grandchildren, but they knew when their grandpa was mad, and nobody ever wanted to make him mad because he was so good to them. JR stopped turning the barstool, and he finally sat down like a young gentleman waiting for his breakfast.

Rowe told JR, "It's good to see you up and early. You normally get up at noon."

JR answered, "I am starving!" And both Rowe and Antonette laughed. Antonette asked JR how was camping and if he slept well. He replied that this was the best camping he ever had, and he really enjoyed the bonfire and roasting marshmallows. The rest of the kids got up shortly afterward.

Mark entered around 0830 am and exclaimed, "That bonfire was great!"

By 0845 am, the rest of the grandkids had filled in all of the barstools next to JR. Mark bragged with excitement about the fireflies they had caught and put into a jar. Antonette was excited and said she wanted to see them again this morning. Mark almost jumped up to go get them, but Rowe said they would do it after breakfast.

Antonette faced the kitchen again and was ready to serve breakfast in the bar. When she turned around with a plate full of food, Rowe was sitting on JR's chair with a smirk on his face holding his fork and knife with a napkin tucked into his shirt.

Antonette put the plate down with an Omelet, sausage, and toasted bread slices and tried to catch her breath. The change from JR to Rowe caught her by surprise, and they all laughed at the little comic transformation. From small JR to big Rowe. Rowe couldn't stop laughing until Isabella asked what was so funny. Rowe helped Isabella to her chair and said that they were just playing games.

Isabella said, "Playing games early in the morning?"

And Rowe said, "Yes!" Isabella giggled and said she wanted to play hide and seek. Everyone laughed, and Rowe said it was too early for hide and seek.

"We all have to eat breakfast first, and then you all need to do your sanitary hygiene!" Rowe also added that he had a big surprise for everyone after breakfast since it had turned out to be a beautiful day, and the weather forecast showed 78 degrees high and a low of 74 degrees. Antonette gazed at Rowe, guessing for an answer, while Rowe looked at her back and just smiled, holding onto his secret.

Rowe told the boys to pack up their tents and that they were going somewhere after breakfast. He said it would be a quick outdoor activity, but they needed to bring sandwiches, drinks, and spare clothes. Antonette was still in a quandary over Rowe's plans for that day. He was not telling her anything, and she was really in for a big surprise.

CHAPTER 4

"So, I recommend the enjoyment of life, for there is nothing better on earth, for a person to do except to eat, drink, and enjoy life."

(Ecclesiastes 8:15)

They drove to Appomattox Boat Harbor in about 20 minutes. The kids were excited and eager to dismount the vehicle, tour the floating docks, the clubhouse, pool, dual boat launch ramp, dry dock, and run on the stage where the bands played during the festivals. Jeff, Elon, and the two dogs were the first to dismount.

Rowe bellowed, "Wait…"

And the boys halted until everybody had piled out of the Suburban. Rowe reminded the grandkids about the rules in the area, to which they all answered in unison, "Yes, Grandpa, we know, we'll be careful."

Antonette had been quiet since they arrived in Appomattox. Rowe was busy watching the grandkids as they roamed around since he did not want to end up looking for them or losing track of them. He finally noticed Antonette's quietness as he missed her voice.

"Hey, are you alright? Was it something you ate earlier? Or what? Tell me, tell me, and I am going to get whoever made you angry today!"

"Nothing. I just feel like I am on top of the world right now! You, the kids, these moments…" Antonette smiled softly; her heart was full for the first time in a long time. Gratitude welled up in her soul and spliced over into a single tear that escaped the corner of her right eye. Rowe wrapped his arms around Antonette, and she kissed him feverishly.

"Can you wait until we're alone?" Rowe asked teasingly. Antonette smiled and tickled him on his side.

Changing the subject, she said, "I didn't know you had a yacht!"

Rowe replied, "Eventually, I would have told you about it. We've been busy, and my hands were full of grandkids and dogs… besides, I wanted to surprise you. Do you like sailing?"

Antonette's eyes widened, "Are you kidding me? I sailed my dad's boat!"

Rowe teased, "That does not mean you won't tip the boat over." And then he tried to get away from her vicious pinch on his arm.

Their attention moved to the kids who were now on the stage. JR was animating Elvis Presley with a stick in his hand, singing his favorite rock music. Jeff and Elon were dancing with Isabella. They noticed that Mark was missing. Rowe asked JR where Mark was. JR continued singing as if he didn't hear Rowe. Rowe touched JR on his shoulder while he was animating his favorite singing idol. JR stopped as soon as he felt Rowe's touch.

"Where is your brother? Where did he go?"

JR's face turned pale, and he said, "I don't know, Grandpa." Rowe got worried and searched the entire clubhouse, still holding Antonette's left hand. Antonette felt queasy as soon as Rowe started walking fast like he wanted to storm the clubhouse. She said a silent prayer to quell the fears of her worst thoughts. There he was, Mark, lost in his own world, playing with the balloons and admiring the hallways decorated with florals and lots of balloons for a wedding.

"Mark! Why are you here and not joining the fun with the others? I said I wanted you to all stay together. Everybody goes with everybody! You got that?" Rowe said sternly.

Mark looked at him earnestly with blue eyes the same exact color as Rowe's, "Sorry, Grand… I had to use the bathroom. I was on my way back to the stage, and I got distracted."

Rowe continued more softly, "Are you okay? Do you like balloons? You seem delighted with these wedding decorations."

"I love it! I wish somebody in our family would get married soon so there could be a big party, with lots of balloons, decorations, music, and tons of food! It would be awesome!" Mark's eyes were shining with fascination.

Rowe and Antonette both did not expect an answer like that, and they both got quiet.

Mark continued, "I am ready to join the others. Are you coming, Grand?"

"Yes, yes, of course, we're right behind you." As soon as Mark closed the door behind him, Rowe cupped Antonette's face and rendered a quick, passionate kiss. Antonette was surprised by Rowe's reaction.

"C'mon, let's go, or else the kids will end up looking for us," Rowe said.

Rowe led the kids to his luxury yacht, with Antonette climbing the steps first to help him hand off the kids one by one. He was the last one to get onto the boat and made sure everyone was safe.

"You have half an hour to check around, and then we are going back home. We'll spend more time here during your summer break," Rowe told the kids as they toured the boat.

Elon quipped, "Grand, my parents said we are going on a Caribbean cruise this summer. But I would rather spend some time with you on your yacht instead!"

Rowe told him that they would have plenty of time to be together when they returned from the Caribbean, as they would be there only for 10 days.

"We have all summer, and you will only be away for 10 days," Rowe said.

"Ten days! That will be too long and boring for me!" Yelped Elon, who liked being with his grandfather more than with his own family. The other grandkids felt the same way. They loved their grandpa, as they thought he was way cool.

Isabella had told him, "Grand, you are the coolest grown-up I know," and it melted Rowe's heart.

Rowe thought that Elon behaved more like his mom, and Elon's mom behaved like Rowe.

Mark, who was busy playing with the floaters, said, "We are going to Rome in December!"

Antonette gasped, "You're going to Rome, Mark?" Mark nodded his head; their family was planning to tour most of Europe. Antonette jokingly asked if she could go along, and she was delighted when Mark said yes, she could come too.

Rowe pretended not to hear their conversation by sitting on the captain's seat while he checked all the lights, and then he followed Mark, who was now playing with the water tubes.

"Grand, can I jump into the water with this today?"

Rowe smiled and gently said, "Not today, kiddo. As a matter of fact, why don't you just slowly put everything back in place so we can hit the road, and we'll come back here when we have more time?"

Isabella said, "I like that, Grand. I will like that very much."

Rowe smiled and kissed Isabella on her cheek. "Alright, it is time to go then."

"Aye, aye, Captain!" exclaimed Antonette with a salute.

Everybody suddenly became energetic and copied her, "Aye, aye, Captain Grand!" And rendered a salute!

It was almost dark when they got back to town, and even though they rarely got fast food, Rowe decided to stop by McDonald's and announced, "Dinner is on me!"

Antonette laughed and whispered, "Gourmet tonight?" Rowe smiled at her and fought the temptation to kiss her again but knew he should not do it in front of his grandkids. Although he had known Antonette for years, still the grandchildren had just met her. He thought displaying so much affection too hastily in the presence of innocent ones might be an indecent role model. Deep in his thoughts, he whispered to himself, *"But the time will come when everybody sees..."*

Antonette asked, "Could you think out loud so I can hear?"

Rowe winked at her and said, "What does everybody want at McDonald's"? And each shouted their food orders in unison.

"Stand down. I will not take the orders until you can talk one at a time." Rowe said sternly. Antonette helped by asking Isabella first and then moved on from there.

Rowe thanked her and said, "I wouldn't know what to do without you by my side. You are good for me." He knew that she was the perfect complement to his personality.

Antonette finally gave her food order, and Rowe was shocked. She just wanted an Oreo milkshake. He obliged and rolled his eyes at her unhealthy choice. It was 7 pm when everyone finally hit home.

"Take your showers before going to bed!"

Everybody answered in unison, "Yes, Grand!"

The grandkids showered and brushed their teeth. They were all tired from the adventures that day and were in bed by 8 pm.

Antonette took a shower, too, with Rowe.

"We're finally alone!" he said as he poured shampoo on her dark hair.

"How could we have missed out on this for so long?" Antonette purred as Rowe massaged her scalp and soaped her body with shower gel.

Rowe kissed her again and made sure the bedroom door was locked before continuing their intimacy. When Rowe approached her, Antonette sat on her knees and took him in her mouth. He groaned with pleasure as she rolled her tongue over him. "Yes, how could we have missed out on this for so long," he repeated.

It wasn't long before the place became quiet, and only the sparrows could be heard. But Antonette did not sleep sweetly that night. Terrible dreams plagued her that night.

It was 5 am on a Sunday, and despite getting a little sleep, Antonette was up bright and early. She was surprised when Rowe woke up and encircled his arms around her waist.

"Good Morning, beautiful! How was your night? He whispered. "Mine was wonderful with you by my side."

"Wait, that is Steve Holly's song. Where did you learn that?" Antonette asked, facing him.

Rowe unlocked his fingers and headed for the bathroom.

"It's always been my favorite song! I like the lyrics and the tune." He sang to her, "And when I open my eyes and see your sweet face, it's a good morning, beautiful day!"

Antonette told Rowe the story from her deployment in Iraq when the boys in the co-ed tent played that music every morning, and everybody wanted to keep listening to it over and over again. One of them had the ambition to be a big singer like Elvis Presley, and he had cassette tapes including 'Good Morning Beautiful' that he played every morning and inspired all the female soldiers who dreamed of a mate who would feel that way towards them someday.

"I am not surprised. It's always been my favorite, too," said Rowe.

"Anyway, why were you up so early? It's Sunday, after all. Aren't you supposed to be sleeping a bit more?" Antonette asked Rowe as they entered the kitchen. She started making omelets again and continued to unpack the sausage links she had brought. Rowe quietly tapped and scrolled on his iPad and answered Antonette without looking up from the screen.

"Nah, I have been an early morning riser all my life. I accomplish most of my tasks before everyone else shows up to work."

Antonette said, "That's nice because I am the same way. I appreciate my acquired discipline in Korea more and more over time and am glad to know we are on the same sheet of music."

Antonette didn't hear a response and noticed that Rowe was intensely scrolling on his iPad as if reading very important news.

"Is there anything wrong, sweetheart?" Still no answer from Rowe.

Antonette started frying her special sausage links, and the aroma suddenly moved Rowe.

"What is that scented, sweet smell? I am suddenly very hungry?"

Antonette served up a plate of two sunny-side-up eggs, sausage, and fried rice.

"What is this? Wow, this looks and smells amazing!" Rowe said as he brought the plate up to inhale the aroma.

Antonette explained, "They are called Longanisa, a Filipino sweet sausage that's been my favorite for breakfast, with two fried eggs and fried rice. You were mesmerized with your iPad while I was cooking. Is everything alright?"

"Yes, yes, I will tell you about it tonight when the kids are gone. But can I have an extra serving of Lonisa?"

"Longanisa… here. Long like in the word 'long,' 'ganisa,' like in ga-neesa." And she added more Longanisa to Rowe's plate as soon as they had turned brown.

Antonette poured orange juice into two six-ounce drinking glasses, one for Rowe and one for herself. After the blessing, they clinked their glasses in cheers, and Rowe forked the Longanisa and eggs. Since he was not used to having rice for breakfast, he barely touched it at first. He loved fried rice, though, just not for breakfast. However, ten minutes later, it turned out he had a clean plate and asked for more Langonisa. Antonette gave him one more and advised that he should not have any more or his stomach would be too full. Rowe asked Antonette where this food came from and expressed his desire that he would like to get plenty more of it. Antonette said she had brought some special foods from her apartment, and enough to last for months.

"Wait until you taste the Tocino!" Antonette exclaimed. Rowe became more inquisitive, asking all sorts of questions about her native foods. Antonette laughed, amazed, and impressed by Rowe's interest in Filipino foods. To help him understand it further, she had her most favorite recipe and ingredients on her phone along with the instructions on how to cook both types of meat, so she emailed it to him.

Rowe said, "I got it." He scanned the recipe and realized that Antonette had put a lot of work into the special sausage.

Longanisa Recipe and Instructions

<u>Ingredients:</u>

- 2 tablespoons soy sauce
- 2 tablespoons vinegar
- 2 tablespoons anisado wine (bitter licorice tasting)
- ½ cup brown sugar
- 1 tablespoon salt
- 2 pounds coarsely ground pork
- 1 pound pork fat diced
- I head garlic peeled and minced
- 2 teaspoons ground black pepper
- 2 teaspoons paprika
- Hog casings about 12 to 15 feet
- 1 cup water
- 2 tablespoons oil
- Required tools:
  - Funnel
  - Fine Kitchen twine

<u>Instructions:</u>

1. Use a bowl and combine soy sauce, vinegar, anisado wine, sugar, and salt. Stir until sugar and salt are dissolved in a bowl. Use a separate bowl to combine ground pork, pork fat, garlic, pepper, and paprika. Add liquid mixture and gently mix until combined. Refrigerate for about 2 hours to allow flavors to meld and to firm up the meat mixture.

2. In a bowl, soak casings in warm water for about 30 minutes. Drain well. In the sink, run warm water through casings and check for spots with leaks, and cut these sections.

3. On one end of the casings, leave about 5-inches on both ends. Do not overstuff casings. Tie off one end into a double knot. Use the fine kitchen twine to tie it.

4.   To make individual sausage links, pinch sausage at intervals of about 4 inches. Gently twist the sausage link at the pinched point in one complete rotation. Repeat the process all the way down the coil but alternating the direction of twisting, towards you and away from you, from one link to the next. Tie off the other end into a double knot or with the fine kitchen twine. Place in a Ziplock bag and refrigerate overnight.

5.   When ready to cook, cut the sausage into individual links.

6.   With a knife, prick each sausage once or twice. In a pan over medium heat, combine links and water. Bring to a boil. Lower heat, cover, and continue to cook until meat is cooked through, and liquid is almost absorbed. Add oil and continue to cook, stirring regularly, until sausages are caramelized. Remove the pan and serve hot.

Tocino Recipe (Sweet Cured Pork) and Instructions

Tocino is a sweet, cured meat typically served as a Filipino breakfast. It is sweet, savory, and tender.

Ingredients:

- 2 pounds pork. You may use a pork butt, shoulder ham, or belly. Cut into ¼ inch thin
- ¾ cup brown sugar
- 1 ½ tablespoons salt
- 3 cloves garlic, finely minced
- 1 tablespoon soy sauce
- 2 tablespoons rice vinegar
- ¼ cup fruit juice, or you may also use pineapple or apple
- ½ tablespoons finely ground black pepper
- 1 tablespoons rice flour
- Natural red food coloring

Instructions:

1.   In a big bowl, combine all ingredients except for the pork slices. Mix until well blended.

2.	Add the pork and mix using your hand. Use hand gloves to avoid stains. Mix for several minutes to an hour.

3.	Transfer to a container with a cover and let it sit overnight on the counter.

4.	Mix a couple of times again before putting it in the fridge. Cure for 24 hours or up to 3 days. It can be frozen afterwards and stored longer.

"It's a great recipe, but I'd rather keep the chef," Rowe said. Antonette blushed, and Rowe reminded her about her face turning crimson when they were in Baghdad. He took her to his CHU, Containerized Housing Unit, and wasn't sure what she was thinking about, but her face had turned bright red. Antonette grinned and was stunned at how Rowe remembered everything.

Rowe continued, "Oh yeah! Did you think I would forget it? I think you smelled my bath towel too. I folded it in half, and I do remember finding it folded three times after you came out of the bathroom. I am very particular about how I do things, and I notice it if somebody touches my things. I am very detailed. And I vividly remember you were quite annoyed when I put the necklace with a cartouche around your neck. Instead of facing me, you pretended to reach for your purse."

"Rowe, that's enough! How did you remember all of these in such great detail?"

Rowe slowly approached her and gently said, "Because I have loved you all these times and can't thank the Heavens enough that you finally came back into my life." Rowe kissed her, but they were interrupted when they both heard a squeal,

"Ewwwww!" It was Isabella standing in the hallway with her doll and Chichi standing next to her.

Rowe winked at Antonette and said, "To be continued," she chuckled and gave him a knowing look.

Rowe approached Isabella and said, "Good Morning, Princess! How are you this morning? Did you sleep well last night?" He scooped her up and took her to the kitchen. "Are you hungry? What would you like for breakfast?"

Isabella pointed at the Longanisa and said, "That!"

"Are you sure? Do you know what these are?"

Isabella shook her head and said, "Nope, but I want to taste."

Rowe said, "Clever girl." And he forked a little piece and fed Isabela.

"Hmmmm, it's really good. I would like some more."

"Say please," said Rowe.

"Plez," pleaded Isabela. "It smells so good."

Antonette smiled and suggested, "I think I might need to cook more of these. If the kids don't finish them, I can always put them in the fridge."

"Great idea! The kids might sleep until 1200 noon. Can they have that for lunch?" Antonette assured him that they could have leftover sausages and fried rice for lunch. The rest of the kids were up at 12 noon, just like Rowe had stated. Everyone enjoyed lunch, and their parents picked them up at 2 pm.

"Bye Grand, bye Nanna, bye! See you next week!" Exclaimed the kids as their parents carefully guided them to the cars. Rowe told Zed and Emy that he was going on TDY for the next two weeks.

Zed asked, "Where will Antonette be while you are on TDY?

"She will be coming with me."

Antonette overheard Rowe, but she did not want to say anything that would appear as if she was contradicting him and just smiled in front of everybody. Emy hugged Antonette, and the gesture was seconded by Zed.

"We do really appreciate that you two have met again, and thank you for being here for dad. We're so worried about him going through life alone, and he looks so happy. We are blessed that you have come into our lives, and we truly appreciate what you've done for Dad and the grandkids this weekend. Please take care, and take care of dad!"

Antonette hugged them back and said, "Don't you worry about anything, and I think I can handle your dad."

With that, the three girls laughed, and Zed and Emy blew kisses to both of them. The grandkids kept blowing kisses as they drove off until they couldn't see figures anymore. The dogs were busy licking Jeff's and Elon's faces and hanging their heads out the window as the group drove away.

CHAPTER 5

"Fight for what is right. Always believe in yourself."
(Castro Sr., Andres L.)

"At last, we are by ourselves again. And where was I?" asked Rowe as he tried to kiss her in the driveway.

"Well, you were supposed to tell me about that intense focus on your iPad," Antonette said as she gently pulled away. "You were obsessed with something until the Longanisa and Tocino's fragrance distracted you. What was it that you wanted to tell me or show me?"

Rowe paused at the steps and then continued. "Let's get inside and lock the doors." They checked the garage and ensured it was secured. Rowe felt that Antonette seemed to be a righteous angel, and he trusted her to see the spy bunker, a.k.a. the Vault. No one else had seen this hidden gem, not even his own children nor grandchildren. It was his playhouse, and now the secret would belong to both of them.

"I would like to show you my secret bunker. Not even my kids know about it, and no one knows what I do down here. What I am about to disclose is a top-secret, and I hope you will understand and accept it." Antonette remained silent, and Rowe led her to the basement, to a hidden door behind the built-in bookshelf and a hallway leading to the top-secret spy bunker.

"Are you ready?" he looked into her quizzical eyes.

"Yes, I can't wait to see it!" she squealed with excitement, secretly wondering if it was really a sex room like in her books.

Rowe unlocked two doors behind another door and locked it back as they went through.

"You have three doors to this room?" Antonette noticed. She was mesmerized as Rowe revealed an astonishing, well-equipped room with fancy spy, cyber, and communication gadgets, computers, and four large television screens ostentatiously pinned against the wall. Antonette thought it was made to look like the situation room in the White House. How Rowe had constructed, it was beyond her imagination. It looked like it was an entirely separate pad from the house. It appeared like a huge vault that held the key to human survival if a natural or any type of disaster ravaged the earth's population. She had never seen anything like it before. There were shelves full of water, MREs, electronics, and medications. It was a beautiful, hidden place underneath his ordinary-looking mansion. It could help to save the human race if the end of the world came. There was nothing else built like it. Rowe teased her that they could play any ball game or a board game there to fight boredom. There was a gym that had almost everything needed for a complete workout.

Adjacent to it was a gorgeous kitchen lavished with a decent bar, a good size bedroom, and a master bath. She could see that the bar had several glasses and just a few liquors, wine, and a cooler with a few beers. She noticed live plants in a fish aquarium by the bar.

"That makes sense," she said. "Live plants provide the fish with a natural food source with the ability to replenish. Plants provide for the aquarium in that they produce oxygen and absorb the carbon dioxide and ammonia that the fish generates. Plants provide shelter and security for the fish. Good science," she observed.

She sat on the king-size bed and was amazed at its softness, the luxurious pillows, and gray linens. Now she had confirmed that Rowe definitely had expensive taste. The bedroom had a small black settee for a good conversation and a little vase with faux silk flowers on top of a black square coffee table.

Rowe asked, "How do you like it?"

Antonette digested Rowe's question as she took in the entire scene. "I like it very much. This seems to be a self-sufficient safehouse, and based on what I see, you could sustain yourself for about six months without going out?"

Rowe always admired her intelligence and ingenuity and murmured, *"I am keeping this woman."*

"I'm sorry? Did you say something?" she said.

Rowe replied, "Yes, it is time. We are expected in the situation room, and I'd like to introduce you to my boss."

Antonette looked confused as Rowe led her to the situation room. Rowe turned on the big monitor, and a few seconds later, a lady was shown on the TV.

"Hello Rowe, and welcome Antonette. Rowe, as you've read in your SIPRNet communication, your passports are waiting for you in locker room Alpha Seven with two backpacks filled with everything you will need. No need to pack. Everything has been packed for you, so you are good to go. By the way, I am HG Hawk, the director of the CIA. We are the best in the universe, Antonette. I was impressed by Rowe's description of you this morning. The CIA is confident of your abilities as they have been proven by your tough challenges and resilience while in the theater of conflict. We did the research, you are an incredible soldier, and we are humbled that you are joining our team. You are joining our team, right, Antonette?"

Antonette was silent and not sure what to say. She was trying to remember something. The name, the CIA… and she finally figured it out. HG Hawk was in her dream! HG Hawk, the President, and the others in the Situation Room were in her dreams! She looked at Rowe with confusion as if hoping for further explanation of what was transpiring.

HG Hawk continued, "Your code name is Alex. I know it was your code name in Operation Iraqi Freedom."

Antonette was bewildered at this mention, "How do you know about my code name?"

"We are the CIA, and nothing is impossible for us. We can do anything and get anything. All you need to do is accept the mission, and we will continue with the briefing. For your country, the people of the United States, and Rowe, will you accept this assignment, Alex?"

Antonette asked herself silently, *'For Rowe? For my country and the people, yes, of course! What do these people mean that for Rowe, I should be accepting this assignment?'*

"I am honored, Madam Director, for this opportunity, but I would certainly like to think about it for a while, and could I get back to you on that, please?" Antonette finally replied.

HG Hawk knew that Antonette would ultimately accept the offer. A true soldier would never back down from this operation now, especially since she had seen Rowe's impressive top-secret situation room. Hawk knew that Antonette would understand the importance of this mission.

With that, the briefing began, and Rowe received the details of the job that needed to be done and the exit strategy. Everything was communicated in the 30-minute briefing.

Antonette preceded Rowe up the stairs, went straight to the kitchen on the main floor, and took a bottle of water out of the fridge. She almost drank the whole bottle straight. She looked for a spirited drink but didn't find any. Rowe kept very little hard alcohol at home, except for those hidden in the secret bunker. Antonette took a grip on herself and finally faced Rowe straight in the eyes with crossed arms.

"Well, well, well, I guess I'm going to put my leave in for the next two weeks, and you?"

Rowe answered, "I am ready to send."

Once again, they stared at each other, and Rowe reassured her silently that everything would be alright. Antonette felt comfortable in his gaze, and she knew that Rowe was telling the truth. At least they would be working together just like they had before. She would watch him constantly and felt that she could adapt quickly to this mission if she worked next to him. She asked Rowe if this was like the movies with Sylvester Stallone in Expendables with other seasoned movie actors and actresses. Rowe chuckled and said this would not be that hard. They were not going to the field; they would just be the ears and eyes of the soldiers in the field.

Antonette felt relieved, "That sounds exciting!"

"It is indeed! Just wait, you'll see!" Rowe said excitedly, with the adrenaline already filtering into his system. "Don't worry, I trained with the famous 5th SFG (Airborne)," he added casually.

Antonette now realized why Rowe had acted the way he did; heroic, strong, agile, courageous, and capable of doing almost anything.

"That is so amazing! You never told me!" She exclaimed, knowing what extreme training one had to endure to join that elite group.

He had learned to use small arms, anti-armor, and weapons such as howitzers and heavy mortars. After graduation from Special Forces training, Rowe had earned his 18X military occupational specialty. He was also trained in Fort Benning, Georgia Infantry School, and had his first permanent change of station at Fort Bragg, North Carolina.

"That is where the Special Forces pipeline begins and ends for those seeking Green Beret and Special Operations careers," he explained.

Rowe was part of the 5th Special Forces Group (SFG) (A), one of the most highly decorated United States Special Forces groups in the U.S. Armed Forces.

"The history of the 5th SFG (A) goes back to the extensive action in the Vietnam War, and played a crucial role in the early months of Operation Enduring Freedom (OEF)," Rowe explained. "The 5th SFG (A) is designed to deploy and execute nine authorized missions: unconventional warfare, foreign internal defense, direct action counterinsurgency, special reconnaissance, counterterrorism, informational operations, counterproliferation of weapons of mass destruction, and security force assistance. They are primarily responsible for operations within the Central Command (CENTCOM) area of responsibility as part of the Special Operations Command, Central (SOCCENT). The 5th SFG (A) specializes in operations in the Middle East, Persian Gulf, Central Asia, and the Horn of Africa (HOA). With two of its battalions, they spend about six months out of every twelve deployed to Iraq as Combined Joint Special Operations Task Force – Arabian Peninsula."

Antonette was overwhelmed with the detailed explanation of the 5th SFG. She was too stunned to speak when Rowe sat next to her at the table and asked if she had found out everything there was to know about him yet.

"What do you mean?" she gasped.

"You know I can read your mind, right?" Rowe told her. "Do you remember when I easily found your living area in Baghdad?"

Antonette replied, "Yes, I am still wondering how you did that?"

Rowe confessed, "Because I had been there before. It used to be my headquarters in my prior deployments. I kept it secret from you and your friends because it was sacrosanct to keep it confidential. It's now unclassified."

Antonette felt embarrassed and said, "I do remember giving you a photo of the SFG compound in VBC because you said you would like to remember that place for the rest of your life. Little did I know that you had been there multiple times on your SFG tours!"

Antonette replayed the memory. She had been deployed to Iraq as a civilian contractor. She never missed attending Catholic services on Sundays and sometimes on Saturday evenings, but at that time, she had decided to attend the mass on Camp Slayer. When the service was finished, she thought she saw a familiar face, and they hugged each other. They weren't expecting to see each other again. But of all places, they met for the third time in war-torn Iraq. They went for lunch at the Camp Slayer dining facility. After their long conversation was over, they agreed to meet the following week again, and Rowe had picked Antonette up from 'The Zoo,' where she used to live and work. They toured the IZ (International Zone) in Camp Slayer, Baghdad, and took pictures with ruined buildings in the background. They were very happy until Rowe told her that he would be leaving Iraq in three weeks.

Antonette had instinctively known that their reconnection was temporary. Rowe had to redeploy to the U.S. because his contract was over, and his wife was very sick. With her friends, Antonette went to the U.S. Military Sadr Air Force Base Airport in order to say goodbye. Rowe was clearly sad to leave, and she too could feel it in her heart.

Antonette felt sorry for him, "The least I could do was to kiss him," she thought. She knew it was wrong and had never crossed that boundary with Rowe because of his marriage. Yet, that didn't deter the way that she felt about him. She was torn and confused. Rowe hugged her tightly, and he kissed her while looking deeply into her eyes as if to say, *"This isn't the last time."* Antonette gently circled her arms around his neck, and they had a passionate kiss in the presence of her friends, which was the closest intimacy they ever shared in a combat zone, inside the wire. It tore Antonette's heart to see Rowe leave Baghdad without her. Once again, she held it in her silent freedom. She cried herself to sleep that night and asked if it was God's will for them to see each other again.

"Well, thanks for that photo. I still have it to this day," Rowe said, interrupting the memory. "Here, let me show you my iPad. It's there, and all my pictures while I was with the 5th SFG (A)." Rowe pulled up another folder, "Here are the pictures that I took of you in VBC. Remember when we met for the third time? I treasured the moment when I picked you up from The Zoo, going to Mass together, a tour of the IZ, and of course, my brief evening before I bid goodbye. You just don't know what I went through after we parted ways. I had a rough time, and I really didn't want to discuss it with anyone. It's painful and more difficult to bear than going through rigid SFG training. Emotional pain is harder than any physical pain. As Special Forces, we went through psychological evaluations all the time. And what I went through when my wife got sick was almost beyond my training, and I almost lost it. I am grateful that I held onto my faith. When you saw me at church, I didn't let you see that I was already suffering severely at that time."

"Why did you join the AG Corps?" asked Antonette.

Rowe proceeded to tell Antonette about some of his experiences.

"5th SFG (A) in Somalia. Have you heard of Black Hawk Down? I was part of ARSOF, short for Army Special Operations Forces in Mogadishu, and we performed multiple successful missions in Somalia, including the capture of top commanders of a Somali warlord, Mohamed Farrah Aidid, a rogue paramilitary clan leader of the United Somali Congress. During Operation Continue Hope, the violence in Somalia increased toward us, or the coalition forces, peacekeepers, and, oh yes, including the international journalists. I will never forget Aidid. I was furious that he caused my first injury in battle. The extremists seized humanitarian aid packages. Our Intelligence determined that the instigators were members of Aidid's Somalia National Alliance, and of course, you know what happened next? It led to the Battle of Mogadishu in October 1993. As I said, I took my first shots in Mogadishu, and my injury was aggravated by my multiple Airborne jumps. Have you heard of our hero, the warrant-officer pilot of the black hawk helicopter, 160th Night Stalkers, who was shot down by an RPG or rocket-propelled grenade? Two helicopters were shot down on that day, one with our hero, and I was on the other black hawk, with Steve Glidewell and others. Nineteen were killed, and Steve and I were among 73 who were wounded in action. We were lucky to be alive when that chopper went down, but we did surveillance on our hero's location. We never leave our comrades behind, no matter how much it costs." Rowe continued.

"Steve, our hero, and I were in combat operations Prime Chance, Just Cause, and of course, the Desert Storm, and Gothic Serpent, where our hero was briefly held prisoner for 11 days. I was shot in the arm, and they took our hero and held him POW. Steve took great care of me, and I thought it was the end of the world for us. There was a lot of small arms fire as soon as we crashed, and we tried to protect ourselves. The gunfights went on for about 20 minutes, and we were lucky to survive that. I was first shot in my left arm and then another one on my right thigh, but I was lucky enough to survive. They were not bad wounds, and I was able to recover and continue with my mission. Those were my unforgettable battle wounds. We conducted medical and airfield assessments under Operation Provide Relief, which turned into multiple humanitarian missions such as helping with the distribution of food, and well, we empathized with local factions and clan elders. We, the Civil Affairs and Psychological Operations Soldiers, or as we called them PSYOP, worked independently and made us an effective force multiplier as part of an international coalition. Some of our troops got injured in the landmine attacks, and that's when the U.S. built "Task Force Ranger," a 440-member collaboration of U.S. Special Operations personnel from the Army, Air Force, and Navy, to go to Somalia."

Antonette listened closely to every word. She had no idea that Rowe had seen so much action and had been on that many chief missions.

"I also had multiple deployments with 5th SFG (A) in Kabul, Helmand, Kandahar, and other nooks in Afghanistan searching for the bad guys that beheaded our journalists and the capture of Osama Bin Laden crossing Pakistan. And multiple deployments in Iraq. I was deployed in the Persian Gulf to oust Saddam Hussein when he invaded and occupied neighboring Kuwait in August 1990. Saddam defied the U.N. Security Council to withdraw from Kuwait. He ignored President George H.W. Bush's warning to leave Kuwait or suffer the consequences. I was part of Red Dawn at that time and worked with the 101st Airborne Division Air Assault's 3/187th 'Rakkasans' infantry. Those guys were fierce! They were almost equal with us, 'almost.' They were well trained and used some of our training facilities back on base. I enjoyed working with them when we raided Saddam's dark hole and found him with no resistance on his part. Boy, did we relish our victory! I do remember the celebration the next day. General Petraeus was so proud of us, and he called my commanding officer to congratulate each one of us. He did the same thing with the Rakkasans. He made a personal visit and congratulated them for a job well done."

"It sounds like you were rarely home," Antonette said. She knew the difficulty of being deployed with children waiting for you back home.

"That is correct, and I'm making up for it with my family now," Rowe said wistfully. "After I was shot in the right leg in Somalia, I recovered from that, but then my lower leg and ankle were injured by my airborne jumps in Iraq. The doctors put a screw to hold the lower leg bones together while they healed. I am better now, but I certainly can't do airborne jumps anymore or everything I used to do while being with SFG. I told myself it was not the end of the world, and I ended up talking to one of the recruiters. He mentioned that I could switch MOS, Military Occupational Specialty code, from 18X to 75 series, which has been changed to 42 series, an administrative MOS. I laughed out loud at first but then agreed – so I ended up becoming 75 series, which has been changed to 42 series, doing soldier assignments."

Antonette found it hard to ignore Rowe's remarks and said, "Easy there, buddy, what was wrong with administrative MOS?"

Rowe stated that there was nothing wrong with it, but he found it so hard to accept to do administrative work after being active in Special Forces. He didn't want to drive a desk.

Antonette replied that she understood, and sometimes it is easier to accept things that cannot be changed. Her answer mystified Rowe because this was also one of his mottos that he often referred to when in the struggle. Once again, he held her tightly and kissed her passionately.

As they cleaned up the dinner dishes that night, Antonette was thinking of Rowe's rough time at war and was bewildered by Rowe's experiences as a Special Forces warrior. She could not believe Rowe was a wartime hero. However, she told Rowe that she was still embarrassed and upset by his great pretense when they were in Baghdad.

Rowe said, "Could you please forgive me? If that beautiful Egyptian necklace won't work, tell me what else I could give you to make up for it."

He was surprised when Antonette said, "What about a dozen more children?"

Rowe jokingly said, "I am up for it."

With that, they laughed and kissed, but Antonette felt that there was more that she needed to know about him. Rattling off a lot of questions now may not be the best move. She silently said to herself, *"Of course, in time, at the right time, I will uncover all of his mysteries."* There was more to learn about him, but what about enjoying the time now, living and enjoying being present in her own life each day with him? Antonette sat next to Rowe on the sofa while they both read a book and thought that being near Rowe was a life worth living. She was happy, and at least she wouldn't be alone like a hermit in her apartment and always going places by herself.

Antonette suggested that they go to her apartment and get more of the longanisa, tocino, and lumpia shanghai that filled her entire freezer. Rowe agreed to help her since it appeared that everyone enjoyed it, and the family would visit again after their mission. They both immediately got up, and Rowe drove her to the apartment. They emptied the refrigerator and freezer. Rowe told her that he could not wait to taste the shanghai lumpias, with pancit noodles that Antonette had promised to cook him at the house.

When they finally finished securing the place, Rowe looked at Antonette and asked, "How long are you going to keep this apartment?"

Antonette's answer was quick and brief, "As long as I work in Richmond. I need a place to stay." It was midnight, and they were outside her apartment.

Rowe already knew that he didn't want to lose Antonette again. He could feel his heartbeat closer when he was next to her. He asked Antonette if she could give up her apartment and live with him instead. Antonette did not expect Rowe's question in the middle of the night and while they were working on bringing the food home.

"Don't worry. I will still cook you egg rolls and pork bellies even if we are not living together forever." Rowe gave a good laugh and then quickly transformed into a serious conversation with Antonette.

"I knew you'd say that. Antonette, look at me. Don't you think it is time to give ourselves a chance? We… We were madly in love, and got separated by war, and saw each other and lost each other again. Please…?" he was looking right into her eyes without blinking.

Antonette had a strong sixth sense. She could feel that Rowe was up to something bigger than she had imagined. There was something he was not telling her yet, and she just knew it instinctively. She wanted to scratch that fantasy daydream because she felt comfortable living independently. But she liked Rowe's family, and she would miss his grandkids if she continued living in her apartment. She had fallen in love with his family as easily as she had fallen for Rowe. She might end up seeing them on the weekends if they lived separately for a while.

She told Rowe she'd think about it. And then they were both silent for the rest of the ride back to Rowe's house. They carried the food into the house and filled the refrigerator and the freezer.

"We have enough to feed a small country," Rowe teased Antonette, and they took the overflow to the spy bunker freezer. It was a huge freezer and had enough space for more longanisas, tocinos, pork bellies, lumpia shanghais, and pizzas.

Rowe said, "I am buying tickets to Rome in December for you and me, my kids and grandkids. Would you be merciful and join us?"

Antonette couldn't help smiling at the word he used. "Merciful - That word is for God to be merciful; I don't deserve that term! Do you remember the saying, I desire mercy, not sacrifice?"

Rowe said, "Yes. Jesus said, 'I desire mercy, not sacrifice. For I have not come to call the righteous, but sinners. If only you had known the meaning of 'I desire mercy, not sacrifice,' you would not have condemned the innocent. And to love Him with all your heart and with all your strength, and to love your neighbor as yourself, which is more important than all burnt offerings and sacrifices.' Those words originated from the books of Matthew 9:13, Matthew 12:7, and Mark 12:33."

Antonette slowly closed the fridge and looked up at Rowe.

"Rowe, that was very noble. I am humbled. Those words have always inspired me. How is it that we share the same favorite song and favorite Bible verses?"

Rowe replied, "My mother almost made me a priest after high school. I was an altar boy; did I ever tell you this? I just didn't feel that calling and felt that my special gifts were to be used in a different way. So, I joined the Army after studying engineering in college because I didn't want to be a priest."

"Really?" With disbelief, Antonette put her right hand over her mouth because she had almost become a nun. Antonette thought she had the calling and was invited for a Retreat in the convent. It was run by the nuns, of course. Ultimately, she wanted to have a family and chose not to become a nun. Antonette couldn't believe the coincidences in their lives. Their parents had instilled deep spirituality in their lives that had carried both of them on a trajectory to this point in time.

Rowe took advantage of Antonette's vulnerability after disclosing the story that he was an altar boy. He knew how much she adored them from the time they attended Mass together, and he had never told her about that part of his life.

"Antonette, I would love for you to join us in Rome," he pleaded.

Antonette was almost in tears when she saw the look in his eyes and realized he was dead serious about the invitation. She was still working on shoving the rest of the meat in the spy bunker freezer.

"There you go. The last of the meat. Well, what were you saying again, in Rome? What are we going to do in Rome in December? Wouldn't it be more enjoyable in April?"

Rowe was quick with his answer, "We can go back there anytime you like, after this trip."

Antonette wanted to scream "YES!" but she held onto it.

"Let me sleep on it, please." She gave a sweet smile.

"I didn't know you were this hard to persuade," said Rowe.

"But I am with you now, so let's enjoy this present moment while we can," said Antonette.

"Does that mean you're coming with me to Rome?"

"I am going to take a shower," said Antonette, pretending to ignore Rowe, but deep inside, she was screaming a big fat 'Yes!'"

Rowe persisted in an answer.

"You know, I overheard you when Mark said we're going to Rome, and you asked if you could come." You said, "Yes, I'd like to come!" Rowe looked at her enticingly while she gradually moved upstairs and then tried to run away. Antonette darted down the hall, and Rowe finally caught her in one of the bedrooms.

"I got 'ya!" he grabbed her waist, and she squealed, then laughed. Rowe kissed her passionately, and they moved over to the bed. He slowly kissed Antonette on the back of her neck, sending lightning down her spine. Rowe and Antonette stayed in that bedroom all night. Somehow, he knew exactly how she wanted to be touched and met her every wish without either one speaking a word. Antonette likewise used her sixth sense to know exactly what Rowe wanted, and he groaned a deep and hungry growl as he exploded inside her. They lay in each other's arms until both drifted off to sleep, not even thinking about the mission that was ahead of them.

"Yes, I will go to Rome," Antonette whispered in Rowe's ear when they woke up the next day.

Rowe went to work and filed his request for two weeks of leave. He said he would be back, and his Veteran colleagues said they would cover him but, at the same time, reminded him of the goods they wanted upon his return.

Rowe laughed and teased, "That's bribery!"

They all laughed, as Rowe had always brought some interesting things for them anyway. When he had returned from his previous trip, he gave them an ivory tooth from the Horn of Africa. His men treasured it to this day. They told him to take care of himself and that they wanted him back soon. They were getting used to Rowe's excuses, but they really didn't know what he was up to on these long absences.

One of his friends bellowed, "I am afraid of what I don't know!"

And they all teased him and laughed about it. But as fellow veterans, they understood and respected Rowe's confidentiality and privacy, so they left it alone.

For Rowe, working there was just an undercover job. HG Hawk placed him there for a reason and had an MOU (Memorandum of Understanding) with the Agency's director. Only Hawk, Rowe, and the director knew about the clandestine operation.

As he returned home, Antonette told him she had filed her two-week leave of absence too and had said they were going on a vacation. She had accumulated a lot of it as she had transferred some leaves from her old job. She had a good boss who told her to take care of herself and to return safely.

Rowe then took the surprise out of his pocket and handed it to Antonette. It was a beautiful little red box. Rowe got a thrill out of surprising Antonette with unexpected gifts. He enjoyed watching her reaction and how it inflated the expectation of what was inside the box. Antonette was super surprised.

"What is this?" Her eyes were blazing with excitement with a broad smile that her face could not contain.

"Just open it." he bit his lip, revering in her anticipation.

Rowe smiled as he watched her open the box. It was a beautiful pair of princess cut diamond earrings, at least half a carat.

Antonette gasped and wrapped her arms around Rowe, who was pleased with her delight. She put them on immediately.

"Princess cut diamonds for my princess." He said with all the love in his voice.

"Rowe, you are truly my Knight in Shining Armor!" she squealed.

They kissed, then laughed and kissed again. Rowe was ecstatic that Antonette would be going to Rome with him and the family.

CHAPTER 6

"The true soldier fights not because he hates what is in front of him, but because he loves what is behind him."

(Chesterson, G.K.)

They retrieved their passports and equipment the next morning from Alpha seven as HG Hawk had described and proceeded to the gates, first-class seats. They arrived at Kuwait International Airport at midnight and were bused to Ali Al Salem Air Base, which was about an hour ride.

This was Antonette's first mission with the CIA. She was alert, and vividly remembered the first time her unit, the 101st Airborne Division Air Assault, was deployed to Iraq and staged in Kuwait at first, prior to Iraq. She sat right in the front seat with her rifle like a sniper. She was laughing silently at that image of herself, and Rowe noticed it. She just winked at him, saying she was okay and just reminiscing about the past. He held her hand and put it on his lap. It felt good to be with her man, her beloved. She would follow him to the ends of the Earth. Silently, they knew that their purpose was to help humanity by combining their special gifts.

"It feels good to be together," Rowe said blissfully.

"I forgot that you could read my mind. I better be careful of what I think." She smiled at him.

Rowe smirked and enjoyed playing with Antonette's soft hand until the bus came to a grinding halt.

They arrived at Ali Al Salem, and after they had introduced themselves to the greeters, they were blindfolded and taken to their mission site for the next couple of days. When they removed their blindfolds, Antonette thought it looked like Rowe's spy bunker, only smaller but still highly decorated with intel communication equipment. There were lots of sandbags in every corner and bunk beds. Each desk had two monitors and a secure desktop, and the TVs were as large as 85 inches, four TVs total in that room. She had thought they would be working in a mock

Pentagon situation room, but she finally admitted this was far from it. They were assigned to the same shift, as promised by HG Hawk.

The next day they were briefed intensively on what had happened, what was currently happening, and what was going to happen. Silently, Antonette said it sounded familiar, although what was about to happen was all new to her. This was a rescue operation, and the two souls depended on their collaborative skills. But her faith and confidence in Rowe were making her even firm and strong, and she promised herself that she could do this mission successfully. Suddenly it reminded her of the time she was learning to drive a stick shift in Iraq for the first time. All it took was a vote of confidence, and then she had mastered it and gained everyone's confidence that she could do just about anything if she put her mind and heart into it. This had been true her entire life.

The following day, they boarded a C-17 to Qatar and were once again blindfolded and then led to their new worksite in Qatar. This time it was larger, and there was more equipment to use and more sandbags. Remote surveillance had become Rowe's specialty, and he was excellent at it. He could also fly UAVs or unmanned aerial vehicles. He did it in Bucca, Iraq, before he became a Fed. Rowe noticed that there were very few cleared translators on the site, and cameras surrounded the place.

On their first night shift, both Rowe and Antonette began their remote surveillance in gathering intelligence so the U.S. SFG could rescue two American POWs. They sized up the situation and made mental notes of the layout and terrain. Neither of them took their eyes off of the screens as the SFG waited for the right moment to proceed. Antonette had 'that feeling' and instinctively knew that something was about to happen.

"Watch your backs," she said as Rowe scanned the screens.

They saw four enemies coming and warned the SFG of the imminent attack. Six more tangos were approaching from the left and right, and the troops fired at them. *Tarratatatat!* Very sharp and loud bursts of machine guns hit the tangos. Rowe and

Antonette said that nobody was inside the room, so the SFG warrior leader kicked the door with his automatic weapon drawn and ready to fire.

"Veer to the left," Rowe commanded.

The next SFG warrior quickly took the steps while the other covered him from any oncoming tangos.

"There are two men upstairs, assumed to be the package." Rowe guided them with confidence.

More troops went up, and four were left below the steps. *Tarratatatat!* More machine-gun bursts and the tangos were down. They saw two bearded men on the cot wearing dark clothes with their hands tied. The SFG leader asked who they were, what their names were, and whether they spoke English. The rescuers were testing them to find out if they were the package of the mission.

The SFG leader asked one more time, pointing his gun at the bearded men. One of them finally spoke in American English.

"Untie me, fuck you!" he scowled.

"Get us the fuck outta here!" the other one added, shouting.

With that, the leader determined that they were the objects of the mission and sliced the ropes binding their hands with his tactical knife.

"It's clear to the left," Rowe said, and they trusted his words. "Go, Go, Go! More tangos heading your way; hit the air!"

The last two men out the door burst their machine guns on the incoming enemies. *Tarratatatat!*

"Go, go, go!" The leader yelled as they loaded into the Black Hawk.

They were safe with the American POWs. But it was not time to celebrate yet. Sensors blared inside the chopper as it gained altitude. *Wooosh!* The Black Hawk pilot carefully maneuvered and evaded an oncoming surface-to-air missile.

"Holy fuck! That was close!" The pilot said quietly to himself but remained outwardly calm and in control in front of the group. After it had cleared the Black Hawk, Rowe and Antonette assured

them that no other incoming missiles or RPGs were detected and they would guide them to safety. Rowe's mic was still open, and he was still monitoring the screens when suddenly someone yelled in the background from the worksite in Qatar.

"Grenade!"

Rowe reacted instantly and grabbed Antonette. They dashed farther away and dodged behind a pile of sandbags before the grenade exploded. Rowe knew they had two to six seconds before the grenade exploded, as he learned it from his Special Forces missions.

Meanwhile, the Special Forces had delivered the American POWs to safe ground. While the medics evaluated and treated their wounds, they were all wondering about the grenade explosion in Qatar. The Special Forces were worried about their excellent guides, their eyes and ears: Rowe and Antonette, who had helped them to carry out the mission successfully.

HG Hawk and her chief of staff were speechless, they had heard the blast through Rowe's open mic, and this was an unexpected event. The rest of the staff in HQ who had monitored the rescue on TV were in a similar state of shock. They had another TV monitoring Rowe and Antonette's worksite, but the connection had been severed, and static filled that screen.

They were all quiet except HG Hawk, who barked out orders to keep trying to reach the agents, Rowe and Antonette. She was deeply worried and perturbed; a feeling of dysphoria washed over her. HG wanted all resources deployed to find out where they were and have her agent team rescued as soon as possible. Her men had found and arrested the terrorist who threw the grenade into the situation room. It had been reported that there was a spy inside the remote surveillance worksite, but they hadn't been able to locate him. None of the guards securing the perimeter had noticed the spy approaching the worksite. He had walked by and casually tossed a grenade where Rowe, Antonette, and other troops were working.

HG Hawk's perturbation was relieved when she received word that the troops had rescued all of the people from the worksite blast. Rowe and Antonette were slightly wounded, but miraculously they were alive. For treatment, they were medically evacuated to the base hospital and then to Landstuhl, Germany. Evidently, they were required to don protective wear to reduce human casualties associated with explosive ordnance disposal. They were wearing bomb suits that protected their head, neck, thorax, and lower extremities. These were the product of confirmed repeatability and robust testing to evaluate the suits.

Rowe, Antonette, and the others suffered only minor or quaternary injuries from the grenade blast. They were medically evaluated to examine minor cuts and burns, checked for crush injuries such as hypertension or breathing problems from the smoke, and assessed for any possible brain injuries. Seven days later, Antonette and Rowe returned home. The doctor had allowed recovery from home; they would be medically evaluated every week until they had fully recovered from minor concussions.

It was a remarkable accomplishment to all who had labored in this undertaking to rescue the two hostages. What an achievement it was! HG Hawk was the one most grateful for the successful mission.

They received an invitation from the White House and a high recommendation from the CIA Director, HG Hawk. The Special Forces and the POWs had joined them on the stage in the recognition ceremony. Both Rowe and Antonette's families were filled with pride as the President, and the First Lady were donning their Presidential Medal of Freedom with distinction.

"This was a delicate situation. It took dauntless and dedicated people to support the troops amidst danger to accomplish this rescue in unfriendly territory. Your loyalty and selfless service will be forever remembered," the President said as he honored Rowe, Antonette, and the rest of the 5th SFG and rendered the POWs with medals as well.

Everyone applauded as the President ended his speech. After the speech, Hawk approached Antonette and Rowe and congratulated them on a job well done. HG Hawk told Antonette that she never doubted her talent and knew that she would 'handle' any challenges of the situation well.

And then she turned to Rowe and said, "Well, you proved your mettle. We knew that nothing would prevent you from heroic deeds, especially with your loved one sitting next to you."

"Thank you! We are proud to serve our nation," Rowe said.

"We were happy to help," Antonette added.

"Congratulations to both of you again." HG Hawk said as she turned to leave and then whispered,

"We'll see you both in a few months."

Rowe whispered something in her ear that Antonette couldn't hear.

HG Hawk winked, and with thumbs up, she said, "I got 'ya!" and then left.

"What was that all about?" Antonette demanded.

"A follow-up mission," Rowe replied mysteriously. "C'mere, let's join the crowd and dance, shall we, my little heroine?"

"Whatever, Shaq Diesel," she retorted. Rowe burst out laughing and grabbed her hand.

They danced with others on the floor to celebrate freedom and revel in their victory. With hearts full of gratitude, they thanked Heaven for their quick recovery.

CHAPTER 7

"True love waits. The heart aches through distance and tears and separation. But the embers of a true love's flame will always burn in the hearts of two souls who have loved each other timelessly."
(Arnold, Barbara D.)

As they were standing by the Fontana di Trevi or Trevi Fountain, the most famous water fountain in Italy, the serenades started playing in the background. The music paused, and Rowe knelt down before Antonette. Antonette gasped and covered her mouth, as this was the moment she had dreamed of so many times.

"Antonette, you are the love of my life whom I have trusted since the war in the middle east that brought us closer together. You have been my wings of inspiration and my reason for living. I want you to be my wife in God's eyes and people's eyes. I never want to lose you again, ever. Will you marry me?" Rowe proposed as he gazed into Antonette's eyes.

Antonette's tears welled. She yanked Rowe's handkerchief from his breast pocket before he could react, and smeared it with mascara-stained tears, then laughed at the result. Rowe laughed. He had always loved Antonette for her antics and her sense of humor. He would love to be part of her laughter forever if she accepted his proposal.

After wiping her tears away, Antonette finally composed herself and said, "Yes, of course, my love Rowe. You are the best thing that ever happened in my life after the war, and I thank God for finding you again. As you said, I will never lose you again. I accept you as the love of my life and am honored to become your wife."

With that, the serenades proceeded with their music, and the dancers showed up and formed a circle around Antonette and Rowe. Antonette thought it was like a fairy tale or a dream, and she did not want to wake up from it. But Rowe told her it was real, grabbed her by the waistline, and kissed her passionately until Antonette agreed that everything was real indeed. The scene was surreal, though, with all the music, dancers, and strangers happily surrounding them. But it was truly happening, and what could be more romantic than getting engaged by the fountain in Italy, with the Vatican overlooking and blessing their newfound happiness?

Back at the hotel, Rowe's children and grandchildren did not have any idea what was going on by the water fountain. They thought it was like any other regular evening where people gathered by the fountain, danced and celebrated each day and night joyfully. It didn't occur to them that their dad had formally proposed to Antonette, and they were now celebrating with each other and passersby at the Trevi fountain. If only they had checked it out, perhaps they would be celebrating with them all night long in front of the fountain, but Rowe had wanted this sacred moment to be just between him and Antonette and to share the news with the rest of the family the next day.

It was 10 am on Sunday, and Zed went to the hotel's restaurant downstairs to join the family for brunch. She found the family waiting except for her dad and Antonette. They waited for about 15 more minutes, and the couple had still not shown up. It was quite odd because neither of them was ever late. There was an increasing concern about them being late for the scheduled brunch as the minutes ticked by. Emy and Zed decided to go up the elevators, found their suite, and knocked on the door to Antonette and Rowe's room. Nobody answered. They were agitated and rushed back down the elevators to ask for help from the reception desk to unlock the room and to check on their dad and Antonette's status. Once they reached the desk, they saw their dad and Antonette strolling through a revolving door with Antonette's left arm tucked in Rowe's right arm, looking far smitten with each other. They seemed to be exultant and didn't care about the world or the time or things around them. It was now their world, relishing every moment they had missed for the last 12 years. Zed and Emy were tearful just from watching the sweet couple with tender feelings for each other. They looked so much in love, feeling incredibly special with one another, and wonderfully validating their feelings for each other. They didn't want to admit that they had been worried, looking for them and wondering why they were late for brunch.

Instead, they both greeted the couple with open arms and said, "We miss you both. How was the weather outside?"

Antonette was the first to hug both women and thought it was so endearing to see them this morning. "Good morning, my beauties!" she said lovingly.

But Rowe knew his kids very well, so he said, "We just stepped outside to breathe some fresh air. We haven't forgotten about the brunch, and we're both doing fine!"

Zed and Emy blushed, and Rowe said, "Let's go to the table and join the others." Once again, he offered his arm to his new fiancée, who lovingly obliged and tucked her left hand into his elbow.

Before sitting down, Rowe quipped, "How is everyone doing this morning? Why are you all looking agitated? Is there something wrong?" They finally answered and told the truth, that they were worried when the couple had not come down for brunch on time because Rowe had never been never late on any occasion. He was always about half an hour, in fact. Zed apologetically said that when they did not show up 15 minutes after the hour, their concerns heightened, and they had knocked on their suite several times. They went to the desk to ask for help to unlock the door, and that's when they had showed up at the entrance doors.

Instead of getting upset for not trusting them like adults, Rowe complimented them on their resourcefulness. Then he laughed and apologized for not letting anyone know that Antonette and he had decided to take an early morning stroll by the Trevi Fountain. His kids said it was alright, and they were just happy to see them looking so relaxed and in love.

Rowe positioned himself in the head chair, with Antonette to his right, tapped the glass with his spoon, and said, "Everybody, can I get your attention please… last night, who went out and checked the commotion by the Trevi Fountain?"

No one raised their hand.

Rowe continued, "Well, I proposed to Antonette last night…" Rowe paused and looked lovingly at Antonette, "…And she accepted!" Everyone gasped and clapped.

"Congratulations! Oh my God, Congratulations!" And then they noticed the beautiful 6-carat diamond ring that was perched elegantly on Antonette's left ring finger. Rowe had an exquisite taste; it was a unique three-stone halo diamond engagement ring that sparkled like the sun and expressed their commitment to each other. Antonette still could not believe she was now formally Rowe's fiancée.

John raised his mimosa glass, and every adult on their table copied him. "I'd like to propose a toast. Here is to a very happy engagement and a lifetime of love, cheers!"

Zed followed, "Cheers to the two of you and to the love you two share!" And everyone said, "Cheers!"

Emy raised her glass and said, "Dad, Antonette, here is to the wonderful two of you, so lucky to have found each other again!" "Cheers!"

Armand raised his glass and said, "Here is to your happy engagement!" "Cheers!"

William raised his glass and also proposed a toast, "Here's to celebrating your engagement!" "Cheers!"

Rosgil raised her glass, saying, "I wish you all happiness on your engagement!" "Cheers!"

Rowe was about to speak when Mark raised his tiny glass of water and proposed a toast.

"I can't wait for the wedding, balloons, and flowers!" Mark said enthusiastically.

There was laughter, and everyone said, "Cheers to that!"

Everybody lined up to congratulate the newly engaged couple, hugging Antonette and then their dad. Everyone was so happy that their dad had finally proposed to the woman he had loved for so long. The children and grandkids had immediately loved and accepted Antonette as part of the family wholeheartedly. She was loving, kind, talented, humorous, and perfectly suited for their dad and their family. Their dad needed such a loving woman to move on with life after the loss of their mother, and they seemed to be compatible at all angles. They not only loved each other incessantly but also had a common ground by both being zealous patriots, and they often spoke the same military language. They were recipients of medals for saving troops in a rescue mission and survivors from the grenade blast in Qatar. They were the indivisible heroes and would finally become husband and wife.

Rowe's children had grown up in a military community while he was in the Special Forces Group, and they were known as "military brats." Rowe thanked God they had grown up without major issues. There were the usual parenting challenges, and Rowe had always participated in their lives when not on missions.

As they waited for brunch to be served, Rowe remembered when William had a fight with his classmate. He had to request leave from work to attend to his son's school issue and resolved it right there. Rowe had such a good attitude, and if not for him, William would have ended up in detention for a week. William had a fight with his classmate, which was clearly not a fault of his own. His classmate teased him and called him "Gringo", a term used in Latin America or Spain to refer to a foreigner, especially one of U.S. or British descent. But the truth was, William was born in the United States, just like his father. Rowe met his late wife in Puerto Rico, they got married, and he had brought her over to the United States. William's classmate had been facetiously calling him Gringo and was looking for a fight. William ignored it a couple of times but fought back on the third tease. Rowe thought it was fair for William to have defended his honor, but did not say it. He apologized to the principal and asked that the other child should stop calling names. It was racial and not good for the school and the community, especially since they were inside the military compound. The principal apologized and promised to add it to their school policy that racial slur or such behavior would not be tolerated. It would be strictly followed, and whoever committed such an act would be suspended from the school. Rowe was quite satisfied with the decision and thanked the principal profusely. Rowe took his son home and had a man-to-man talk with him. Once again, Rowe had become their hero.

Rowe thought about the trouble they had with his daughters when they were typical teenagers. At times, they were disrespectful to their parents, and Rowe knew they had a bad circle of friends. But he kept the lines of communication open, huddled up with his two girls, and discussed their attitudes. They changed and matured gradually as they grew older and eventually apologized to their parents. They felt guilty as they started having families of their own and promised to raise their children with good attitudes. The girls had also been taking such great care of Rowe since their mother passed away to show how much they loved and respected him.

Rowe's granddaughter Isabella pulled his shirt and snapped him out of the memory.

"Grand! Can I be at the wedding?" she asked.

"Of course, you will be the flower girl!" Rowe said, and he proceeded with the wedding plans announcement.

Rowe continued, "I know you have been waiting for this, and don't tell me 'no' because I know you..." and everyone laughed. "I know you are all excited to plan for the wedding. We'd like to start with 'Operation Wedding Plan' after we come back from this vacation. Zed will be in charge of the planning, being the oldest child, and she can delegate duties. But I would like to remind you to keep it modest, and invite our relatives and friends, including a few relatives from distant places such as Puerto Rico and the Philippines."

They all smiled, as they all knew it was not at all going to be simple because they wanted it to be the wedding of the century. Although Rowe and Antonette were in their 50s, their wedding would be in the Headline News because of their military achievements and because Rowe had been a popular figure due to his innovative inventions. Despite Rowe's advice, the children had already started planning to keep it simple. But they were all thrilled and couldn't just wait to get back home to dig into it.

"Emy will be taking care of the media publicity. She and Armand can handle the catering and help with the menu." Zed exclaimed. Armand knew exactly the perfect chef for the reception and mentioned that he had met him at one of the fundraising events in Georgetown, Washington, DC. They had five more days left and couldn't wait to return to the United States and continue their wedding plans for Rowe and Antonette. They spent the next 5 days touring Italy, visiting all the amazing water fountains, and taking tons of pictures.

On the last day of touring, the whole family went to Trevi Fountain one last time. Antonette wore light-colored blue jeans, a black jacket, RayBan sunglasses, and a baseball hat. Rowe had worn dark jeans and a ridiculous T-shirt that said, *"I proposed at Trevi Fountain."* Antonette teased him about it, but he said he didn't care. He felt so proud that he had finally done it. He had almost spilled the secret and proposed that night when Antonette had made it challenging to accept his invitation to go to Rome. He was so glad he held onto the secret and that he had gotten his wishes because he needed nothing more but Antonette by his side.

After a full day of sightseeing, the family slowly walked back to the hotel, dazed by the excitement. They were all talking nonstop about the wedding plans as the group filtered into the lobby of the hotel. They all went to their rooms; Zed kicked off her shoes and flopped on the couch in the sitting area while the kids went to their bedroom area. John, her husband, opened the fridge for iced water. He asked Zed if she wanted iced water too and then hollered to ask JR, Mark, and Isabella.

JR said, "I would just like some bottled water, dad."

John called Mark, "Hey Mark, what would you like to drink? Mark? Maaaark? Mark! Where are you?" John went around the entire room and even checked outside the room but didn't find Mark.

"What's going on?" Zed asked when she saw him frantically looking out in the hallway. John was now clearly agitated and said the unthinkable; Mark was missing. It was one thing for him to wander off occasionally at home, but in a foreign country, John felt sick.

"He is not in the room and nowhere to be found." He hollered.

"Oh my God! How could this happen?" Exclaimed Zed.

Isabella asked, "Where is Mark?"

JR was getting upset, "What do you mean, where is Mark?"

"Okay, calm down, everyone. Let's call Grand and let him know Mark is missing," John said, but Zed was already in tears. Her hands were shaking as she picked up the phone and dialed her dad's room. She told Rowe that Mark was missing, and the phone became silent.

"Mark is missing," Zed repeated, sobbing. "I was holding his hand when we toured the water fountains, and I don't remember when he got loose. I suppose it was when I was taking pictures." Rowe advised her to calm down. "Okay, slow down, and let's backtrack. You said you held his hand as we toured all of the water fountains. Did you check to make sure he's not downstairs in the lobby? You know how Mark is. He is always curious about things."

Zed's eyes were red and swollen from crying. Her husband was upset too and wanted to run outside immediately and look for Mark before it got dark. They called Emy and Armand and their youngest brother William and his wife, Rosgil. Rosgil stayed in the hotel with the other children since she was pregnant and already tired from the day of walking. She asked William to call her with any updates, and her husband agreed.

Rowe and Antonette thought about what places Mark might try to visit. Antonette asked Rowe what Mark's favorite place in Rome was? Rowe said that he particularly liked Trevi and also the fountain where the James Bond film Spectre was staged. Antonette then suggested they go there to see if Mark was wandering around that area. They phoned Zed and John and said they would go to the Fontana dell'Acqua Paola or Big Fountain, where the movie was filmed. Zed mentioned Fontana dei Quattro Fiumi. Mark seemed to be fascinated by the four river gods representing the Nile, the Danube, the Ganges, and the Rio de la Plata, reigning beneath a towering Egyptian obelisk.

Rowe concurred and said to go for it and hope that Mark was there. The group split up and scoured the fountains for Mark, but he was nowhere to be found. They had agreed that they would all meet at the Police Station if that failed. Deflated and worried, they found themselves at the police station, and nobody could believe they were about to report a missing boy. John tried to calm Zed, who was now hysterical by this point. Rowe talked to the Commander and described the day's events. He gave a description of Mark and said that they appreciated any support in finding Mark. When word spread through the station that an American boy was missing, one of the Inspectors quickly informed the Commander that there was a little boy named Mark matching the description, who had gotten separated from his parents sitting in the corner of his office.

"Would you like to follow us, please? I think we have found your Mark!" The commander said with a big smile.

Everyone rushed to the path led by the Inspector, and they were all relieved and so happy that the boy was indeed Mark! Zed ran to Mark as soon as they saw him.

She hugged him hard, kissed his forehead, and said, "Where did you go? I was so worried for you. We were all worried. Please don't do that to us ever again!"

John and everyone else hugged Mark. Isabella asked Rowe to put her down on the floor so she could hug her brother Mark too. Zed asked him again where he had been and how he got separated from the group?

Mark answered, "I am alright, mom. I just wanted to go back to the Obelisk for one last look, and when I turned around, everyone was gone. I approached a policeman when I got lost and asked him to take me to the Hotel. Instead, he took me here and told me to wait. I knew you would come for me, and I was never worried. I am alright. I knew you would come." He shrugged calmly.

Rowe saw the gentleness in Mark's face, the calm, serene, and innocent look in his crystal blue eyes. He knew God's Angels were always with him. He had known that he was divinely protected since Mark was a little boy. He had seen the signs that vividly indicated that Mark indeed was different and special.

Rowe mentioned to Antonette that Mark seemed to be attracted to religion as a career.

"He's always been attracted to anything that alludes to religion. Mark has always been interested in holy relics, reading the bible, attending Sunday school, and being an altar boy. He liked doing research studies at a very young age."

Antonette felt excited, "I love that! What an awesome gift!" And she whispered to Rowe, "I would support him fully if he wanted to become a priest." Rowe was not surprised by Antonette's offer. They were both religiously inclined and would love to have a priest or a nun in the family, or priest and a nun. It would be such a blessing.

Rowe finally said, "Alright, let's thank the Inspector and the Commander for their help. I think we should take Mark back to his favorite Obelisk one more time as a group since it was so important to him. We can take some pictures for Mark's future book, 'The time I Got Lost In Rome,' and then we will get back to the hotel for dinner. I am getting hungry now."

Everyone laughed and said in unison, "We all are!"

Rowe offered an envelope to the Commander as a donation for the poor. The Commander said he didn't have to do it, but Rowe was persistent enough, and he finally accepted the offer. Antonette embraced him for it. They had both planned to sponsor several charities at home in the very near future.

CHAPTER 8

Two days after they had returned home from Italy, Rowe reported to duty, while Antonette worked from home in Richmond. The jet lag had finally subsided, and they briefly talked about Antonette giving up her apartment, which would require her to pay a two-month rent penalty for breaking her lease. Rowe wanted her to move in now, instead of after the wedding. They were both ecstatic and looked glowing as they went back to their regular lives in the wake of their engagement. When he came home that day, Rowe wanted to surprise Antonette with another gift, but first, they needed to eat as they both were starving.

"What should we have for dinner?" Rowe asked.

"I am craving pasta!" Antonette said, and got to work in the kitchen while Rowe went to the den to check on a business transaction from the day before.

Antonette made spaghetti with meat and a homemade tomato sauce that she had cooked earlier in the day. She prepared some salad, and made Faggioli soup. The soup filled the kitchen with a delicious rich aroma and had white and red beans, ground beef, fresh tomatoes and tubetti pasta in a savory broth. She also prepared garlic bread with cheese.

Rowe suddenly felt very hungry. "That smells so amazing!" Rowe said as the aroma pulled him towards the kitchen, "Let's eat! Now!"

Rowe set decorative bowls on the table and Antonette filled them with soup. While Rowe warmed two dishes slightly in the microwave, Antonette heaped generous servings of spaghetti on each. She took the salad out of the fridge and sprinkled fresh parmesan on top.

"Mmmmmmmm! Where did you learn to cook like this?" Rowe said after trying the soup.

"I learned the fundamentals of Culinary Arts in Virginia. I used the remaining GI Bill after I had earned my master's degree. I finally indulged in a fun course, and I totally loved it," she said as she garnished the spaghetti with fresh grated Romano cheese and a little bit of fresh parsley. After they had blessed the food, Rowe looked around the table and said, "My love, I can't ask for more. This is simply amazing!" Antonette smiled and gave Rowe a kiss accompanied by a hug before they started to eat.

"Wow, that's a special spaghetti sauce!" Rowe exclaimed. "What is the secret ingredient?"

"I'll never tell!" Antonette said with a wink and agreed that they would have it once a week, and she would also think of other pasta varieties. She loved cooking, and even more, she loved cooking for Rowe.

"There is something about feeding the people I love that makes me so happy," Antonette said.

After they had finished dinner, Antonette made some tea and decaffeinated coffee. Then she surprised Rowe with cheesecake and blueberry sauce that she had made in the morning for dessert. She also had some vanilla ice cream in case Rowe wanted some. Rowe's eyes feasted on the cheesecake and ice cream.

He said, "Mira, I can't resist!"

Antonette said, "Gotta' have some sinful desserts once in a blue moon."

Rowe rubbed his belly but insisted that he still had a little room for the cheesecake with blueberry sauce. Antonette smiled as she put a small slice on the dessert plate, and they both shared it.

"There's more cheesecake in the fridge," she said with a big smile. Rowe laughed at her challenge and said, "We better save the rest for tomorrow." Then he sipped his decaf coffee while Antonette finished her hot tea.

After dinner, Rowe helped with rinsing the dishes and putting them in the dishwasher after dinner. Before Antonette could turn around from drying her hands on the kitchen towel, Rowe wrapped his arms around her waist to keep her still. He pulled something from his pocket and placed a small velvet red box in her hand.

Antonette said, "Oh mi amor! What is this?" She turned around, slowly opened the red box and tried to restrain her excitement. It was a beautiful diamond tennis bracelet.

Antonette blushed as Rowe looked into her eyes and offered, "May I?"

Antonette nodded as Rowe took the bracelet out of the box and put it on Antonette's right wrist.

"Rowe, this is beautiful! I don't know what to say!"

"Say nothing else other than you love me."

"I can say that without a bracelet, you don't have to bribe me for it!" Her cheeks flushed even more.

Rowe laughed and said, "Oh, how I missed you, girl. You always crack me up!"

And then he looked into Antonette's eyes and gently kissed her on the forehead, on both cheeks, and finally kissed her lips, full of passion biting her lower lip gently. Antonette wrapped her arms around his neck, and he lifted her off the ground. They both remembered the night in Baghdad airport; it was just like when they had kissed goodbye. Except for this time, it was not a goodbye, and they would never be separated. So, they are no longer two but have become one flesh. Therefore, what God has joined together, let no one separate." (Matthew 19:6).

"I don't feel like watching TV tonight. Let's go to bed. What do you say?" asked Rowe.

"Well, as long as you carry me, then I shall say, Aye, aye, Captain!" Antonette replied with a salute.

Rowe scooped her up and carried her to their bedroom. They picked up where they had left off in Rome. Both were still grateful for this moment, to be here in a peaceful land without the sounds of gunfights outside the wire. The past was never far from their minds, but they were both learning how to live in the present. To live each moment in time as if it was the only thing that mattered, to live with grateful hearts for the joy in each day.

Zed and Emy had been busy since they arrived in Virginia. They had all finally agreed to choose one aspect of the wedding to coordinate, but they hired a wedding planner to free up some time and energy. This would allow them to focus more on entertaining guests on the day of the wedding. They wanted the ceremony and reception to be remembered for a long time since it would probably be a while before there was another wedding in the family.

William had said that his wife was feeling tired with the pregnancy, so they were taking it easy but more than ecstatic to help with choosing the floral arrangements. Emy suggested a location for the wedding and disclosed to everyone that their dad would be marveled.

Zed guessed "Fort Lee."

But Emy said, "Nope! Actually, it would be inconvenient if we were to use Fort Lee. Can you imagine having to provide the Visitor Center on base with a list of people attending, and they would all have to show their military ID cards or be sponsored by a military cardholder?"

Both Zed and William agreed. William guessed some potential wedding places too, but Emy said it was none of those.

"Ok. We give up." Zed and William gave the hand gesture.

Emy triumphantly said, "Appomattox Boat Harbor dock, of course! They have everything there, the awesome clubhouse, a romantic outdoor wedding venue, the stage for the band, and it will be perfect for my guys to cater the food!"

Zed exhaled a big sigh of relief, gave her a hug, and kissed her sister on the cheek. It was perfect. Emy returned the hug and kissed Zed on the cheeks; they first laughed, then cried tears of joy. William joined their circle, and the three of them hugged and kissed each other's cheeks.

It was as if they could feel their mom in spirit, and she was happy knowing that they were taking care of their dad; and that the children had received the gift of a loving woman in their lives too. They formed a circle of best friends' arms and stayed that way for about 10 minutes. They cried, laughed, and prayed that God would bless their mom so she would rest well in Heaven. Zed said a quiet prayer and asked God to bless them too and guide them to be their dad's best supportive children, and to bless their kids, in addition to Antonette.

"Amen." the group said as they dispersed.

Zed called Suzanne, the wedding planner, and told her where the wedding would take place. Suzanne had a lot of questions about the number of people invited and what kind of an event they wanted.

Zed told her it would be an opulent, luxurious, star-studded wedding and that she couldn't wait to see the elaborate pavilions.

"I can't wait for all of the guests to witness the ceremony where Antonette and Rowe finally exchange their vows. They seem *indivisible* through their long love story of meeting and becoming separated, then reuniting. With their selfless service to their country, it's time to give back to these heroes and recognize them with an ostentatious wedding." Zed told Suzanne.

Rowe and Antonette would show the world their love for each other by finally saying "I do" in the presence of family and friends after 12 long years of separation.

Suzanne was amazed and said she was ecstatic to decorate the place. She'd take care of everything, the pavilion, the clubhouse, and the wedding. There would be climbing plants covering the arbor arch, beautiful flowers, balloons, live music, delicious food, and champagne everywhere. Zed told her to invite no more than 400 guests, including Rowe's friends from the PX. She told Suzanne about Rowe and Antonette's amazing story of reuniting at the PX that day. Suzanne was charmed and impressed and promised Zed that everyone would have a wonderful experience at the wedding. All the family had to do was show up and enjoy the reception!

Zed replied, "Inshallah," as she learned from her father from his multiple deployments in the Middle East a long time ago. She added, "It sounds too good to be true," and they both laughed. Zed gave the details to Suzanne that her sister Emy would be taking care of the layered wedding cake from her bakery, and Will, her brother, would provide the menu soon. Suzanne showed a list of bands, and Zed was so excited to look at the selections. It would be nice to find good music performers and add to the entertainment. She asked Susanne if they could have surprise firecrackers on the boat with the words, "Best wishes and Congratulations, Rowe & Antonette!"

Suzanne covered her mouth and exclaimed that it was an amazing idea and would be euphoric. They both giggled and continued with more wedding plans for Rowe and Antonette. Zed told Suzanne that money was not an issue and that her dad and Antonette deserved the best. Suzanne replied that she was not worried about that, and they would be happy with just the outcome. She reminded Zed to order nice wedding weather and good wine, and they giggled again.

"I will ask the Blessed Mother for the good weather. We know Jesus would give His mother anything she'd ask of Him. If we run out of good wine, though, I'm asking Jesus for that one!"

To which they both said, "Amen!"

The day came to try on the wedding dress. The seamstress was recommended by Suzanne, the wedding planner who had told Zed and Antonette that she had known her for 34 years. When Suzanne had said that she trusted the seamstress for a perfect fit, everyone believed her.

Antonette looked at the wedding gown, and it was even prettier than she thought it would ever be. She listened when the seamstress said to put it on slowly and carefully. The gown had an A-line / Princess cut with tulle, long sheer sleeves with lace, and a beautiful lace form-fitting bodice. The seamstress was awestruck by Antonette's beauty in the gorgeous Lalamira wedding gown. Antonette didn't recognize herself as she stood in front of the mirror. No doubt the gown was gorgeous, and she restrained her emotions while the seamstress was working on fitting it perfectly to her frame. There would be one final fitting, and Antonette thought she wanted to make sure the dress would still fit perfectly.

"It's easier to take a little in at the final fitting rather than try to add fabric after I do these alterations." The seamstress advised Antonette as she showed her where the train should be attached and detached. Antonette got the hint and knew that she could not gain any weight between now and the wedding, but it was alright if she lost a few pounds. The seamstress spread out the train and said, "Ah, Senorita Antonette, this is simply gorgeous!"

It took them about two hours to find what needed to be trimmed, taken in, and let out in different areas of the dress.

"How long would you like for the sleeves to be? The seamstress asked.

"Very long," Antonette said with a straight face, and they both laughed. "Actually, I wanted a thumbhole to keep the sleeves in place, so I do not have to wear gloves."

The seamstress agreed, saying that it made perfect sense, and added that Antonette was actually the first to have a wedding dress with thumbholes. The seamstress was fascinated by the idea and added it to her catalog for future sales. They finally finished, and Rowe picked her up from the bridal shop at noon and asked what she would like for lunch.

"How about a small salad?" Antonette sadly said that she was immediately on a diet to make sure she would fit into the gown and look amazing for the wedding.

Rowe chuckled and said, "Women, women, women! You look beautiful just as you are, don't change a thing!"

Antonette just smiled and said, "You're just jealous that I have restraint."

With that, Rowe became defensive and said, "Me, jealous? Mama mia, I am happy with my tuxedo. By the way, just wait and see."

Antonette smiled and calmly asked, "Really? How did that go anyway? Did everything fit, or does some need to be adjusted?"

Rowe said, "Um, as a matter of fact, I need to be on a diet too and lose a few pounds. Too much spaghetti, I would say. I blame your good cooking!" Antonette laughed, so they agreed to eat healthy together until the wedding. They each had a low sugar detox Kale and Apple smoothie and a small salad for lunch. Their day went by really fast as the two tried to suppress their excitement about the wedding. As they drove home, Antonette was wondering how the wedding ring would look with her engagement ring. They had stopped at the jewelry shop before they had parted ways to try on their wedding clothes. The contour wedding band with channel set stones and milgrain beadwork was just as brilliant as the engagement ring.

They had agreed on protein and vegetables for dinner. Antonette served Salmon over salad greens with walnuts, kalamata olives, goat cheese, and a sesame dressing. Afterward, they enjoyed decaf coffee and tea as they discussed their workweek and some wedding plans. They went for a 2-mile walk after dinner and would continue to do so with the motivation of fitting into their wedding clothes. They used to do it during their military career as well, running or walking to lose weight. Doing it together seemed like much more fun now that they had a common goal to work towards.

"The house is really quiet without the grandkids," said Antonette once they had returned.

Rowe agreed and said, "I don't miss them as much now that you're here with me."

"That's not true! I see your face when Isabella likes to hold onto your pants, saying that she will love you forever if you carry her?" Antonette said as they headed to the bedroom.

Rowe laughed and turned on the TV while Antonette went to rinse off after the walk. He looked at movies briefly, flipping the remote from one channel to another before switching to Fox News. They were talking about troops withdrawing from Afghanistan.

"They have been saying that for 20 years, and we're still there," Rowe said, clearly disturbed.

"WHAT?" Antonette yelled from the bathroom.

"The news was talking about troops withdrawing from Afghanistan, and I said that they have been saying the same thing since 20 years ago, and we're still there." He repeated.

Antonette finished her shower and said, "That's so true. We'd like to have our troops back. We can help our Afghan allies even from here. But the thing is, the food and other items left there might be intercepted and would land in the wrong hands. Where are the superheroes when we need them?" Antonette said emphatically. "Why can't I be Superwoman? I want to be a Superwoman, dammit!"

Rowe chuckled and said, "Then I would like to be a Superhero too, so both of us will be guardians against terror. Yep, two retired vets turned into Superheroes. I like it!"

They both silently wished they had supernatural powers to be used for the greatest good and to protect our Freedom. In their 50-year-old bodies, their patriotic hearts were still 25. Rowe and Antonette had been passionate warriors and wished they could continue as public servants by being superheroes. Something deep in their souls made them want to save people and save the world. They were zealous to help protect people from harm and wished they could have some sort of special power to purge evil and have peace on earth. They both knew that they already had extraordinary gifts, but neither was sure how they could be used for the greater good. Indeed, by combining their unique gifts, it would lead to positive outcomes, just like in Qatar.

Finally, Antonette walked out of the bathroom and wore her bathrobe to the kitchen to warm some milk. She didn't hear Rowe following her to the kitchen, who surprised her by kissing her ears, the back of her neck, and slowly going down to her small back until the bathrobe fell off to the floor.

"This is why I don't miss the kids when you are here," Rowe said in a deep voice. He turned her around, facing him, and admired her naked body before he cupped her right breast and then the left while kissing her lightly on the mouth and gradually went down to kiss and gently bite her nipples. He wasn't satisfied with that and went further down and kissed her abdomen and then parted her legs and kissed her there. Antonette was helpless. Rowe pressed Antonette to the edge of the kitchen counter and began to make love to her. She gave a deep moan as he made love to her until they both came simultaneously. Rowe kissed her nipples again, her neck, and then her lips.

"I love you. I wanted to do this to you in Baghdad when we were in my chu," he said, looking into her eyes. "Too bad you distracted my thoughts with those shirts. I also wanted to kiss you… if you had turned around after I clasped your necklace, I might have done it. Forget all the rules. I wanted to make love to you then and not stop until we were both exhausted and drained…." Antonette just looked into his longing blue eyes and kissed him passionately.

Antonette remembered when she met Rowe the first time. They both were attracted to each other the first time they met in Fort Jackson, South Carolina. But Antonette restrained her silent freedom to want a relationship with him because he was married. She did not want to break any relationship. She had once read: "A house built on another woman's tears won't stand."

They were then separated by war and life. When they met again in Baghdad, something was different that time. They could have met anywhere, but of all places, they met again in Baghdad. In a war zone infested with insurgents, where one had a bounty on their head. They were so happy to see each other again. By then, they knew that there was something special between their souls. But Rowe was still married, and so she held back. She had been divorced for two years, but she was not about to get involved in a complicated relationship. She thought it would be too much for her to have such a relationship in addition to being at war in a war-torn country like Iraq. As much as she wanted to just live in the moment, it would be an awful distraction in support of the OIF. It would have shattered her mind if something had happened to him while they were still going through the war. She believed in the Golden Rule and still did. If she were in his wife's shoes, she wouldn't want anyone breaking her marriage. But his wife was ill, and Rowe and Antonette had spent a lot of time together as friends gaining a deep emotional intimacy that neither had expected or prepared for. They both saw a glimpse of a possible future together, but neither understood the timeline. Would it happen? How long will it be until we see each other again? Would Divine Timing ever be in their favor?

There was no physical intimacy except for when they had kissed goodbye at the airport in front of a group of friends. Antonette had learned to quietly cherish her admiration of Rowe. She embraced her silent freedom and had learned to survive in tough situations. As Rowe left Baghdad, the uncertainty of not knowing if they would ever see each other again tore at Antonette's heart. It split her heart into shattered pieces to see him leave without her, and at the same time, it cracked her heart wide open. Life was not fair; she had mumbled as she watched him go. And in the days that followed, her soul ached at the loss of Rowe, and she cried from a deep well inside her heart that had been closed off upon her divorce. Their separation broke her heart wide open as she realized that it was possible to love again. And through that dark time, she talked to God, became even closer to Him, and laid the deepest parts of her soul bare for Him to heal.

Now that they were both single, Antonette had worked on her darkest shadows, and it just felt right to give herself freely to the man she had loved for such a long time.

Her past thoughts were distracted when Rowe whispered in her left ear that he could read her mind and stop thinking. He continued to make love to her, this time on the dining table, and then they ended up on the sofa. After they were exhausted, Rowe took her to bed, but they awoke in the night and made love again. Antonette said she'd have to take off work tomorrow as she wouldn't have any strength after their passion. Rowe chuckled and said he would be doing the same thing. They marveled at each other's naked bodies and explored everything. They intertwined both legs, and Antonette placed her right leg in between Rowe's and moved it against him, which aroused him, and he started again. They finally finished, and both went into the kind of deep hypnotic sleep that can only be created when you are laying next to the one you love dearly, physically depleted.

Both of them had the same vivid dream that they were superheroes in a war zone like Iraq and were saving lives. Later that night, there was a terrible storm. The house shook with the thunder and lightning that blazed through the windows, startling them both awake at 0333.

CHAPTER 9

"Each of you should use whatever gift you have received to serve others, as faithful stewards of God's grace in its various forms."

(1 Peter 4:10)

Rowe and Antonette had decided to combine their individual God-given gifts in order to lift up humanity with the power of their *Indivisible Love.* They had already agreed to unite as husband and wife, but Rowe wanted more. Rowe had offered a job to Antonette so they could spend more time together as they prepared to become united as husband and wife. Antonette initially pushed back and said that she liked being independent by having her own job. Rowe replied that she would be on a guaranteed salary. Therefore, she would maintain her independence and level of responsibility by playing her role. He admired her broad set of skills, which he knew would contribute to the business's success.

"I'll think it over," Antonette said casually.

Rowe was now familiar with how difficult Antonette played, but he loved her for what she was. That kept them inseparable because Rowe thought they really had many things in common. They were compatible in so many ways, with so many synchronicities.

One thing he had always loved about Antonette was her good sense of humor. He remembered a long time ago when she was demonstrating in front of their training group. Antonette knew exactly how to deliver her speech while inserting ice breakers that kept the audience laughing and engaged. She enjoyed being funny and making people laugh and told the class how medicinal laughter was. Rowe watched as the audience transformed from laughter to seriousness and back to laughter while Antonette naturally captivated the group. Oh, how he adored her! Her performance was beyond par, and he had fallen more in love with her that day. His imagination was taking him to another dimension while watching how dynamic Antonette was with her class demo. Little did he know then that he would one day pursue Antonette until she said yes. She was not an easy woman to catch, and he felt challenged by it.

He decided to offer her to become a partner in his company, not just an employee. Since they were not married yet, they could each contribute cash, property, and skill in exchange for an interest in the profits of the business. They would work together to produce the financial results of the business and share the outcome—partners in business and partners in life. A true-life partnership where each would fully support the other, and they would make decisions together as a team. Each would have a 50% allocation based on their ownership share. Rowe knew that this was an exceptional business proposal for Antonette. But he also knew Antonette could grow his business exponentially and organically with her skills.

Rowe had decided to give multiple surprises to Antonette before the wedding. He had a surprise gift for Antonette every day for twelve days before the wedding, just like Christmas! He hid a red box under her pillow on the first day while he pretended to read a Jack Carr novel. He was immersed in the book and didn't realize that Antonette had gone back to bed. He heard a shriek from the bedroom and momentarily panicked, dropped his book, and ran into the bedroom, thinking maybe Antonette had seen a huge spider. Antonette had the habit of turning her pillow before she went to bed. That night, she was surprised to find a little red box under her pillow. She let out a weird scream, covered her mouth, and then touched the velvety box.

"Rowe? What's this, sweetheart?" She said as Rowe bounded into the room, realizing she had probably found the surprise.

"Oh, it's been there since this morning. Why don't you open it and see what's inside the box?"

Antonette complied and gasped as she saw the south sea pearl and diamond stud earrings. In the middle of the box, there was a white cultured pearl necklace, and underneath that was a matching pearl bracelet. Antonette cupped her mouth and was almost in tears.

Rowe said, "That will look great on our wedding day."

"How could you…" Antonette said as she pictured the jewelry set with her gown, it was perfect. When they picked out the wedding bands, she glanced at them at the jewelry store but had said nothing to Rowe that she thought they were beautiful.

"Well, I did have to rob a bank," Rowe quipped.

"That's not what I meant. When did you get these?"

Rowe was ready with his answer, "Oh, I picked those up from the jewelry store after I tried on my tuxedo. I thought they would look good with your gown." Rowe noticed Antonette's every move, and he had seen the pearls catch her eye even so briefly and couldn't resist spoiling her.

Antonette rolled in the bed next to Rowe, "Thank you, my love," she said, clutching him like a little girl. "And did you check underneath your pillow tonight?"

"No way! No, you didn't!"

Antonette teased, "Go on. It's been there since last night; would you like to check it out?"

Rowe looked surprised and hesitated for a moment, then decided to check underneath his pillow. He found a velvety dark navy-blue box. He opened the box and found a mickey mouse watch. He burst out laughing, and they both laughed until happy tears streamed down their faces. And then, he noticed in the corner that there was another opening, and he slowly removed it. It revealed an elegant luxury watch.

"Oh, my, my, my…! what is this?"

"Don't wear it until the big day comes," she said. Rowe listened to her while he admired the Rolex Submariner.

"It looks like a very expensive watch."

Antonette said, "I robbed a different bank."

Rowe laughed so hard and hugged Antonette, who was watching him through the little girl's eyes. He made her feel that way and loved her unconditionally the same as he loved Isabella.

"Well, well, well, I can never outwit you, can I?"

Antonette said, "Nope! I won't let it happen!" And they both laughed.

The following nights there were more surprises for both of them. It was like a scavenger hunt adventure, as they found treasures in hidden places. One night, they laughed so hard when each found new underwear as their surprise gift. Antonette giggled and blushed when she saw the new lingerie that Rowe had gifted her. It was sheer pink with lace, Rowe said she'd look beautiful in it, and he couldn't wait to see her in the sexy babydoll set. Antonette gifted him with a pair of boxers that had the words, "I am the man." Rowe burst out laughing and tried them on with excitement. They both had fun trying on their new undergarments and, even more fun, slowly taking them off of each other.

On the night before the wedding, Rowe gave Antonette a big box. Inside the box, Antonette found a light, quality, concealable, tactical enhanced multi-threat vest level IVA, National Institute of Justice certified made by DuPont Kevlar. It was a heat-resistant para-aramid synthetic fiber with a molecular suture of many inter-chain bonds that made it incredibly strong yet lightweight to wear. It was best known for its use in ballistic body armor and had many other applications because of its high tensile strength to weight ratio. Rowe wanted the best bulletproof vest for his beloved, for he had one too, courtesy of the CIA.

To Rowe's surprise, Antonette was even more excited at this gift than the lingerie or jewelry. She jumped up and down and absolutely loved her new body armor. She tried it on, and it fit perfectly on her slim body. She said she couldn't wait to wear it on their next rendezvous with destiny.

On the same day, Antonette gave a wonderful small box to Rowe wrapped in gold paper and a red ribbon. He opened it and adored what he found inside. It was a silver medallion with the image of St. Michael, the Archangel, with a sturdy neck chain that he could wear anytime, especially during battle.

On the back of the medal, it said, "*St. Michael the Archangel, defend us in battle. Be our protector against the wickedness and snares of the devil. May God rebukes him, we humbly pray; and do thou, O Prince of the heavenly host, by the power of God cast into hell Satan and all the evil spirits who wander through the world seeking the ruin of souls. Amen.*"

Antonette said, "*At the end times, the Lord said, at that time there shall arise Michael, the great prince guardian of your people; it shall be a time unsurpassed in distress since nations began until that time. At that time, your people shall escape, everyone who is found written in the book will be delivered. Multitudes who sleep in the dust of the earth will awake: some to everlasting life, others to shame and everlasting contempt. Those who are wise will shine like the brightness of the heavens, and those who lead many to righteousness, like the stars for ever and ever"* (Daniel, 12:1-3).

Antonette put the chain around Rowe's neck, kissed him, and said, "May God protect us always." Rowe humbly said, "Amen." They hugged for a long time like best friends who had known each other for many lifetimes. The scavenger hunt adventure had made them both feel invigorated. Some gifts touched their hearts, some excited, and some made them ready to conquer and save the world again. They both appreciated the material gifts, but each knew that the greatest gift was to be in the union.

Antonette finally agreed to become Rowe's business partner, and they got to work with the attorney and accountant to iron out the legalities of making it happen. Antonette and Rowe were now life partners in every sense.

CHAPTER 10

"And above all these put on love, which binds everything together in perfect harmony."

(Colossians 3:14)

The day had finally come, and everyone scurried to make it to the wedding ceremony by the Appomattox River. Antonette looked alluring in her wedding dress. Her hair was tied in an elegant, braided bun decorated with lace and florals, and a delicate little curly strand of hair was by her left ear. She was wearing the set of pearls gifted to her by Rowe. It looked magnificent and perfectly complimented her Lalamira wedding gown. The long sleeve lace wedding dress came with thumbholes, just as requested. It was off the shoulder slightly and showed her cleavage but not too much. The detachable gown train gave the final detail of elegance.

Rowe's children and guests thought Antonette looked gorgeous in her dress, and the pearls drew attention to her statuesque neckline. There was a subtle gasp from the crowd, and she appeared at the entrance. Antonette's right hand was tucked into her oldest son's arm as he walked her down to the red-carpeted aisle. Ironically, he was also named JR, so they all called him "Big JR." Antonette could see Rowe waiting patiently on the platform with the priest, their best man, and the rest of the wedding party. The men wore sharp charcoal gray 3-piece tuxedos with a white shirt and a pink tie. The women wore beautiful long simplistic pink chiffon dresses with spaghetti straps and silver strappy heels. The guests were wondering where the hundreds of white and pink roses that decorated the arch had come from, and the white and pink balloons that perfectly completed the elegant scene. Antonette's grandson Evan was one of the ring bearers, as well as Zed and Emy's sons, JR, Mark, Jeff, and Elon. They all served as ring bearers, and Isabella was so excited to be the flower girl, tossing pink rose petals on the aisle. Both Antonette and Rowe had requested the wedding singer to perform "Over the Rainbow" before the wedding started, which truly set the tone for the unusual 7 AM sunrise ceremony. It was an unusual wedding song, but it suited their fairy tale romance.

Big JR kissed his mom on the cheek and handed off the bride to the groom. As the ceremony began and sunlight streamed through the flower-covered arbor, Antonette and Rowe were overwhelmed but controlled their emotions. They exchanged promises and rings. Antonette was calm; Rowe couldn't wait to kiss her in public. He wanted to call her his own but not in a distorted objectified ownership way. He wanted the world to know that she held his heart, and he held hers. Through unconditional love, they belonged to each other while still maintaining their own silent freedom. The nuptial ceremony concluded, and the audience was expecting a first kiss that was sweet and full of promise. Everyone was tearing up just thinking about it. Rowe looked deep into Antonette's eyes, and they both smiled. Rowe gave Antonette a sweet first kiss dip as he laid her backward in his arms and she leaned back and slightly lifted her right leg. All of the cameras were flashing and rolling for a picture-perfect scene, and everyone gushed over their first tender kiss as husband and wife. Such a kiss inspired some of the guests to pucker up and drop a kiss on their partners during the wedding.

Antonette's youngest son Chris was responsible for filming the wedding. He had four assistants who ensured that all angles were recorded. Chris perfectly captured a banner that was pulled behind a helicopter showing, "Congratulations and Best Wishes, Rowe & Antonette!" The guests below had heard the sound of the helicopter blades and had plenty of time to read it clearly as the helicopter passed through the serene sunrise. A few of Rowe's military guests had momentarily taken a mildly defensive stance at hearing an unknown helicopter approaching.

Rowe observed this and whispered to Antonette, "I guess someone should have warned them." And they both chuckled.

"Oh, Ah, Wow!" They all marveled at the air sign, and it surprised both Rowe and Antonette the most. This was an unexpected part of the ceremony, but then the fireworks started and gave the guests another surprise. Rowe and Antonette were delighted by their family's creativity, and a buzz of energy captivated the entire city at seeing the helicopter and fireworks.

After all of the photo-ops for local magazines and the wedding pictures were finished, Rowe and Antonette were circulating among the guests. From a distance, Rowe recognized a familiar face and the person who was holding Antonette's hand.

"Hello HG, we are so delighted that you made it!" Rowe said as he approached.

HG Hawk thanked them for the invitation, and the three chatted for about 15 minutes before HG wished them the best with their wedding gift and then excused herself. But she stared at both of them in a way that only the three of them understood. Rowe and Antonette then led the enthused guests to the club, and they enjoyed the toasts from the best man, Dexter, and fellow SFGs who roasted Rowe. The crowd roared with laughter as his face turned bright red, and he couldn't help but laugh at some of the stories.

After dinner, Rowe and Antonette opened the dance hall for everyone. Rowe surprised Antonette with his dancing dexterity.

"Is there anything you're not good at, honey?" Antonette teased.

Rowe laughed and said he was really terrible at some things, and she was yet to find out what those things were. With that, they both laughed, causing heads to turn as they twirled effortlessly around the dance floor. After everyone had enjoyed dinner and dancing, they cut the cake, and Antonette cut a massive piece of cake for Rowe, much bigger than what he had cut for her, and the guests laughed. As the party came to its end, Suzanne, the wedding planner, announced the tossing of the bouquet and gathered all the single women to get ready. Deidra from the PX caught the bouquet and was thrilled. She was the first one who had signed up when Rowe came back to the PX and told everyone to give their information to Dexter if they wanted to receive an invitation. Deidra was so excited that her picture would be in the magazines that featured the glamorous wedding. She envisioned the headlines, "Wedding of the Year, and they lived happily ever after." And she was proud to be the woman who caught the most coveted bridal bouquet. She was ecstatic and gave them both hugs; Rowe and Antonette were so happy for her.

Antonette and Rowe saw how their families had helped in different areas. Krishna had helped Suzanne decorate the tables and wedding takeaways and ended up helping at the bar. She was certified in bartending, and so was Chris. They were both experts at mixing drinks. They each jumped in and started making their signature cocktails, laughing with the guests. Her second son, Pat, and Abi were responsible for the logistics of making the stage safe for the band to play. Antonette's oldest son, Big JR, and Jodie were pitching in where help was needed keeping the cards and gifts organized. The children from both sides had finally met each other and tried to catch up, talking about Antonette and Rowe and other topics at hand.

Antonette could tell from a distance while she was entertaining guests that Rowe was also falling in love with her family, just like she was in love with his family. Rowe had invited Antonette's children and their spouses to his yacht and graciously extended his invitation to come over to their house and to make themselves feel at home.

"There's enough room for everyone to stay overnight whenever you like," he offered.

Rowe's attention was focused on pleasing his new children-in-law, and he had paid for all of their plane tickets and a 5-star hotel for Antonette's children. He organized all of their logistics so they wouldn't have to worry about getting to and from the airport.

Antonette had told him they could afford to buy their own tickets and pay for their lodging, and Rowe respected it. However, he pleaded with Antonette to allow him the opportunity to take care of it. He reminded her how she had wanted to pay for all of the camping gear when she met his children. In the end, Antonette yielded because she had become familiar with Rowe's persistence; she knew he would pester her until she said yes.

Antonette's kids were all hanging out on the yacht and asked Rowe where their honeymoon would be.

"Iceland! I would like Antonette to experience snowmobiling in summer and dip in their spring waterfalls."

Antonette's youngest son Chris mentioned that he'd been there previously and enjoyed all of the activities, including the over 44,000 steps they had to climb to get to the top of the waterfall.

Rowe said they might want to skip that one. He had been there before and walked in the mud following the water trail up to the falls.

"It was a great hike, a little treacherous though, but I would recommend it to young people like you." Rowe joked.

"You guys are still pretty young at heart, it seems to me," Chris said, and everybody laughed.

Rowe then smiled and added that they also wanted to try a warmer climate and would go to New Zealand in the near future. The warm climate would probably be better for hiking adventures.

"How long were you planning to be in Iceland?" Asked JR, the oldest son. Rowe said they would stay there for a week after first visiting Hampton, VA, for a few days of sailing. They also planned to spend a few days in Wisconsin Dells to see the glacier-carved sandstone formations when they returned.

"That is a marvelous idea! I have heard that it is a beautiful area!" The middle son Pat exclaimed. Everyone agreed and wished them so much joy and told the newlywed couple to be safe in their travels.

Rowe asked what they thought of the wedding reception.

"Are you enjoying yourselves?"

Everyone thought it was great, especially the banner in the air pulled by the helicopter and the fireworks. They expressed that everyone was friendly, and it was nice to become acquainted with their extended family and learn about what each did for a living. They had even invited each other for a visit to enjoy Michigan's northern climate, Texas weather, or northern Virginia. They felt like they had all known each other for a long time because everyone seemed to be cheerful and genuine.

Rowe asked the kids to keep the Honeymoon itinerary secret from their mom. Antonette did not know their itinerary, and he wanted it to be a surprise. The kids all promised it would be kept secret and confirmed it would be a grand wedding gift. They assured him that Antonette would be ecstatic about it because she loved nature and traveling. Rowe felt that Antonette's children were so much fun and authentic, and Antonette's children had a mutual impression of Rowe. He was modest, and his stalwart morals defined what kind of man he was, a good citizen and role model. Antonette's kids thanked Rowe for being good to her, as she deserved the best after enduring hardships and life challenges. She had persevered and deserved nothing but a glorious true love relationship. They also told him that she was a survivor.

He looked at them and nodded, confirming and saying, "Yes, and what a survivor." Rowe was standing at the edge of the boat, looking out at the water, thinking about Antonette. She had captured his heart so long ago, but he never had sex with Antonette until they had found each other the fourth time as single people. They were both ready for the type of love that would fill that vacuum of emptiness left in the wake of their own separate tragedies. Love would always prevail and rule over the universe of negativity. Their sex that first night had taken their relationship to the next dimension. It brought them to a new level of commitment and unity. They felt their world had changed from the 'me' world to an 'us' world.

"What are you thinking about?" Antonette said as she came up behind him and wrapped her arms around his waist.

"You," he said and hugged her as they enjoyed a long passionate kiss.

It was time to say goodbye, and Rowe left his yacht, giving Antonette a chance to chat alone with her kids. Rowe understood private matters and respected Antonette's need to connect with her children alone for a while. He went back to the clubhouse and joined Zed and the rest of his own family in entertaining their visitors at the reception.

"Where did you find this guy? He's a multi-billionaire, for God's sake! He owns a lot of successful business companies and has holdings in my company," said JR, a certified public accountant for a major firm. When he heard his mother was getting married, he had researched Rowe's businesses and background.

Antonette was stunned at what she was hearing.

"I didn't know about all of that. Sure, I knew he was successful when we reunited, but I had no idea that he was a multi-billionaire? After years of separation, we found each other again, and I was not interested in his money. I just loved the man I had found before, and my love for him had never changed since then. He is still the same man like the one I had loved before, and that's all that matters to me. I am even giving up my independence not only for the two of us to be married and live together, but we have also decided to become business partners. I never trusted anyone enough to give up my independence. I don't even know our honeymoon itinerary."

JR said, "You are a saint, Mom." He added, "We know about your honeymoon itinerary, but we made a promise to keep it secret from you."

"It is a sacred promise to Rowe that we can't break and a matter of trust," Chris added.

Antonette was overwhelmed at what her kids had said, but it felt good. To have her kids view her as a saint was a little much, but regardless, she accepted the compliment. She was happy that they had bonded with Rowe. She had made a lot of sacrifices for her children, and to bask in the glory of her children's admiration warmed her heart.

She said, "Praise be to God! And I am not worried about the itinerary as long as I am with Rowe. I trust him with my life."

Rowe returned with Isabella on his hip to tell Antonette that a few people wanted to say hello back to the reception. The kids hugged their mom and shook hands with Rowe as they departed.

"Don't worry, I will take good care of your mom," Rowe said as he carried Isabella. "Say bye, princess."

Isabella said, "Bye. I will come here all the time and taste Nanna's egg rolls."

They all laughed, and Antonette's children said in unison, "Yes, she can cook!"

Antonette was pleased that Rowe seemed to enjoy her children, but it came as no surprise because she had loved his children as if they were her own from the moment they had met.

CHAPTER 11

"When they met, it was as if their souls each felt an imaginary missing puzzle piece clicking into place."

(Arnold, Barbara D.)

After they had said goodbye to all of the guests, Rowe told Antonette that he had a surprise for her. Antonette was wondering where they would go for their honeymoon. Rowe had kept it secret till now, and what an exciting way to start their new life together. He would keep her guessing which added to the thrill, and he just loved watching her innocent face.

Rowe drove them to a small remote airport. They went through the gate, the guards saluted him, and he saluted them back. He pulled the Suburban into a parking spot right next to one of the hangars. Antonette did not see any houses but a few small planes inside the airplane hangar. Rowe held her hand and led her towards the hangar. He told her to wait for a minute and then talked to a man standing by the single-engine plane.

The man handed something over to Rowe and said, "You got your baby!"

Rowe laughed and invited Antonette to the passenger seat. Antonette remained silent until Rowe asked, "Are you hungry for anything? By the way, you look gorgeous in your wedding dress! Your picture is all over the news!"

Antonette smiled and knew that Rowe was just teasing her. But truly, Rowe knew people in the media for publicity, as he had dealt with them before when an article about the best weapons for the American troops was published. He was on the headline news and on the front of several magazines at the time. He also knew how to deal with the media, which sources were to be trusted, and who published tactfully.

He almost said, "Money talks." But caught himself and preferred to keep quiet. He did not like bragging at all; it was one of his most valued principles. Still, Rowe wanted to impress Antonette so much, to show her his power. But he also knew that he had to keep his ego in check, especially with Antonette. He knew that her unconditional love for him had nothing to do with his money or his power. This is why he loved her so.

Antonette looked around the plane, it was a newer plane, and it looked impeccably kept.

"It must have been expensive to rent this plane," she said matter of factly. She had suspected but didn't know that Rowe was a licensed pilot until now. *More surprises, of course*! She told herself silently.

"I bought this plane after I retired from the Army," Rowe said.

Antonette gazed at Rowe and thought about what her children had told her.

"What else didn't you buy, Rowe?" She asked sarcastically, with a hint of disbelief in her eyes.

Rowe laughed and said, "Let's get going. I don't want to be late. I am glad you came back into my life, Antonette. You have made me feel brand new like I have an entirely new life and future."

"Rowe, when I met you, I loved you instantly. My soul gravitated towards yours like a magnet, and it was inexplicable. I kept it to myself because you were not available to me, but I never stopped loving you from the first day we met."

Rowe hesitated and then decided to confide in Antonette. "Last year, lots of things were running through my mind. I thought of crashing this plane and ending everything. I didn't think I could take the emotional pain of loss anymore. Money doesn't buy happiness. But then I thought of my kids and grandkids, and I couldn't do it and put them through another tragic loss. I pulled deep on my faith and my hope that maybe the future would be better. I stepped closer to God, He promised me a wonderful gift in the future, but I had no idea that it would be you returning to my life."

Antonette was shocked by Rowe's admission. "Rowe, I didn't know that you had been suffering so greatly. But I am here now, and if you ever plan to put this plane down, I am going down with you. I will be with you until the end of the line."

"Wait, isn't that a line from Captain America's movie?" Rowe tried to add levity to the tense subject.

Antonette continued, "I don't know how else to put it. I just want you to know that I am here now, and nothing bad will happen to you anymore. If you hold onto your faith in God, He will rescue you as He has rescued me so many times. He always makes a way, even when we can't see the road ahead." Antonette continued on about spirituality and then started talking about life after death and how he should never want to end his life no matter how much his soul was hurting.

Rowe said, "Those days are gone. God saw me through those dark days. Now we have found each other again, and because of you, I found life again. I believe in love again. You have rejuvenated me, and I will never allow anything to harm you." Rowe wanted to get moving but didn't want to be rude, so he grabbed her gently and kissed her with passion to close the subject. He believed what she had said, and it was so powerful. There was something about Antonette that made him believe her when she said that he would be safe and protected from harm as long as they were together, and they were together with God at the center of their relationship. Somehow their union had brought them each even closer to God; it was a sacred connection. They were *Indivisible*.

They kissed again passionately. Rowe ran his hands lightly over Antonette's breasts. Rowe wanted to make love to her right there in the airplane, but they were distracted by the arrival of another single roaring engine. Rowe regained his focus and revved up the engine. After leaving the hangar and receiving the signal from the tower, he executed a perfect takeoff as they soared into the air.

They arrived in Hampton 20 minutes later, and Rowe adeptly parked the plane. He helped Antonette dismount and led her to a limousine waiting 50 meters away from the hangar. Antonette felt out of sorts because everything looked strange, she didn't know what to expect next, and Rowe was not telling her anything at all. The limousine stopped in front of the Madison Hotel. Jeffery, the chauffeur, removed several bags of luggage from the back. Rowe had a good chat with him before they thanked each other, and Antonette saw out of her peripheral vision that they did the hand sign. Antonette wondered if Rowe owned that limousine too and if the chauffeur, who looked more like a heavyweight fighter, was his employee or another friend. The suspense of what Rowe had planned was killing her.

"I did not know you have so many friends," Antonette finally said to Rowe.

Rowe grinned and said softly, "You haven't seen anything yet."

"Excuse me? You're killing me with all these surprises, honey, and I can hardly bear it anymore. What do you have packed in all of that luggage, and how do I know whether I will have everything that I need for the trip?"

Rowe told her that if he forgot anything she needed, they would buy it along the way. Then he finally confessed that after Hampton, he had planned a trip to Iceland.

Antonette's eyes glowed, "I have always wanted to go there! What are we going to do there, will there be snowmobiling?"

Rowe looked pleased with himself, and Antonette couldn't wait for him to reveal more of his 'Top-secret Honeymoon plans.' They checked in at the front desk and were shown to the Honeymoon Suite. Rowe scooped Antonette into his arms at the door to their room. She laughed and held onto his neck as he carried her into their suite and locked the door behind them.

"I know you're dying to hear the details of our trip, but I would like to hear your questions one at a time, just so it will help me organize my thoughts."

By that time, Antonette was focused more on changing her outfit and said, "I think I need to change clothes."

"May I help you undress? I think it would be quicker." Rowe chirped.

"Why would it be quicker?" asked Antonette.

Rowe joked that he wanted to rip off her dress and ravage her. Antonette, while totally wanting to be ravaged, disagreed with that idea. She loved the wedding dress so much, and it was too beautiful to be destroyed.

"Of course, I won't destroy it! How about if I just use my teeth to undo the zipper?" Rowe said, and they both laughed.

He loved her dress too and unzipped her slowly and gently slid the dress to the floor. With that, he grabbed Antonette by her waistline and teased her with a slight kiss and a bite on her lower lip. Antonette circled her hands on Rowe's neck and kissed him back passionately. A longing, sensual kiss that Rowe would die for, and he became hard immediately. Rowe bent down and kissed her there, pulled the lace slip over her head and pushed her back onto the bed. They made love until the sun went down, and they decided to order room service instead of the dinner reservation that Rowe had planned. The next two days were filled with sailing adventures, and Rowe took Antonette around Hampton, showing her all of his favorite restaurants.

On the third day, the chauffeur drove them to Dulles Airport for the flight on Icelandair. They had both packed a small piece of luggage, as they wanted to enjoy the benefits of traveling light. Rowe had the rest of their belongings sent back to Richmond with the chauffeur.

They arrived in Iceland about 6 hours later at the Keflavik International Airport. Rowe and Antonette saw a familiar, tall, muscular man with a bearded face waiting and holding a placard with their names.

"Weren't you at our wedding? I believe it is… Steve. That's right, Steve?" Antonette said as they approached the man.

Steve was delighted to hear that Antonette had remembered his name.

He said, "Welcome to Iceland!" Rowe and Steve hugged and did the hand sign. Antonette had seen the same hand sign between Rowe and Jeffrey, the chauffeur, and Dexter at the PX.

"Let me take you to your hotel," Steve said with enthusiasm. Rowe and Antonette followed him to his SUV, an Iron Blue Dacia Duster 4x4. On the 30-minute drive to Reykjavik, Antonette noticed that Steve and Rowe seemed to be old friends. Their mannerisms and speech patterns were very similar.

They pulled up to the hotel. Steve gave them a map and a myriad list of activities, the number of their group, and the details for snowmobiling.

"Steve and I were in the SFG together. And now he's running a successful business in this country with his brother and brother-in-law." Rowe explained to Antonette.

"You know, you both talk alike. So, I figured you might have been in the same service at one time," Antonette observed.

Steve answered, "You're a smart lady, Antonette. I caught that at the wedding, and I knew you would figure out what was going on soon enough."

"Did you mean that I would figure out that Rowe would have his buddies from SFG planted at various places throughout our entire honeymoon? It was a little hard to miss!" Antonette said with a chuckle.

"It takes one to know one," Rowe said, then hugged and kissed Antonette in front of Steve. Steve laughed and advised that they should rest early for the night and get energized for the next glorious day's activities.

"I know it's your favorite part, Rowe, so you can snowmobile as long as you want to, buddy! We are going to drive you to Hercules, and then we will drive you over to the ice. You can start with the group but go out on your own later as long as you want to. It's my wedding present!" Steve said with a huge grin.

"You didn't have to do that!" Rowe exclaimed. He was reeling with joy.

"Right, just like you didn't have to buy a wedding package tour to send my wife and me to Hawaii, Philippines, and Down Under, for our wedding present. It's the best present we ever had, and my wife treasures it to this day, especially the trip to Baguio City and Banaue's Rice Terraces, the eighth Wonder of the World! You will get to meet her tomorrow night, Antonette, and you will love her, and she's just as adorable as you are!" Steve said.

Antonette blushed and said, "Wow! Thanks, Steve. I can't wait to meet her."

"She didn't come to the wedding because she was helping our fourth daughter with a newly born child. Our new granddaughter's name is Kristine."

Antonette replied, "That's fabulous, Steve! Can't wait to meet her and your family!"

"Only my daughter Ice is here with us, and my son-in-law has been helping me with the business. The rest of our kids are in the UK and Sydney, Australia. I'm not sure if Rowe told you that I met my wife Reyna here in Reykjavik. She was one of the tour guides on my first trip here and I was fascinated by her agility and beauty. I chased her, and it took me three different tours to Reykjavik before she finally said yes! When we got married, Rowe was my best man. I have been here ever since, happily married. We have two sons and two daughters and five grandkids, and I am sure more are coming!" Steve finished, and they all laughed.

True to his words, Rowe gave Antonette the thrill of her life the next day. Steve took them to Hercules, which would take them to the snow. Antonette thought she should have guessed that Hercules was the name of the big bus. She was astounded how the surroundings suddenly changed into all pristine white snow. Rowe grinned as they both collected their snowsuits and helmet and headed to their assigned snowmobile.

"Let's slide to pick up our snowmobiles!" Rowe suggested.

Antonette was excited and said, "Let's do it!"

They asked somebody to take their pictures as they slid like small children to their snowmobiles. They made their way over to their two-seater snowmobile, which they could both ride together. There were 12 pairs in their group, except for two who were traveling solo. Antonette and Rowe's snowmobile was second to the tour guide. They finally started the motors, and Antonette could tell how much Rowe loved snowmobiles as he started theirs. They cracked the ice as they drove through it, and Rowe increased the speed.

"Yoo-boo!" Here we go!" Rowe exclaimed as their group snowmobiled in single file across the frozen snowy terrain. Antonette had never gone that fast on a snowmobile. The adrenaline from the speed along with the beautiful scenery, made her giddy. The snowmobiling group tour lasted for an hour, and Rowe told Steve he couldn't get enough of it. He took Antonette out for another hour, and they had never felt very close as they sped across the ice with Antonette's arms wrapped around Rowe's waist. *We will remember this day forever,* she thought as they pulled back into the parking area where Steve was already waiting for them.

"Wooohooo!" Antonette yelled as they arrived.

Steve laughed and said, "We can do it again tomorrow while the ice lasts. Antonette, are you up for it?"

Rowe said, "Oh yeah, she's up for it."

Antonette laughed and said that Rowe's enthusiasm was very much contagious and so she would go for it. They agreed to come back tomorrow and do it again.

Steve said, "That's the spirit. Did I warn you about Rowe? He likes to drive on open terrain that does not require a road or trail. We had an operation in Alaska called Operation Skylight, and we drove through the ice. Rowe was ahead of everyone else and had to come back to rescue us. We snowmobiled all day, up at the crack of dawn."

Antonette said, "Oh my gosh. That sounds like a lot of endurance!"

Steve and Rowe laughed and said at the same time, "Tell me about it," and they all laughed again. Rowe reminded Antonette that Steve was on his team in Somalia from Black Hawk Down, and Antonette was awed.

They saw where the others would camp that night and saw the waterfalls next to the walking path. It was indeed beautiful but treacherous.

Rowe was marveling at the idea, "So it would be about 50,000 steps? OK, I've been there, done that. I got a brown shirt. Best of luck to you guys and gals, and enjoy while you can. Have a great hike, and see you again later."

And everyone headed for their tents. For Antonette, it had already been the experience of a lifetime, snowmobiling at the height of summertime! Then Rowe, Antonette, Steve, and his wife Reyna all ate dinner at a local restaurant. They enjoyed a simple but hearty lamb soup with potatoes, turnips, carrots, and fresh herbs, which was served with warm rolls. The comfort food felt good, and the group shared a lot of laughs over Rowe and Steve's adventures. The four friends became an instant family that night.

Two days later, they kayaked through the glaciers. Rowe filled their green jug with the water by the glacier. He drank some and offered it to Antonette, and she gladly took a sip of the water.

"It tastes different from the water in the United States," she said.

"Much cleaner," Rowe added, and they both felt excited about the new experience. They spent the night camping and hoped to catch a glimpse of the Aurora Borealis. Steve said they were visible, especially on a clear night like tonight, even though they could see it better during winter. They were both in awe as soon as they saw the Aurora Borealis. It was a greenish glow across the sky and quick to disappear, about 30 seconds. But they both managed to get pictures as a souvenir.

"What a paradise," Antonette said and looked at Rowe. It was as if they were the only two people in the world that night, just the two of them together under a magical sky.

They stayed in Reykjavik for one week, hiked to a volcano eruption site, and enjoyed the hot springs. Rowe and Antonette said goodbye to Steve and his wife at the airport. Antonette hugged Reyna and said they would be back again, maybe in December, to catch more of the Aurora Borealis. Reyna said it sounded great, and they were welcome to stay at any time. Antonette had found another great friend in Iceland, and she treasured Reyna in her heart.

They headed back to the States and eventually landed in Milwaukee at General Mitchell International Airport. They rented a Jeep Wrangler to explore the town before driving to their rustic cabin and getting into the waterpark activities. Antonette let Rowe show the way, unknowing that this was Antonette's playground while stationed at Fort McCoy, Wisconsin, in 1997 for four years.

Rowe told Antonette, "You know I can read your mind, right?"

Antonette blushed, "I keep forgetting." And they both laughed.

"Would you like to visit the old Fort McCoy and see if it has changed? What about going around Beloit after that?"

Antonette was ecstatic and grabbed Rowe's arm, "Could we please?"

"Aye, aye, Captain," and Rowe gave Antonette a joy ride to Fort McCoy to let her reminisce about the past.

New buildings were constructed, the PX had been expanded, and the gym was also reconstructed. They drove through her old unit and went into her very own building. It was in the same building where she had watched the horrible terrorist attacks on New York's twin towers. She would never forget that day. There were multiple deployments after 9/11, including her unit, the 101st Airborne Division Air Assault in Iraq. She found Rowe for the third time in that war-torn country. They also drove by the parking lot where she slipped and fell to the icy ground at Fort McCoy. It iced terribly on Fort McCoy during that particular winter. It was the place where Antonette learned to walk on ice and to layer up to stay warm. They also passed by the building where she lived for four years and then drove through the recreation center where she led the Hawaiian Luau during her time. She wondered if the same people managed the same building but knew they were probably long gone. Then they passed the chapel where she used to attend mass, and she reminisced about the time when she volunteered to take charge of egg hunting for the children. She also volunteered every year to sell wines during the Annual Dog Summer Concert at the Constitution Park and remembered getting a free tee-shirt every year and getting to meet the celebrities. Those were fun days, she said. Then they stopped by the training building and stepped into the dining facility for lunch. Rowe and Antonette enjoyed eating at the mess hall, as it brought back the old days in the military for both of them. Antonette did not recognize anyone anymore. It had been 25 years since she left Fort McCoy, and there must have been a rotation of assignments. Before exiting the post, they drove by the Headquarters Building, where the Commanding General office was. It had also been newly reconstructed.

They left Fort McCoy and toured Sparta and then Tomah, Wisconsin. She showed Rowe where she used to wait for the Amtrak every two weeks to visit her family in Michigan. And then the last building they visited was the Veterans Affairs Medical Center in Tomah, where she had volunteered to help in any place they needed her. She talked to the Veterans and drove them to Sparta and sometimes to Walmart near the hospital.

After they had seen everything, they proceeded to Beloit, Wisconsin and Rowe took Antonette to revisit all the areas she had been to with her family when they met halfway between Michigan and Fort McCoy, Wisconsin.

Antonette thought Rowe had a golden heart, showing her all of the old places she had lived while stationed in Wisconsin. Rowe knew how much she would enjoy this side trip, and she loved him even more for the kind gesture. They visited the University of Wisconsin in Madison and then decided to go back to their lodge.

Antonette told Rowe the story about driving through a flying turkey, which broke her windshield. When the cops came, they told her she couldn't take it home as they were considered an endangered species. Antonette silently cracked up at their statement and thought the cops just wanted to take the dead turkey home and cook it.

Rowe quipped that she might be right and said, "Abuso de el poder," abuse of power.

Antonette understood his Spanish very well and replied, "Tienes razón mi amor," you are correct, my love.

Rowe marveled at Antonette's knowledge of Spanish. She said it was her second language back in the Philippines. Rowe felt excited and suggested that they should visit the Philippines soon, and Antonette agreed. Her family would be exhilarated and so happy to meet Rowe. They could not come to the wedding and have been asking her to revisit her first home.

The rustic lodge they stayed in was beautiful and with modern amenities like a hot tub which they were both grateful for after a long day of traveling and driving. They both slept hard and woke up the next day excited to visit the lagoon with Tommy, another SFG from back in the old days. Tommy took them to different nooks of Wisconsin Dells, and then they had a 25-mile helicopter ride over Devils Lake and State Park and Baraboo Bluffs. It was a magical land, and they were both thoroughly enjoying the final phase of their honeymoon.

CHAPTER 12

"I am my brother's keeper."

They had four more days to go in Wisconsin, but something was wrong. Antonette was getting ready for their day trip to the waterpark and saw Rowe on the phone outside the cabin. He was pacing back and forth with a furrowed brow; she knew that look. He asked Antonette to follow him to the bathroom and turned on the showerhead when he came in. Rowe was literally whispering to her, and Antonette had to read his lips. He told her it was finally happening; he had received a call about troops coming home from Afghanistan. Some of his SFG buddies had formed a covert operation, and he had promised to work on remote surveillance for them.

Rowe had asked about the status of their communication equipment and the Ret. Col Post had said it was not too shabby. Ret. Col Post said they would appreciate remote surveillance until they reached Hamid Karzai International Airport, where thousands of people had gathered over the past two weeks in a desperate attempt to evacuate on C-17s out of the Taliban-controlled country. The Ret. Col Post said this massive effort could be possible with the help of the unofficial heroes inside the airfield who had challenged orders not to help beyond the Kabul airport perimeter. They needed Rowe's eagle-like cyber watch for protection. Ret. Col Post told Rowe they would wade into sewage canals if necessary and potentially use other alternate unnoticeable routes like tunnels and pull certain Afghan targeted people who were flashing the fruit image on their phones. It was considered an impossible endeavor, but they wanted to rescue these people who were the ones who had helped them succeed during the previous missions in Afghanistan. They simply had to fulfil a promise not to leave any man behind. The Green Beret retired, and counterinsurgency adviser in Afghanistan told Rowe he'd be thrilled to join the rescue effort, for he believed the Afghans they were rescuing had demonstrated loyalty and a strong vision of American democratic values. It sounded strange, but it was the truth. Rowe promised Ret. Col Post said he could depend on him, and they talked about the timeline.

"Leave it up to me. I have access to the IP line and the capability to make this happen," Rowe said.

Ret. Col Post replied, "You're a good soldier and a great hero, Rowe. I owe you one."

Rowe had always befriended people no matter their status in life by doing favors without expecting anything back. As a cardinal rule, he believed that all people should be treated with the same amount of respect and dignity; and that one should do the right thing without expectation of anything in return. He believed in the phrase, "*I am my brother's keeper*," and lived by it, looking after his fellow brothers and sisters in their time of need or struggle through their bravery and responsibilities.

"We need to leave Wisconsin right now," Rowe said with determination. Antonette, carrying the same values in her heart, agreed. They hurriedly packed their bags and traveled on the next flight back to Richmond.

Rowe made several phone calls as soon as they reached home; the first one was to HG Hawk. She was distressed about what Rowe asked for and said, "This is dangerously impossible and might have nasty repercussions."

We blew up a heavily fortified CIA base in Kabul so its contents would not fall in the hands of the disturbed Taliban militants. After destroying the base, we shepherded hundreds of Afghans, mainly due to reprisals. We knew how it worked, just like what happened in Iraq. Several Kabul airport attacks have killed 13 U.S. Marines and about 60 Afghans. Two suicide bombers and shooters attacked crowds of Afghans flocking to the Kabul airport trying to get into the C-17 flights, and they killed some of our Marines and some Afghans.

"Whoever is leading this insane operation, your men better know what they are up against." HG was highly concerned.

"They are my fellow SFGs and the SEALs," Rowe said curtly, interrupting HG.

HG Hawk respected the SFGs and the SEALs. They were very skilled and adept at cutting through the madness. The special group had made all of her missions successful; they were reliable and loyal, like Rowe. They always had her back, and she owed this to them. She knew that Rowe was excellent at what he did and had sacrificed his own safety so many times in these kinds of operations. If not due to his physical limitations, which had sidelined him into becoming a surveillance expert, he would be out there in the field with his fellow SFGs and the SEALs to face the Pakistani militant groups and disillusioned Taliban fighters. But she added that something was waiting for him afterwards, bigger than this operation. In the end, Rowe convinced HG Hawk to help him.

Rowe answered without hesitation, "Count me in." Then HG asked, "What about Antonette?"

Rowe assured her that they were in it together. He wasn't sure if he heard it right, but he thought HG Hawk said, "Fuck, I love you guys!" before she hung up the phone.

The operation successfully transported more than 800 Afghans. Rowe and Antonette's surveillance allowed the group to dodge heavily militarized Taliban checkpoints through Kabul airport, using images that convinced the Taliban they were on their side. The Afghans showed the guards their iPhones or photos of a sweet rugby football-shaped melon, a favorite fruit in Afghanistan. The name of the fruit was also the same password given to US military members at the airport working unofficially in tandem with the heroic veterans.

Rowe was monitoring all the activities from his secret bunker at home. He took a bathroom break after he was sure that Ret. Col Post's group and the rescuers had securely boarded one of the C-17 flights. Antonette took over the controls until Rowe finished and then took her turn to use the bathroom. They were both glued to the screen while intensely monitoring the rescue operation, and both wished they were there in person. Antonette felt lucky to be assisting Rowe as they worked together in this daring effort. They were committed to helping others and not leaving anyone behind on the battlefield. This was a principle that they had always lived by and would continue to live by forever, *"I am my brother's keeper."*

After that, they went on a few other missions for HG, each one successful due to their teamwork. Some were more dangerous than others, but they were an *inseparable* team and always came through victorious.

CHAPTER 13

The Headline News showed, "There are at least 100 casualties from yesterday's bombing." Rowe turned up the volume and caught the broadcaster's last sentence.

"Who are we fighting now?" Antonette asked Rowe.

Then he turned the channel on to CNN and then switched to FOX News.

"Texas is mourning the loss of its 100 casualties due to two suicide bombers. The terrorists have claimed responsibility and warned that there would be more. We are in a state of terror, infiltrated by terrorists and causing havoc in American lives." Antonette watched in horror with her hand over her mouth.

Rowe's iPhone rang; HG Hawk told him to meet at the Situation Room now.

"Mi Amor, meet you downstairs, Ahora!"

Rowe raced down to the S room, followed by Antonette. They quickly flipped on the lights and TVs and fired up their desktops. HG Hawk appeared at once.

"There has been an infiltration of terrorists. I'm sure you have already seen on the news that two separate suicide bombers killed about 100 Americans in Manhattan Mall and Brookfield at noon today. Another two suicide bombers killed 32 Americans and injured 60 others when they forced themselves amidst the shoppers in San Antonio Malls at 1300 hours. One suicide bomber blew himself up at La Cantera, and the other inside the North Star Mall.

Another incident in Liberty Mall, Philadelphia, reported multiple car explosions. The FBI also spotted a man planting an improvised exclusive device (IED) on 23rd Avenue in New York City last night, arrested him, and the FBI detonated the bomb. The IED perpetrator was identified as KAKO and was taken to a secluded location for further investigation. But another one remained at large and successfully planted the bomb on Peoria Street, which killed a couple walking to dinner.

Rowe and Antonette recalled their military experience with IEDs. An IED is a homemade bomb or destructive device to destroy, incapacitate, harass, or distract. They are used by terrorists, suicide bombers, and insurgents. They come in many forms ranging from small pipe bombs to sophisticated devices capable of causing massive damage and loss of life. They can be delivered through a package, a vehicle, placed or thrown by an individual, concealed on the roadside, or a carcass in the middle of the road.

IEDs were used during the Iraq War that began in 2003. They became popular a few months after the U.S. troops arrived in Iraq to capture Saddam Hussein and find weapons of mass destruction (WMD). Rowe and Antonette both remembered this timeframe during their service. The number of IEDs had increased in Iraq, especially during Ramadan. Which is the ninth month of the Muslim year, during which strict fasting is observed from sunrise to sunset. The troops had hoped that the killings would stop due to the sacred observance of Ramadan, only to be disappointed because the killing did not stop. Instead, the number of casualties soared due to the surge of IEDs planted just outside the wire of US-led coalition bases. It was horrible.

The amount of IEDs used in Afghanistan had increased since 2007, and the number of troops killed by them by 400 per cent. The number of wounded rose by 700 per cent. They caused a crippling effect, if not loss of life. It was the leading cause of death among the troops in Iraq and Afghanistan. The IEDs consisted of different components: an initiator, switch, primary charge, power source, and container. They may be surrounded by or packed with additional materials or enhancements such as nails, glass, or metal fragments designed to increase the amount of shrapnel propelled by the explosion. The magnetic ones were tough to spot and easy to employ. They were small and magnetic bombs which had become the militant tool of choice in Iraq and Afghanistan. They were also called sticky IEDs that could be quickly tucked under a car bumper and held in place by magnets. Any vehicle could be turned into a car bomb or used as an assassination tool, making stopping the bombs much tougher.

"Tell me about the device they detonated," Rowe asked HG.

"The FBI took the IED after detonating it to examine what type it was. The terrorists used fertilizer, gunpowder, and hydrogen peroxide as explosive materials on this IED based on their search. Explosives used a fuel oil and an oxidizer, which provided the oxygen needed to sustain the reaction. A common type of IED, called ANFO, is a mixture of ammonium nitrate, which acts as an oxidizer, and fuel oil." HG showed them pictures of the fragments and chemical analysis on the screen.

They were intensively studying the IED data when another headline news popped on the TV. They reported incidents in Texas, California, Pennsylvania, New York, New Mexico, Atlanta, Georgia, and Florida. In New Mexico, a Facebook feed with videos revealed that multiple cars had run over IEDs, two 4x4s and several cars were destroyed on the highway. One vehicle suffered secondary explosions, creating a massive dark smoke that halted other vehicles and made the roads impassable. The incidents happening simultaneously put the media into a frenzy, and they reported it as another terrorist attack similar to 9/11. It became chaotic, fear gripped the Nation, and people did not know what to do; complete panic ensued.

"There have been similar incidents in Germany and the United Kingdom," Rowe announced after seeing more live images on social media.

HG Hawk cursed and was yelling. "Fuck, what the fuck is going on? How the fuck could they be here on our soil?" She called her Chief of Staff and told him she wanted all corners in the building secured and covered. She flicked the button and saw Rowe and Antonette waiting for her to return, aghast, but they seemed to understand what was transpiring entirely. Rowe advised HG Hawk to brief the President that he should give a direct order for people to get off the streets and stay home immediately.

"No one should be driving until the ramblers are ready. Most people don't know what to do or what the hell is going on. Tell the people to lock their doors. It is the time to defend themselves from the infiltrators for those with guns. The tangos don't have uniforms, and they're dressed like us. People will not recognize if the enemy is knocking on the door. Don't get too close to anyone you don't know; they might be suicide bombers. Don't pick up anything; it could be an IED. Been there, done that, got a brown t-shirt. It's infuriating that they have brought this war to us on our turf. We are in a state of terror; the best thing to do right now is to tell everyone to stay off the streets and don't travel until the threat has been neutralized." Rowe urged. "Get the electronic jammers to neutralize the threat; tell the President to do it now!"

HG Hawk said, "You got it. I'm on it!"

Rowe explained, "Electric jammers or crew vehicle receivers or jammers (CVRJs) are vehicle-mounted electronic jammers designed to prevent IEDs' detonation, which is often triggered by off-the-shelf technology like cell phones. Such devices counter existing and evolving radio frequency (RF) threats by jamming each threat's transmitted RF signals. Such a system has demonstrated superior performance in Iraq and Afghanistan despite the number of casualties. With CVRJs, the foot soldiers were well protected against IEDs, magnetic and non-magnetic."

After she hung up with the President, another incident shocked the group. HG received word from Intel that an IED had blown up the vehicles occupied by the Vice-President and his secret service entourage right at Connecticut Bridge near St. Thomas More. They found the Vice-President still breathing with an unrecognizable face and blown left leg. They medically evacuated him via helicopter, fast and furious, to save his life. The blast killed his driver, and there were no survivors from the other secret service vehicles. Reports were flooding in from all sources; another report was that the KAKO had killed the owners and occupied the Valdez gas station on Massachusetts Avenue. The terrorists had reached Washington, D.C. and were causing loss of lives and significant destruction of our Nation's Capital infrastructure. The Pentagon was frantic. The Marine Expeditionary forces (MEF) based in Quantico were activated, along with the 101st Division Combat

Aviation Brigades (CAB). They were the first troops deployed to secure the bridges, including the William Howard Taft Bridge.

It had been less than one hour since the start of the attacks when another incident rocked the Americans to their core. The company's CEO, who had created and manufactured the lifesaving jammers, was driving to work when an IED killed him. The electronic jammer used to counter magnetic IEDs was his brainchild. The jammers were used heavily by the troops in Iraq and Afghanistan while fighting terrorists there, and they had saved many lives. His car exploded when he ran over some type of object on the road. The terrorists had planted an IED on the street just outside his home and waited for him to drive over it before detonating. His employees were emotionally crushed, and America mourned his loss.

"Who has been supplying the equipment for the terrorists? Is it the Russians, again?" Antonette asked HG, but there was no answer.

She was screaming at someone on the other end of the phone to get the Tanks, and HMMWV (High Mobility Multi-Purpose Wheeled Vehicles) mobilized to assist the CAB as soon as possible.

The terrorists quickly infiltrated the country, and now news reports added incidents in Virginia, North Carolina, New York, San Francisco, California, Oregon, Washington, Oklahoma, Nashville, Tennessee, and Wisconsin. The narrowing media broadcasters had reported more incidents, and social media was flooded with live streaming video coverage of the chaos.

"Fuck! We can't just sit here; get us a team. We have to do something!" Rowe barked at HG as he watched his beloved country slowly turn into ruins at the hands of terrorists. Antonette knew that Rowe was angry, as he rarely cursed.

"Hold tight, be ready. I think I have something for you." HG said, and the screen went dark.

Rowe and Antonette called their children and told everyone to stay home, be careful, don't let anyone in, and don't let the kids go outside until further notice. Rowe's friend Steve would arrange safe travel to an undisclosed location for everyone. They had all learned to keep plenty of food and water on hand for emergencies, so as terrifying as this news was, they felt prepared. Some of their neighbors called the incidents 'isolated' attacks and continued their business because they didn't realize how widespread and dangerous the threat was.

CHAPTER 14

"So do not fear, for I am with you; ... do not be dismayed, for I am your God. I will strengthen you and help you; I will uphold you with my righteous right hand."

(Isaiah 41:10)

In broad daylight, terrorists grabbed a five-year-old girl from the street, put a blindfold on her, and demanded the FBI for helicopters, food, money, and free Jihadist prisoners. She had been taken to an old building in Dupont Circle.

The FBI Director sent Agent Cooper to negotiate with the kidnapper. HG Hawk was stationed on-site near the scene's perimeter and intervened.

"We have it covered, Cooper; let the CIA handle this", Hawk barked. There had been hot discussions between the two, and HG Hawk said that the infiltrator was considered an international matter.

"This is bullshit. It's a domestic affair and therefore on FBI turf," Agent Cooper insisted.

The CIA chief of staff had a terse conversation with Hawk earlier, insisted that it was the FBI's jurisdiction, and told her to back off the mission. HG Hawk faced her stubborn chief of staff with a cold gaze and said, "This is CIA, not FBI, and you know it! Now get out of my face and let me do my job!" He saw the look in her eyes, knew she was right, and didn't want to tangle with her, so he consented.

After talking with Agent Cooper, the FBI Director, Arthur Seelig, had a one-on-one with Hawk. Both were defending the United States of America, and they should work together, but the CIA would take the lead. HG Hawk said if they wanted to stay and help, they could. But this was a major operation under the control of the CIA.

"We're on the same team, dipshit," HG hissed.

Seelig spat on the ground and realized that HG Hawk was correct. They both needed to work hand in hand to defend the nation in a state of terror. Seelig agreed, then turned and walked away; he kicked an empty can that exploded just a few feet away. HG Hawk was blown backwards to the ground by the force of the explosion, and a small piece of shrapnel landed on her left bicep. She was momentarily stunned but jumped into action when she saw what had happened to Seelig. He was bleeding profusely, and both legs were gone. She used her belt as a tourniquet on the stump of one leg and grabbed another belt from a colleague for the other leg, saving Seelig from bleeding out in the street.

"Ambulance! Help! Get somebody here, now! Call for help; please help!"

A helicopter ambulance arrived a few feet away from HG Hawk's location and, after clearing the road, medically evacuated Seelig, who was semi-conscious on a stretcher. HG Hawk was dazed and shocked; she covered her mouth with her right hand, choked back hot tears, and then suddenly threw up behind a tree.

"Clear the roads! Clear the roads! Don't let anyone get closer. Shoot them if you have to. We don't know who's with us and who's against us. Clear the fucking roads now!" She ordered.

Her thoughts then returned to the hostage situation. She was seething that it was a child. "We needed somebody to rescue the girl!"

Everyone was deployed to different places, and the Special Ops were still on rescue missions in Pakistan and Iraq. The CIA's COS said they needed more troops to rescue the girl. Although Hawk had dismissed her COS earlier, she thought he was right about this. They needed more manpower to rescue the girl. But they needed someone to come in at the top floor who would not let the tango ascend.

HG Hawk determined that if they couldn't get more troops here quickly, only one man could do this rescue mission effectively. She took out her cell phone and made the call.

"Rowe, I want you to get your ass out here. I need you on a rescue mission. One of the terrorists has a five-year-old girl hostage, and he's making insane demands from our country. You are my only hope. You are the only one I know who can pull off this mission." There was silence on the other end. Rowe was fuming and picturing a small girl like Isabella in the hands of a terrorist.

"Did you hear me? We are sending an attack helicopter to your lawn as we speak." HG had an unusual quiver to her voice. Rowe picked up on it immediately.

"Hawk, are you alright? What's the matter? What else is happening down there?" Rowe always trusted his gut and had never missed on anything so far. He had always trusted his instincts, and they had served him well.

"Seelig was blown up, makeshift IED in a soda can. I don't know if he will make it," HG disclosed. "The enemy is watching us, Rowe!"

Rowe asked, "What? He was blown up by what? What the hell happened?"

HG Hawks was quivering again, "I was just talking to him, he turned around and kicked an empty can, and the can exploded a few feet away from us. It was closer to Seelig; otherwise, it would be me missing both legs", and she felt like vomiting again.

"Hawk, listen to me. Listen to me! Stay away from the road. Don't let anyone get close to the scene; you got that? No one! You don't know who your enemies are in this chaos. You can't recognize them because they don't have uniforms, no codes, no names. They blend in and can plant IEDs anywhere. Did you hear me, Hawk?"

"Rowe, I have already given that order to my men and women," HG said calmly. Please just get the fuck here now, and rescue that poor girl before the terrorist blows himself up and kills the girl and our troops holding the building! He knows he's trapped, and the negotiations are failing. Here are the grid coordinates...."

Rowe wrote them down and said, "Got it, I'm on my way."

Rowe unlocked his closet and retrieved his garments. He took the body armor with a knife, an M4 5.56mm carbine with PEQ-2 infrared spotlight, laser designator, waterpark, SIG pistol 9mm, extra mags filled with ammo, and smoke grenade, hand grenade, and his Kevlar.

Antonette was standing in the bunker next to Rowe; he had instructed her on all surveillance equipment before their last mission. She alone would be his eyes and ears for this rescue.

"I will return to you, Mi Amor." And briefly hugged and kissed her with passion. "My life depends on your eyes and ears. If you want me to come back to you alive and in one piece, you've got to do your job!"

Antonette nodded and cleared her eyes from the welling tears. She went back to the computer after Rowe left, closed the secret entrance, and focused on the job. Once again, she cherished her silent freedom and said Rowe looked like a magnificent Spartan, succinct. He looked great in his battle rattle uniform, and she could visualize what he looked like on his active SFG days.

"I love him. My Lord, please stay with him," Antonette said aloud, and she pushed her deepest fear of losing him to the far recesses of her mind. She needed to entirely focus on her job and not let the fear consume her.

Rowe carried his night vision goggles in case it was dark inside the building. 'Anything can happen at war', he said to himself. He exited the spy bunker and found the Black Hawk helicopter on his lawn just like HG said it would be. With adrenaline fueling him, Rowe boarded the chopper like nothing was wrong with his bad leg, and the pilot pulled up. He liked riding in a Black Hawk. It was always a thrill. It had been a while, and the ride gave him flashbacks of Operation Enduring Freedom in Afghanistan, Iraq, the conflicts in Panama, the Persian Gulf, Kosovo, Somalia, and many more. He thought he should partner with the current original manufacturer and offer some of his innovative ideas to help the troops. His mind was always about the troops, the soldiers, the military, freedom, and Antonette and his family. Those priorities were his sole purpose of existence.

The Black Hawk helicopter was explicitly designed for a fight. They can reach a top speed of 190 mph and are operated by two pilots and two crew chiefs, one being the door gunner. They can accommodate up to 11 troops in full gear, and the Special Ops models could be outfitted with up to 16 Hellfire missiles and air-to-air weapons like the AIM-92 Stinger missile.

The pilot dropped Rowe off at the rooftop helipad where the girl was held. The gunner took a defensive position. The pilot yelled, "Will wait here for 10 min unless you can make it shorter!"

Rowe said, "See you in five" and simultaneously raised his left hand with an open hand, "five."

He tactically disembarked with M4 ready, tugged the door open, stepped into the stairwell, and heard the little girl's pleading.

"One tango, and the girl. No one else in the room," Alex guided him. But her instinct said that danger was near, and she continued to scan the monitors for more tangos.

"Please let me go. I want to see my mommy!" the girl sobbed.

Rowe slowly descended the steps and saw the terrorist in a room, holding the blindfolded girl on the neck with 9mm in his right hand. The terrorist did not have a mask or any face cover.

As soon as Rowe saw the terrorist, he said, "Let the girl go!"

The terrorist talked to someone on the radio and stopped for a few seconds.

"Rowe? Is that you?" Rowe froze. He knew that voice, but it couldn't be.

"Omar? What in the fucking hell are you guys doing in my country?"

Omar laughed and told him, "We will make this our land. We brought the battlefield here since you took most of our good men. We are the new offshoots. We are the KAKO who believe in Jihad, the supreme belief! You should have just left our men alone in Afghanistan! We followed our people, and we have good logistics support, you know from whom!"

"Okay, Omar. Just let the girl go; this is between you and me." Rowe said cautiously.

"Rowe, Rowe, I should have killed you when I had the chance. You didn't believe me when I said we could do anything, and now we have brought the battlefield to the USA. It is our time, Rowe," Omar said, waving the 9mm around.

Rowe was buying time until he could get the perfect shot without harming the girl.

"Omar, I am not here to negotiate. Either you give the girl to me, or you die. And you will not be alone to die. Your fellow KAKO will also die in vain. No bribery here. Either you give the girl to me, or I will shoot you in between your eyes."

Omar hesitated and knew that Rowe would deliver what he promised, accurately and swiftly, as proven in the past. Rowe had a reputation as the 5th SFG's remarkable asset because of his laser sharp shooting skills. He could also read minds, which Omar did not know, and Rowe realized that Omar was becoming terrified and ready to detonate explosives on his body.

Rowe maneuvered down one more step and kept Omar engaged, "How many are you? Where are your men? You know you can't win this." Rowe challenged.

Omar said, "Ah, you will be surprised. We have covered mostly all the USA, soon to be ours. It is 100,000 of us, enough to put your country in chaos. We have taken over submarines and airplanes. We are big Rowe. We will take over the USA; there is no stopping us now."

Rowe felt a chill down the back of his spine. Submarines? Airplanes?

"How many submarines, Omar?" Rowe thought he must be bluffing.

Omar laughed at Rowe's inquisition. "Rowe, you Mother Fucker.... you will all die."

"Let the girl go, Omar. Don't do this," Rowe said as the girl screamed and sobbed.

Omar replied, "Or what, Rowe? Are you going to shoot me? I am well equipped and not afraid to die. I have explosives all over me, and you all will die with me!"

Rowe hesitated and said slowly, "You don't have to kill yourself, Omar. You made a mistake, but it can be undone. I can get you immunity."

Omar answered, "No, Rowe. Not for me. Allah will be at my side. I will be a hero, and I will take the girl with me."

Rowe leaned closer, *'just one more inch, and I'm shooting this sad excuse for a man between the eyes,'* Rowe thought.

"Let the girl go, Omar, and take me instead; it would be more impressive to take me down with you than a fucking toddler," Rowe goaded him.

Omar raised his right arm, and Rowe saw a cell phone in his hand and was about to press the button. Omar said, "That's a good switch, but I am used to your bullshit Rowe. We can do anything in this world, you know."

"Goodbye, my friend." Omar shifted his position and was about to spin, but Rowe was quicker and had already fired.

Thug! Thug! Omar dropped to the floor before he could finish his words.

"So can we," Rowe said calmly as he slid down the rest of the banister. He told the girl not to worry, moved her away from Omar and told her to stand still for just a minute. He was glad she was blindfolded and hadn't seen Rowe plant two bullets directly between Omar's eyes, blowing out the back of his skull. Rowe deactivated the explosive vest on Omar's body and destroyed the phone.

"You are in good hands now; you are safe," he said as he grabbed the girl, and they started to ascend the staircase to the roof. The girl was still sobbing and asking for her mom. Rowe spoke to her gently and told her not to worry and that she would see her mom soon after a short ride on a fun helicopter.

"What is your name?" Rowe asked the girl as he wiped her tears.

"Shirley," she said and stopped sobbing, then hugged Rowe as he removed her blindfold.

"Well, Shirley, you are with the good guys now, so you don't have to worry. We will get you to your mom."

The girl was about Isabella's height but one year older than Isabella. Rowe hugged her tightly and headed up the stairs.

"Alex, I got the package. How's my perimeter?"

"Rowe, you are clear. The tangos are down. Wait. Wait, someone is going up… it is, ah, it is a tango. Repeat, I confirm. Two, two tangos! One in 30 seconds, the other in about 90 seconds."

Rowe went back down the stairs and quickly tucked the girl behind a large wooden box; both dropped down, "shhhhhh," he held up his finger.

"Wait here," Rowe said to the girl, frozen in fear. Rowe stood up and moved swiftly towards the door.

One of the tangos appeared in the doorway with his weapon drawn. Before he could fire, Rowe kicked him in the face, and the pistol went flying across the room. The tango recovered quickly and lunged at Rowe. They fought Shotokan, and Rowe could tell that they were well trained in various Martial Arts. They traded blows and blocked each other's advances. Rowe missed a block, was knocked backwards and saw his opponent reach for a knife. But he regained his stance, moved in quickly and broke his opponent's neck. Alex was biting her nails, listening to everything and her focus was locked in on the infrared images on her screen.

"Tango number two at your six, approaching the door," Alex said, keeping her voice calm and steady.

At that moment, the second tango showed up and fired a shot that narrowly missed Rowe. The girl screamed behind the wooden box and ran for the stairs, which drew the attention of the tango. Rowe dodged to the right behind a metal pole and deftly drew his 9MM. Rowe shot him twice in the forehead before the tango could turn his head back in Rowe's direction. Rowe was known to be most effective under pressure. Two tangos down. It was quiet, and Rowe listened for more footsteps. He started counting… One thousand one, one thousand two, one thousand three. None, no movements, no sounds. Nothing.

Alex said, "Nothing moving towards you. Rowe, are you okay? Rowe!"

Rowe said, "Mi Amor, that was close!"

Alex said, "There are U.S. troops on the first, second, and third levels; all three levels are clear. Those two tangos were flushed out and were trying to escape to the roof!"

Rowe ran towards the stairs and scooped up the girl, "Thanks, Alex. I got the package, and we're moving. What does the sky look like?"

"The Black Hawk is still waiting on the Landing Zone."

"Alex, did my chopper leave the area when I disembarked?"

"Alex said, "No. No compromise. I magnified the scene, and it's all the same people, the pilot, his crew, and our people on the roof. You are clear to deliver the package."

"Aye, aye, Captain," said Rowe. It dawned on Antonette that this situation had reoccurred in her dreams, so she scanned the perimeter and beyond the perimeter very closely. But the perimeter and beyond the perimeter was clear. No RPGs. She felt so much energy, drew deep into her intuition and asked God to help her protect Rowe with her superpowers.

Antonette smiled and said to herself, "My Lord, please keep my love safe and bring him home to me. Thank you for letting me see those tangos on my radar in time to warn my love. All glory to you, Lord."

She contacted HG Hawk and reported, "Hawk, this is Alex. Repeat, this is Alex reporting. Guardian's mission was accomplished, and he got the package. I repeat, the Guardian got the package. Alex, out."

They strapped the girl into a seat of the Black Hawk, with a crew member sitting next to her and put protective earphones on her head. She stared off into space in shock and seemed oblivious to her surroundings.

Meanwhile, now inside the Black Hawk, Rowe said, "That was close! I had to shoot! He was about to detonate an explosive vest!"

The pilot asked if he was all right, and Rowe replied that he was.

The pilot said, "We heard you encountered more tangos inside, but your time was excellent, sir!"

Rowe said, "It's nothing like the old times. Easy peasy."

The pilot laughed and said, "Ain't that the truth."

Antonette, still connected and listening to Rowe, thought she said it to herself, but actually, it was out loud, "Hmm, and a little arrogant. But I love the way he fights," which made both Rowe and the pilot laugh.

As they flew towards HG Hawk's location, Rowe's memory of Omar brought him back to when they were at Helmand and Bagram. Omar was one of their interpreters. They became buddies, and Omar always brought gifts to Rowe like Kabuli Palaw, an authentic Afghan rice dish with succulent lamb, carrots, raisins, and apricots. This elaborate dish came in many flavors and was cooked with a unique blend of spices that created a fantastic feast for all the senses. The Kabuli Palaw that Omar brought was not spicy like Biryani but had an elegance to it, with glistening carrots and raisins and then the tenderness of the lamb. It was mild yet very flavorful. It had hints of cardamom, cinnamon, and saffron. Rowe told Omar he had culinary talent.

Omar laughed and said, "My wife cooked it." And they both laughed.

Rowe said, "You could have said yes, and I won't even know the difference." And they both laughed again.

Omar also brought the national drink of Afghanistan, called *doh*. It was a legion of sour, salted beverages popular throughout central and eastern Asia. It was a combination of yogurt, whey, club soda, lemon juice, mint, and salt. The salt served as a valuable rehydrating agent in warm climates, such as Afghanistan. Rowe had quickly learned to love it.

It was accessible to like Omar, but Rowe was careful not to fall into Omar's generosity. There had been several deaths in the past due to trusting the unknown enemy.

Rowe thanked him profusely for the treats and sometimes offered him cigarettes. Omar told Rowe about his family. He had a wife and four children, two boys and two girls. He wanted to provide for his family, so he applied as a terp (interpreter). He was highly endorsed by his local government, had a top-secret clearance, was hired, and embedded with the 5th SFG (A). He had also said the Taliban had come to his house several times and threatened his life and family. Rowe listened to Omar's story and empathized with him. But it was part of his training not to trust anyone on the battlefield, and his instinct said, 'be careful'.

And true enough, Omar had sold them out. There was an enemy attack one night, but the 5th SFG had suppressed the Taliban. Rowe saw Omar running out to the side gate. Omar looked back and saw Rowe running after him. Omar disappeared in the dark, and the 5th SFG lost track of him. Maybe Omar had no choice; maybe the Taliban had threatened his family again more forcefully. Rowe would never know.

At another time, the 5th SFG was conducting surveillance when they encountered the Taliban in the mountains. There were heavy gunfights, and Rowe's buddy got shot. Rowe had stopped to apply a tourniquet to his buddy's leg and was about to carry him across his shoulder when Omar suddenly appeared in Rowe's path. Omar had an AK-47. The other Taliban members nearby yelled that they needed to leave and called Omar to rush. Omar had stared at Rowe with a cold gaze as if their friendship had never existed. Rowe knew that Omar could quickly have shot him, but instead, he fled and left Rowe to attend to his buddy. Rowe did not want to kill Omar since Omar had once spared his life, but anything can happen in war. Omar had taken the wrong path, and Rowe had no choice. Rowe remembered the sound of the rescue UH-60 Black Hawk approaching to evacuate him and his injured buddy.

The sound of the whirring blades flickered into Rowe's consciousness and started to pull him from memory back to the present.

"We're here!" the pilot said and snapped Rowe from his thoughts as they descended. The Black Hawk landed safely, and Rowe handed the girl over to the CIA waiting on the ground.

Antonette, back in the bunker, breathed a sigh of relief. No RPGs had appeared as they had in Antonette's nightmares.

"Thanks, Rowe. I owe you one," said HG Hawk.

"I was the right person for the job. I knew the tango, Omar. How's Seelig?"

HG Hawk covered her mouth and shook her head.

"I'm sorry, you did all you could to save him," Rowe offered. "You have a bigger problem on your hands than you realize; there are more enemies here than we thought. According to Omar, at least 100,000. He could be bluffing, but I wouldn't discount it. You need to advise the President now to have his friends in the Pentagon hurry up with their jammers, or we'll lose our American Freedom and possibly tip the scale of World Freedom in the wrong direction!" And he told HG Hawk everything that Omar had said. She already knew about the submarines from Intel, but not the number of enemies who had been planted throughout the States.

HG Hawk got a chill in her spine after listening to Rowe's intel report, but she stayed calm. Indeed, she had a lot on her hands, and she trusted everything she had just heard.

"Get the President on the phone," she commanded her assistant.

HG Hawk said she had one more favor to ask. This time it was for Antonette, and she would discuss it after he had returned home. Rowe wondered what mission would be better for Antonnette than him; perhaps the role required a female.

The Black Hawk landed on Rowe's lawn, the same place where it had picked him up, and Rowe navigated his way back to the house tactically. The Black Hawk stayed, and Rowe knew why but was still curious about the new mission. Rowe closed the door and found Antonette waiting for him at the bottom of the stairs with water, a towel, and a dry shirt to change. They hugged and kissed.

Rowe said, "I am a little arrogant?" Antonette blushed; she didn't realize he had heard her.

Rowe quipped, "You murmured in the mic, and I heard it. I am glad that I am just a little arrogant, not too much. I am pleased to hear that." And he kissed Antonette on the forehead. He was truly a hero, and she adored him even more after seeing how he fought the tangos. Antonette asked what he wanted for dinner.

"What about pizza? I always crave pizza after kicking ass."

"Ok, You're the man," Antonette said, and they both laughed.

The red phone buzzed, and the monitors flickered into focus.

CHAPTER 15

"Now faith is the assurance of things hoped for, the conviction of things not seen."

(Hebrews 1:11)

"Congratulations again, Rowe, job well done," Hawk said. Without wasting any time, she said, we need to rescue the President from Camp David and take him to the White House. This time, Alex will do it."

"What! Why Alex? I am ready to go," Rowe quickly protested. He knew that Antonette was capable of anything, but he didn't like her going into such a dangerous mission without him by her side.

"I know, that would make a lot of sense since you just finished a heck of a rescue mission. But Alex knows her way around Camp David and the White House since she had worked there before. There is no need for further introduction to the layout. Alex is already familiar with it. Besides, you will be with her anyway; you will be her eyes and ears. Do you have any questions about Operation Shangri-La, Alex, Rowe?"

Both answered, "Negative."

HG Hawk continued. "Good. The Black Hawk is waiting for Alex, so gear up; we need to roll fast."

Antonette and Rowe kissed one more time, and Rowe said, "Come back to me alive and in one piece, please?" Antonette answered, "Inshallah!"

She put her night-vision goggles over her head and geared for battle with the special Kevlar gift from Rowe. She tactically navigated her way to the Black Hawk. Riding in the chopper gave her flashbacks of the air assault flying above Babylon in Iraq. Oh, how she missed it. She adored their training exercises. It was exhilarating and the best part of her tour in Iraq air assault from a Black Hawk! Antonette briefly thought that she should write a book about her four deployments.

"What is your name, sir?" Alex asked the pilot as they headed for Camp David.

"Michael, but everyone calls me Mike," he responded.

Alex smiled to herself. Who else would be better off taking her to a battle than Saint Michael the Archangel? She knew immediately that the mission was Divinely protected. There were three of them in the Black Hawk that evening; Michael, the pilot and two crew chiefs, one of whom was the gunner. She was the fourth, and the President would be the fifth passenger. There was room for the President's aide and service detail if they could save them all. Alex silently started to say the Rosary as they cruised at 130 mph.

"Ma'am, did you say something?" Michael asked.

Antonette replied, "Are you ready for this?"

"Been ready all my life. We also have two Apache escorts complete with Hellfire missiles, 30mm cannon, FFAR (folding fin aerial rocket) rocket pods, FIM-92 Stinger anti-air missiles," the pilot assured her.

"Well, alright! Then let's do it!" Antonette said enthusiastically.

They were escorted by the two Apache helicopters and also a medivac UH-60 that was outfitted with two medical litters, which they were hoping they wouldn't need. After a short flight, they approached Camp David.

"I don't like what I see; watch your backs," Rowe's voice crackled over the mic.

The helicopters touched the ground just as they saw the President running down the back steps of the lodge near the pool, with his bodyguards surrounding him. The original plan was for Alex to stealthily enter Camp David before any tangos arrived and extract the President from the safe room there. Something had gone wrong. The attack on Camp David had already started, and the operation launched into a contingency plan.

Alex leapt out of the Black Hawk and covered the President and his security detail, firing at the enemy as the escaping group ran towards the chopper.

Rowe's mic crackled again, "Alex, there are four tangos to the left!" She quickly turned and fired her weapon. Tarratatatat!

"Got 'em," she said.

"Six running towards you now. Tarratatatat! They all scrambled into the Black Hawk, Alex bringing up the rear and covering the group.

The gunners took care of that group, who had fired into the security detail and wounded one of the secret service members running right next to the President.

"Egress, repeat egress, get out of there now. I see explosives all around Camp David. The tangos are in pursuit! Repeat; the tangos are in pursuit! Two, three, four, I see ten, there are ten tangos. Move now, exfil fucking exfil; they will light up the sky!" Rowe shouted.

Antonette said, "Go, go, go! Let's get the hell out of here now!"

They all jumped in, and the Black Hawk lifted off immediately, but just as they were above the treeline, they felt a massive explosion underneath them that rocked the chopper. Camp David had been partially destroyed by an explosion and was engulfed in flames. The President was shocked. Trees were on fire, and thick black smoke covered the area as everyone in the Black Hawk buckled in for a fast ride back to Washington.

"Oh, my God. What is happening? Where is my wife?" The President asked, suddenly terrified for her safety.

Fortunately, his wife was in the White House safe room. She had hosted the Blue Stars Charity to help the golden families and honor the Fallen Heroes earlier that morning. As soon as the White House security detail had heard about the roadside bombings, they whisked her away.

The President had planned to spend a relaxing day at Camp David working on the finishing touches for a televised speech later that evening. They had been briefed on the unfolding situation and were ordered to stay inside the safe room and monitor the situation from there until the choppers arrived to evacuate them back to the White House. The trip was last minute and not on any itinerary. It was considered a safe place until intel had received word of terrorists winding their way through the walking trails near the lodge. A few had been picked off by security, but too many were approaching. One of the secret service members stationed in the woods had found two colleagues lying in a pile of leaves with their throats cut, and the call for extraction was ordered. The country needed to hear from the President, and he had to be safe in the Situation Room to make a National Announcement to the American people.

"Does anyone have news on the Vice President's condition?" The President asked, but no one had an update.

The President had miraculously made it inside the helicopter without any injuries but was a little dizzy from the adrenaline rush and the explosions.

Unexpectedly, Rowe exclaimed, "RPG! RPG! It's going to be a direct hit. Oh my God! Alex, get down! NOW!"

The pilot heard this and veered the Black Hawk to the left, but the RPG would still make a direct hit.

Suddenly, a radiant light blazed through the sky and miraculously averted the missile away from the Black Hawk. Everyone had braced for impact and saw the explosion in the air. The radiant light then went down, picked up the tangos and before anyone could speak of what had just taken place, the radiant light disappeared with the tangos as quickly as it had appeared.

Everyone started talking at once.

"What the fuck was that?" Michael asked.

"Did you see that?" "What the hell?" The other crew members asked, bewildered.

Rowe, gripping his seat, let out a sigh of relief when he saw the missile strike had been averted. The President, the pilot and crew members were safe, and Antonette was safe. He rubbed his eyes and keyed in his computer to back track what had just taken place above Camp David. He saw the tango release the RPG; it was on a direct track to hit Antonette's helicopter. Then it detonated away from the Black Hawk with no explanation. He did not see anything else, not even the mysterious radiance, no sign, no clue, no proof. He replayed the scene three times, then ran his fingers through his hair and smiled. He kissed his pendant with St. Michael and read the inscription silently. He genuflected on his left knee and tapped his heart three times. He thanked God for saving Antonette, the President, and his men.

He said silently, *"Now faith is the assurance of things hoped for, the conviction of things not seen"* (Hebrews 1:11).

Rowe didn't know that Antonette had given him the pendant because she compared him to another pilot named Michael, whom she knew was an incarnation of Saint Michael here on Earth. Saint Michael, the first pilot, had delivered her safely to her unit beyond all odds while she was fighting the war in Iraq. Now a second Saint Michael was with her on this mission; she knew without a doubt he had been sent by God to deliver them safely.

Meanwhile, still riding inside the Black Hawk, the President looked at the individual across from him after checking himself for wounds and asking the others if they were all right.

"What is your name?" The President asked.

"Call me Lady Savior," a voice said, and suddenly the President saw a blinding, powerful diamond light. He shielded his eyes and couldn't see where the voice was coming from. He couldn't see anything. Everyone in the back of the Black Hawk covered their eyes too. When the light was gone, the President was blind. He was in a complete panic.

"My eyes, I can't see!" he said frantically.

The Black Hawks and its escorts touched down on the White House lawn. The perimeter had been heavily secured and fortified by the Marines, hypervigilant as they stood guard. The President was helped off the helicopter, and Alex guided him to the Situation Room. It was equipped with secure, advanced communications equipment for the President to maintain command and control of U.S. forces worldwide, but it was not equipped for a blind President.

Suddenly, as they entered the Situation Room, the President recovered his eyesight and exclaimed, "I can see! I can see! Oh my God, I can see!"

The gunner explained that the President was blinded by a radiant light while in the helicopter. The President rubbed his eyes, and he could see his COS, the NDI, NSA, and the HSA, who were not sure what the hell was going on with the President. They thought he was delirious due to the explosion.

"He was talking to somebody, and then suddenly, a radiant, diamond-like white glowing light appeared, and we remember the President asking, 'Who are you?' But we didn't hear anything else. It seemed that only the President had received the answer." Everyone just stared blankly at the gunner's story. "He lost his eyesight after the blinding light disappeared, fucking bizarre."

The President's aide agreed, "We saw the blinding light too and shielded our eyes, but only the President lost his eyesight." The secret service agents also mentioned that the RPG was miraculously averted away from the Black Hawk by this radiant light. The pilot added that he saw the RPG on the monitors and thought it was their end. One of the Apache pilots said he saw it coming and knew it was too late for the Black Hawk to dive. Suddenly, a radiant light averted the missile away from the chopper, and it exploded in the air. They also saw the light taking the enemies up in the sky, and then the light disappeared. It was instantaneous! The group with the President was still reeling from shock and relief that the RPG had been averted and were in awe that the enemy had been essentially erased. Then the President had asked someone's name, and they remembered nothing else until they had landed.

"Lady Savior," the President said, I will never forget her name. He told everyone in the room that he felt like there had been a miracle after regaining his sight because he was also cured of any pains. He felt like he was instantly healed physically and spiritually, and he felt only love in his heart. The people in the room looked at him incredulously, but the President was respected and always serious, so they believed every word. The President was grateful to know that there was no loss of life among his security detail but was saddened by the destruction of Camp David and to learn of the two secret service agents who had been killed in the woods.

The head of the NSA was on one of the monitors and exclaimed that this terrorism must be stopped. There was scattered intel about submarines and stolen aircraft, and they needed the President to take command now that he was safe.

Alex and the crew left the Situation Room as soon as they had been debriefed and proceeded to the Black Hawk, waiting on the heavily guarded White House lawn.

"Guardian, this is Alex, over," Antonette said. Rowe's mic came live and replied, "I hear you loud and clear, Alex. Go on."

"Guardian, this is Alex. What does the sky look like?" Rowe replied, "No one touched the chopper, and you're clear from tangos, Alex. No compromise in the cockpit, over."

Once boarded, Alex continued, "Guardian, this is Alex. Mission complete, and package is all in. Repeat, mission complete, and the package is safe." Rowe answered, "Roger, that Alex."

Antonette said, "Over and out," and almost added, "I love you," but realized she wasn't the only one who could hear their transmissions. That would have to wait until she touched down in Richmond.

Rowe replied, "Out." He turned off his mic and said, "I can't wait to feel you in my arms. You are my heroine."

"Great job today, Mike. How about a lift home?" Alex told the pilot, and he jokingly told her to make sure her tray table was upright.

"Smartass," she replied, and they both laughed.

The NDI said, "We are glad to hear you have recovered your vision, Mr. President. There is someone here who wants to speak to you." HG Hawk appeared on the giant monitor, she had dark circles under her eyes, but she addressed the President as if she was not exhausted and bone tired.

"Good Morning, Mr. President. Glad to see you are safe and sound. What we see around the country, and in London, and Paris, is the result of the infiltration of KAKO. Our Intel says it's a new breed of an enemy that believes in Jihadism. Our Intel also collected about 100,000 of them here, spread out in our nation, seeking to destroy American lives and many lives in other countries. My intel says you need to do a formal speech right away and inform the people. Tell them to stay off the roads because of IEDs and defend their homes and communities if armed. They should shelter in place and not drive anywhere until we get our troops equipped with RF electronic jammers to protect them against radio-controlled improvised explosive devices. Yes, Mr. President, the terrorists have brought the battleground to the USA and caused massive loss of lives and equipment. They are spreading fear among the Americans and challenging our people's *indivisible* principles. Our people don't know what to do; we have chaos in the cities. Some people in remote areas are in denial and continue to drive to work, get groceries, and attend meetings… just like what the vice-president was trying to do early in the morning. The people have not seen IEDs before; they will be blindsided. We recommend that you make an emergency announcement within the next 30 minutes if the terrorists try to shut down our communication. And Mr. President, about submarines and aircraft…" then HG Hawk spilled the intel from her source to the President and his group in the S Room. Everyone was shocked. They couldn't believe what they had just heard; how could this happen here?

"This isn't the speech I thought I'd be giving today," the President said, pulled a wrinkled paper from his coat pocket, and then ripped it in half.

CHAPTER 16

"Be joyful in hope, patient in affliction, and faithful in prayer."

(Romans 12:12)

The President announced as soon as the Pentagon and his advisors cleared him. He wanted to inform the people that he was alive and had made it to the White House safely because of Lady Savior. His advisors initially fought against it. What if the American people thought he was crazy or delirious? But ultimately, they agreed that it might scare the enemy to think that we had a superpower helping us, so they agreed to let him tell the public what had happened. Plus, the people needed hope; they needed to know that God was here, and miracles were occurring to help us in our time of distress.

"I saw a miracle today, and thank God Almighty for looking over Lady Savior who rescued us earlier today. We want to seek her help to save the world wherever she is.

I didn't have the opportunity to thank Lady Savior while we were in the helicopter. I remember hearing that we were about to take a direct hit from an RPG. Still, a radiant diamond light was brighter than I had ever seen before, which drew the RPG away from our helicopter and detonated the device! I felt protected; our helicopter was safe despite the potential RPG and the considerable explosion right underneath us that destroyed Camp David. I asked one of the troops who had saved me," the President continued. "The answer was, 'Call me Lady Savior'. A diamond-like radiant light momentarily blinded me, but now I have my full vision, and my aches and pains have healed. Truly a miracle has occurred, and I have a feeling that I have seen America's Guardian Angel." Almost everybody around him was in tears at his public disclosure about Lady Savior. And he continued, "So, Lady Savior if you are watching, we need your help. America needs you. The world needs you. Help us, please."

And then he turned around and faced his people in the S Room off camera.

"About the subs and aircraft," the NSA said, "We're on with the Pentagon, Mr. President. We're getting more details and fortifying a plan to destroy the enemy and prevent American loss of life."

After the public announcement, the media reiterated the President's words: "Everyone stay home, don't drive anywhere until everything is secured. Arm yourselves and defend your homes."

"The president is looking for Lady Savior, who miraculously rescued him from Camp David to the White House. The media continued to broadcast the search for Lady Savior. If she is watching today, we need you, Lady Savior, to help save the country. Save the World. Please continue to shine your radiant light and create more miracles."

It was dark by the time Antonette returned to Richmond. She used her night vision goggles and maneuvered her way back to the spy bunker. Rowe saw everything; he saw her coming down the stairs and waited for her at the bottom of the steps. Antonette hugged him as soon as she descended, and Rowe hugged her tightly. Antonette believed that Rowe truly loved her by the way he held her. No one had ever held her like this; it was all-encompassing and enveloping. She felt safe, loved, seen, and understood all at once. They could each feel their heartbeats closer when they were together. They were *inseparable* and in total unity at that moment. Every cell in their bodies was tingling with energy, and they knew that they were meant to work together for the highest good of humanity.

"Nothing, there is nothing that could take me away from you," she whispered. "Nothing."

Rowe cupped her face and kissed her, saying, "I love you, you, and you. You are my hero. You are amazing and brave, and you saved the President!"

They both hugged again and listened to the news in the background.

"Who is Lady Savior, and where is she?" The reporter asked rhetorically.

Rowe and Antonette sat down, and Rowe had an idea of who Lady Savior was, but he kept it to himself. They heard the sound of the Black Hawk's rotor above them as it lifted, and then it was gone. The helipad was constructed above an impenetrable room; Rowe had designed it that way. A secret underground passage from the bunker led directly to the impenetrable room with a trap door to the helipad in case of evacuation or emergency.

Rowe helped Antonette remove her gear and gave her a bottle of water. He hugged her tightly again and kissed her like he had not seen her in decades. He missed her just in the short time she was gone and admitted that he was scared something would happen to her during this dangerous mission. They hugged for a long time until they heard a cough on one of the monitors. It was HG.

HG was waving her arms around in wild gestures as she demanded answers. She cleared her throat and demanded, "Who the Hell is this Lady Savior in the helicopter? Anyone? Alex, Rowe, did you see anything?" Not waiting for an answer, she said, "Rowe, could you backtrack the video feed and show us the blazing radiant light that the President claimed he had seen, which temporarily blinded him until they reached the White House?"

Rowe complied with HG's request, but he already knew that there was no sign of radiant light. He magnified everything on the monitor so HG could see for herself.

HG quipped, "Well, whoever she is, thank God she's on our side! I'm not one to believe in miracles amidst the chaos, but I saw that RPG heading straight for the President's chopper and then it was gone. One minute, a group of tangos was on the ground, and then they were gone. A miracle is the only explanation for that RPG instantaneously averting a direct hit, and erasing the enemy on the ground.

"It was amazing," Rowe said as he winked at Antonette, and she looked at him with a knowing glance.

"Congratulations, Alex and Rowe, for a job well done! Alex, a heck of a job out there! You guys are *inseparable;* we need you to work as a team on every major mission! You helped save America and restored our unshakeable resolve by keeping the President safe. You are *indivisible,* and the world needs your strength, especially now. We were hoping you could monitor the area around the White House all night, and I suggest you work shifts overnight. My COS will be taking over for me while I close my eyes for two hours. I'll contact you tomorrow, goodnight!"

Antonette and Rowe heard the word *indivisible* echoing in their consciousness all night. It dawned on Antonette that all of this was her dream the night she woke up sweating profusely. Rowe had touched her hair and face and assured her that everything would be alright. Antonette looked up, and Rowe saw tears in Antonette's eyes.

"What is wrong, Mi Amor?"

"It is all happening now. This was the nightmare I had before you woke me up that night. What if the world falls into a dystopian land as I saw in my dream?"

It broke Rowe's heart to see her in tears, and he wiped them away and kissed her eyes, cheeks, nose, and lips. He loved her so much and would protect her with every fiber of his being. "It won't; we're going to make sure of it," he said with resolve.

Rowe volunteered to stake out the monitors the first night, and Antonette brought him more bottled water from the fridge to the situation room in the spy bunker. They hugged and kissed goodnight one more time.

Antonette turned to leave, and Rowe said, "I will miss you!"

"I'm right upstairs, silly. Now do a good job, my warrior!" Antonette said and blew him a kiss as she headed upstairs to shower and go to bed.

When Rowe was left alone, his thoughts circled Lady Savior. He had a feeling that it was Antonette, but neither had discussed the subject. After all, if he could read minds, why should it be a surprise that Antonette had superpowers of her own? And he was unable to read her mind about Lady Savior. It was a successful rescue mission indeed. How many more rescue missions would there be in this chaotic situation? Rowe knew that Antonette could handle herself, but he hoped the next mission would be his.

He thought to himself; the electronic jammers should soon be up and placed throughout the country. He had a prototype in his bunker and was determined to invest in its continued innovation after the chaos was over. The Feds had built thousands of prototypes, which had saved the troops from getting blown up on the battlefield many times. He knew some improvements could be added to keep the troops safe; they just hadn't been added to the prototypes yet. Rowe made a mental note to talk to his friends in the Association of the Old Crows, who were also working on developing Electronic Warfare (EW). They had many ideas for information-related capabilities, such as Electromagnetic Spectrum Operations (EMSO) and Cyber Electromagnetic Activities (CEMA), and Rowe vowed to continue funding their research projects.

CHAPTER 17

HG woke up at 4 am and saw that the enemy was now using a magnetic IED on the TV. The truckers had banded together after that and had already taken down three groups of insurgents on their own. Many cars had been blown to pieces when the IEDs chased and blasted the cars leaving no survivors. Roads in certain areas had become impassable, and KAKO had confiscated some truckloads. The supply chain was already fragile due to the pandemic, and they weren't going to be stopped by a bunch of 'pussy terrorists' as one of them put it on TV. HG laughed out loud at seeing that video and said, "I fucking love you guys; give 'em hell."

There were random shooting incidents in California Beach and shopping malls. The KAKO had taken over a school in Oregon and another in Georgia and used them as a battle station. They had robbed banks and taken over gas stations. Despite her 36-years of experience with the CIA, including the terrorist attack on 9/11, she couldn't believe this was happening in random places all over the United States.

The KAKO shattered people's American freedom and threatened to take over the world. How did the KAKO enter unnoticed into her country? What had happened to the security measures put into place to keep terrorists out after 9/11? These questions swirled in her head endlessly. She hoped for more cyber technology innovation, and she thought of Rowe's company and his brilliant ideas. HG thought of Rowe as a Saint, a Protector of the People and Warriors. He was all about saving the troops, saving America, saving people, saving the universe. The enemy had been lurking, plotting, silently inserting themselves into America. She thought about the submarines and stolen aircraft, which gave her a chill down her spine. She needed Rowe and Antonette's help.

The night shift was up. Rowe stretched and started up the stairs to wake Antonette for the second shift. He saw Antonette coming down the stairs, looking well-rested with a freshly brewed coffee in her right hand.

She said to Rowe, "I made just one cup because you need to get some sleep," and touched his messy hair. Rowe grabbed her waist, encircled his arms around her, and then looked deeply into Antonette's eyes.

"Good morning, sweet lady." He briefed her about last night's activities while he was on shift. Then he took her coffee cup and set it down next to his desk. He scooped her up, laid her down on the king-sized bed, and then rested his head on her belly.

"Rowe, I need to start my shift soon," Antonette protested lightly.

"The world can wait," Rowe said, and she wasn't about to argue with that look in his eye.

He took his clothes off and then hers, and laid naked next to Antonette. He pulled the sheets over them and made love to her, grabbing her hips and taking her from behind. It did not take him long to finish, he was so turned on by Antonette's heroic rescue mission. This was a good thing, because a few seconds after the two of them lay spent in the sheets, the alarm on her watch signaling the start of her shift blared and they both jumped and then laughed. Antonette rushed to put her clothes on, fixed her hair, and grabbed her coffee. Rowe stealthily headed for the stairs, and Antonette caught a glimpse of his naked body and smiled to herself.

"Rowe, my love, you can rest down here instead of going upstairs. You have all the facilities in this self-sufficient room, and I'd like you to be here if the CIA calls."

But deep inside her, she was concerned that their house might be bombed and would hate the idea of thinking Rowe was sleeping in a very vulnerable location. She didn't tell him that; sometimes, she had these thoughts and was afraid it might be a premonition. She also didn't want Rowe to know that she wanted him nearby if there was another terrorist attack. Antonette didn't like showing her vulnerability and preferred to put on a brave facade when it came to working matters. It was occasionally lovely to stop being an amazing self-sufficient woman and let her guard down. Antonette had learned how to take care of herself in war. She was a survivor. She had later learned how to allow herself to be cared for by others and not be afraid to receive and be feminine.

Rowe said, "You know I can read your concerns, right?"

And Antonette blushed and said, "I love you."

Rowe replied, "Roger, roger… I will take a shower down here and rest. No worries."

Antonette put her arms around Rowe's neck, his naked body against her, and kissed him, saying, "Thank you."

Rowe said, "My pleasure, and I love you too."

The next day, Muzabar, the leader of the terrorist group, appeared on TV. He exclaimed that the United States must yield to their demands. They wanted to occupy the White House and demanded that it must be vacated as soon as possible to the extent of eliminating everyone, anyone, if they resisted.

"We will rule the United States. We will capture the situation room and have command and control of the whole world; no one can stop us!" Muzabar screamed at the TV screen. According to one newscast, Iran was on their side, and their satellites were working in favor of KAKO.

Rowe, listening, said silently that Muzabar had overlooked America's unshakeable resolve and freedom to fight. His blood was boiling, and Antonette was just as angry.

Rowe finally let it out. "He has forgotten that the American people are *indivisible.* There is a reason why we are called the United States. America's faith will not be shaken; the US will never surrender to such selfish and cowardly bullies. We haven't forgotten 9/11. We are united in fighting against terror; whatever our differences are, we will come together when attacked. Do not tamper with America's Freedom."

"Try and stop me," Muzabar's final words echoed, and the screen went dark.

"Watch your words, Muzabar," Rowe said sarcastically and looked at Antonette with a cold gaze. She had seen that look before. "The head of KAKO," he added sarcastically. "We are coming for you. Nobody strikes the United States on my watch."

Antonette and Rowe took turns monitoring various locations for the CIA, and their intelligence reports were hampering new attacks in the most critical areas. But it wasn't enough, and they were both itching to be part of the action.

CHAPTER 18

"When you go through deep waters, I will be with you. When you go through rivers of difficulty, you will not drown. When you walk through the fire of oppression, you will not be burned up; the flames will not consume you."

(Isaiah 43:2)

On the third day, the country looked like a battle zone. Buildings had gaping holes from RPGs, wreckage filled the streets, and infrastructure like bridges had been destroyed. Civilians were clashing with the insurgents in small groups to defend their towns. Although the US was winning all small battles, the long-term damage was apparent. Troops were driving HE Cougar Mine-Resistant Ambush Protected (MRAP) Humvees all over the DC area, especially in Dupont, where some insurgents had been hiding.

Although Antonette already knew about MRAPs, Rowe explained it like he was giving a lecture. The MRAPs were explicitly designed to withstand IED attacks and ambushes. There were more than 12,000 MRAPs deployed in Operation Iraqi Freedom in Iraq and Afghanistan from 2007 until 2012. The production of MRAP officially ended in 2012, and our troops and allies were redeployed to their countries. The MRAP All-Terrain (M-ATV) replaced the Humvee in combat roles. In 2015, an award was given to a large business contractor to manufacture the Oshkosh L-ATV, which stands for Light Tactical Vehicle, a lighter mine-resistant vehicle to replace Humvee in combat roles and supplement the M-ATV. "Should I specify the contracted vendor?" Antonette smiled and nodded that she had a good idea who it was.

"Three days! We can't sit here and allow this to happen!" Rowe exclaimed in anger to Antonette as he watched the news and sipped his coffee, his second cup for the night. Every fiber in his being was surging with rage that American Freedom was in jeopardy. He knew that these insurgents wouldn't win. They had chosen to fight an unwinnable war;

darkness shall never overcome the light. Still, they were destroying the country, and it ripped at his moral fibers to watch it happen.

"I am with you; we are *indivisible*," Antonette replied and hugged him, and her silent freedom screamed inside, "*Do something.*"

Later that evening, two Humvees were patrolling the school campus in Oregon. The insurgents threw a rock at their windshield, attacked them, and were poised to slit their throats. Suddenly a radiant light sucked them up like a vacuum, and they disappeared. The troops were stunned. They thought they also saw a man with an edged sword and sandals on his feet, like a gladiator's sandals, but did not see him entirely because of the blinding light. They looked up until everything became invisible. They recalled the President's speech about a radiant light saving him from an RPG, which they had laughed at when they saw the Press Conference. Now the radiant light had saved their lives from the insurgents, who had slit the throats of their comrades-in-arms. The troops reported the incident to their commander.

The First Sergeant (1SG) rubbed his chin, "Did you just witness another miracle?" The 1SG and the Commanding Officer had been following the news on TV about the President's story and more miracles being reported.

The news spread like lightning, and their story was all over the media. The press knew that they had chosen to create discord and instigate fear to get better ratings in the past, but this was not the time for that. The American people needed hope, and they broadcast every miraculous story in an effort to elevate unity in people with messages of faith and togetherness.

"I'll be damned, Lady Savior," HG said when the Pentagon briefed her about this latest story.

But the COS added, "The troops also seemed to have seen a person with a jagged sword but could not specify because of the radiating light."

The President said, "Do we have another Angel other than Lady Savior?" Do we have two heroes? Thank God they are on our side."

"That's what I have said too, Mr. President. I am happy they are on our side. Yes, it appears that we have two Guardian Angels with an unconquerable, *indivisible* spirit." HG replied and had a feeling she knew exactly who they were.

In Rowe's spy bunker, Antonette was up early and prepared to take over the work shift. Wearing a green camo shirt and sipping coffee, she found Rowe fixated on the news about the incident last night and how a superhero had saved the troops.

"Wow… that's amazing!" She exclaimed and winked at Rowe.

Rowe turned around and, seeing her firm breasts under the tight camo t-shirt, said, "Good Morning, Mi Amor. You are looking lovely this morning in your camo shirt. And my imagination is running wild again. But Houston, we have a big problem."

"What is it?"

Rowe continued, "They have been tracking the hijacked subs. One of the States is in imminent danger as a submarine is headed their way."

"Where is it heading?" Antonette inquired.

"Oahu, Hawaii."

Antonette gasped, "Rowe! That's my home. Rowe…"

Rowe said, "I know. Another one is heading to Alaska. They have two hours, Antonette. And we have to deal with hijacked aircraft too. It's a big load."

Antonette looked at Rowe. They kissed one more time and flicked off the monitors—time to get to work.

On that day, the sky was cloudless and a bright deep blue color so pure that only God himself could have painted it. Everyone in Hawaii was in a trance, fascinated by radiating glorious lights moving swiftly in the sky. Meanwhile, somewhere off the Hawaiian shores, a terrorist named Mosher, who had hijacked a nuclear submarine, screamed at the American Navy Captain, Santos.

"What happened to the sonar? Why can't I see anything?" Mohsen yelled, "Fix this now!"

The sonar screen had gone dark. Fakhriz, one of the insurgents, grabbed Santos and dragged the Captain to the instrument panel with a knife to his throat. Moshen took his knife out also and threatened one of the hostages in the corner, who was a sonar technician in second class.

"Fix the sonar, or I will cut both of your throats," Fakhriz screamed.

Captain Santos interjected, "Easy… okay, okay, I will fix it but take your knife away from him first.

"I will slit his throat if you're playing games with me," Moshen became highly agitated.

Captain Santos made a few adjustments and reported that the sonar was working. He had casually disabled one of the settings to make it seem like the sonar wasn't working. If there was a rescue attempt, he didn't want the terrorists to know what was coming.

Mohsen peered at the screen, saw it was working for a few seconds, and then it failed again. Fakhriz positioned his knife on Captain Santos again, digging the tip into his throat, which caused a thin line of blood to trickle down his shirt.

Captain Santos gritted his teeth and wanted to take down the insurgents, starting with Fakhriz. Santos had no doubt the USS Helena (USS 753) would be rescued. He was buying time. He and his crew had been held hostage for 48 hours now. Captain Santos was confident and had faith that there would be a rescue attempt, or they could overtake the terrorists at the perfect moment.

Captain Santos suggested that they surface so they could 'reset the sonar,' which was just a tactic to stall. He knew they would be easier to rescue if the submarine surfaced. After they had reached about 50 feet below the surface, he scanned the horizon through the photonics masts, and they saw the brilliant clear blue sky and blue waters across the ocean on the high-resolution displays. He moved the joystick, and it scanned the sky. Some strange lights were zipping around, which the terrorists overlooked. He quickly focused on the water again.

"Continue to the surface." Captain Santos said as he winked at his men in the corner. The radiant light looked familiar. He had heard about the miraculous rescues that had been happening all around the mainland. Two *indivisible* superheroes appeared as a brilliant light saving the world from the ruthless killer KAKO. He suppressed his excitement and kept a straight face.

"I see no land on the horizon," Captain Santos said to Moshen and turned over the joystick to Mohsen, who rotated it just like Santos as the submarine reached the surface.

"Fakhriz, try it," Moshen shouted.

Fakhriz moved the joystick around and saw blue water. He rotated again and saw another part of the blue ocean. "I see nothing," he said, sounding deflated.

Exhausted and aggravated, Mohsen said, "Fakhriz, be the sonar man and tell me when you see the island!"

Fakhriz agreed, "Naeam syidi!" Yes, Sir!

Fakhriz was another former interpreter for the special forces while aboard the Navy's USS Georgia. It was armed with 155 Tomahawk land-attack cruise missiles and could hold up to 66 special operations forces. He was excited to be helping Jihadism. They were less interested in converting non-Muslims to Islam than expanding their territory for their brothers and children. Soon they would occupy Hawaii and its surrounding islands, and then Alaska and the mainland. He could not wait to see his fellow Jihadists live all over the island, eating fresh coconuts, ripe bananas, golden papayas, and fresh succulent pineapples. He lived in the middle of the desert all his life and living on a beautiful island surrounded by water sounded fascinating. He had fantasized about his new life hundreds of times. It had been his fantasy to live like a king with women dancing to the lively hula music around him, just like in the movies. He couldn't wait to be served meals fit for a new Hawaiian king.

He also thought about his KAKO brothers, who had been busy killing Americans and causing disarray. They were also in London, Germany, and the United Kingdom. Soon they would control the United States and then the World; he thought as he daydreamed about having a beautiful Hawaiian girlfriend.

Fakhriz was lost in thoughts, staring at the sonar screen, not realizing that his people stationed around the submarine were disappearing one by one. He glanced at the high-resolution digital display one more time and was stunned when he saw a face he didn't expect to see. He did a double-take and saw Rowe's face. Rowe looked pissed.

"Moshen, someone is on the Submarine!" Fakhriz shouted.

"Well, go up and check it out," Moshen replied angrily.

Fakhriz rushed towards the sail to verify what he saw. Fakhriz did not know about the lights that had been saving Americans from the KAKO, but he was about to find out in person.

Moshen rushed through the mess area and found his fellow Jihadists bundled together, including their radio communicator, the men he had assigned at the communication mast, radar mast, and weapon sensor mast. Fakhriz was heading towards the sail when he saw Rowe coming at him. Fakhriz tried to land a kick on Rowe's face, but Rowe was quicker. He grabbed Fakhriz's right foot and flipped him to the floor.

Fakhriz yelped as he grabbed his elbow, "How the fuck did you find us in the middle of the ocean, how did you get here, and most of all, how did you get into my submarine?"

Rowe replied, "Your submarine? The last time I checked, this was a US submarine. I should ask you, what are you guys doing in my land?"

Fakhriz laughed out loud and said, "We will kill you all. It's 100,000 of us, and we have surrounded your country by air, land, and water. You're all going to die. We will take over, and we will own this land, United KAKO!'"

Rowe deciphered that this was the second time hearing the number of KAKO in the country. Rowe said, "Not on my watch. You know I cannot allow that to happen. You have chosen to fight an unwinnable war. Who is your financier, and who has been arming you?" Rowe landed another punch to the side of Fakhriz's face.

Fakhriz collapsed under the blow, spat blood at Rowe's feet, and said, "So you can try to stop us? It is our time, and I am sorry, but it *is* happening on your watch."

Rowe had heard enough, "I'm sorry too, and since I cannot get an answer from you, what about taking a long flight to the netherworld?" With that, he gave Fakhriz one strong kick to the temple, and Fakhriz slumped in a heap on the floor, unconscious, no doubt dreaming about pineapples and beautiful women.

Rowe grabbed him by the collar and tied him up with the others. Then he searched for more KAKO inside the submarine. No one could identify him with his mask on. He untied all the American sailors and asked for the ship's captain.

"We are free! Finally, we are fucking free! Captain Santos said. He had been trying to identify Rowe, who was wearing a face covering. "Thank you, our hero, whoever you are. You saved our ship and these sailors!"

Rowe said, "I love the word 'Freedom,' Capt. You got your ship back."

Captain Santos quipped, "The seas may be rough, but I am the Captain! No matter how difficult it is, I will always prevail."

Everyone said, "Aye, aye, Captain!"

Rowe walked through the mess area to leave, and at that moment, a brilliant, radiant diamond light flooded the room. Captain Santos and his crew shielded their eyes, and when they looked up again, all of the insurgents had disappeared. Rowe reached the sail, transformed into a blazing light, and disappeared into the sky.

Those who took pictures of the radiant lights wondered what had happened. The light was just as mysterious as the Aurora Borealis, but it didn't appear in any of the pictures. There were no pictures, no proof of the insurgents who disappeared except for those who were there to witness it firsthand. Captain Santos sent a video-recorded message to the news outlets telling them what had happened, but there wasn't a shred of evidence to prove it.

"For we walk by faith and not by sight," the media reporter said. "The Guardians removed the KAKO from USS Helena and U.S. Navy Los Angeles nuclear-powered attack submarines. The crews of the two USS fleets are now free, and the insurgents are gone!"

Rowe and Antonette were back at the spy bunker, watching the news together as they each drank a large bottle of water and looked at each other.

When HG called, Rowe had just finished eating some scrambled eggs mixed with Antonette's special sausage. "Wow. What an arduous task. Glad that's over with. It is time to have peace in the world."

"Excellent job monitoring and saving the fleets. Did you guys see any super radiant lights on your monitors? Intel said the crew was safe, and the insurgents had just disappeared. And they saw the saving radiance like they had heard about from the President." She further said, "Nobody knows what happened to the KAKO. The Navy searched the waters and found no dead bodies. Look, I'm thankful the miraculous lights have been saving the world, but they need to save a few KAKO so we can lock them up in Guantanamo Bay Detention Camp for interrogation."

Rowe asked, "Don't you have enough terrorists in your hands to get the information you want?"

"This is different, Rowe. We want to know where the money is coming from; we need to find their leader and take him down. We need to bring this darkness to *justice,* and I don't care who the mastermind is. We will unravel this mystery. I want to know how they infiltrated the country and evaded our security systems. It could be Russia behind the curtains or the Chinese; everyone has a motive, but we need to know the source of the financing." HG said with a serious tone.

Rowe would like to have told HG that he and Antonette could get her that information without keeping KAKO on the ground, but he kept it to himself silently.

Instead, he said, "Calm down, HG. You got your hands full, and I think you're exhausted. Is your COS there? Are you getting any sleep?"

"How can I rest? America is not only imminently facing the threat of terrorism today but what happens here affects the entire World. The President has called the allies, and The UK, France, India, Germany, Israel, and Australia have bound together to defeat the KAKO. We will partner with them, as always, to defeat terrorism. Rowe, the world is with us, but I won't rest until we take down the terrorist leader.

"We have had profound success in the fight against the magnetic IEDs they planted on our roads. We are making headway on land and sea. They expected to anchor themselves to American land and rule over us, but their grip is slipping. Their perceptions that Americans are weak and arrogant are perception disqualifiers. They have forgotten that we are called the United States because we truly are United. One Nation under God. We are one; the heart and spirit of the country are *indivisible.* We have a solid foundation for Truth, Liberty, and Justice, and we believe in the Divine. We are *indivisible, indivisible, indivisible!*" She repeated the word three times.

At that moment, Rowe realized that HG truly believed in the supernatural and in Divine intervention, Divine timing. Perhaps the KAKO were here to teach us all a lesson about Unity and Trust.

HG's little speech had triggered something deep inside Rowe and Antonette, and all at once, they saw things from a higher perspective. There were so many stories of unity and compassion in the news. People helping strangers, the images of crying children bringing tears to the eyes of reporters, the sheer grit of the American people who would never give up their Freedom. Antonette recalled one of her favorite quotes by Pema Chödrön from The Places That Scare You: A Guide to Fearlessness in Difficult Times: "Compassion is not a relationship between the healer and the wounded. It's a relationship between equals. Only when we know our own darkness well can we be present with the darkness of others. Compassion becomes real when we recognize our shared humanity."

"War makes people recognize their shared humanity," Antonette thought to herself.

CHAPTER 19

"What shall we then say to these things? If God is for us, who can be against us?"

(Romans 8:31)

HG virtually summoned Rowe and Antonette with another agitating news. "Here is another catastrophe happening at JFK and one in San Francisco. We need both of you to save people at JFK; there is an aircraft that KAKO has hijacked. They have killed the Pilot because he refused to take off and demanded another pilot. We are stalling. Rowe, it looks like they want to repeat 9/11 based on my Intel. They claim they want to fly to Cuba, but my resources say otherwise. They know they are losing this battle, and they are determined to kill as many people and destroy as much of America as possible before it's over."

Rowe got a chill in his spine again and looked at Antonette with a cold glare.

"Not on our watch," he said to himself.

HG said, "Excuse me?"

"What's our itinerary?" Rowe said, very focused.

HG spilled out the details, "Rowe, a Black Hawk will fly you over to JFK, and you will stop the hijacked aircraft from taking off and hitting their target One World Trade Center (OWTC). The Marines will handle a separate issue at San Francisco International Airport."

Rowe leaned over, put his fists on the desk, and said to himself silently, *"They need a miracle; they need the Guardian Angels."*

"If you keep talking to yourself, we will not finish talking anytime soon, and I need you to go and kick some ass at JFK." HG snapped.

Rowe and Antonette grabbed their gear and left the spy bunker; a Black Hawk helicopter was waiting for them on the helipad.

HG respected Rowe and knew that he was wealthy enough to create his own CIA. With Antonette next to him, they were capable of hiring talented young men and women to save the world. They could equip their people and fight against cyber-attacks that threatened America and its allies and improve counterterrorism to prevent what was happening now from recurrence. They could help improve foreign intelligence and have more effective systems in place. Rowe inherited his wealth from his parents, which his grandparents handed down. They migrated to the United States from Italy, saved every penny, and invested in profitable portfolios. He refused to squander their money into vainglories. Instead, he invented weapons to protect America and the troops. He had the idea of marketing weapons to be sold overseas, weapons that would not work if used against Americans.

In the Black Hawk, the whirling rotor put Rowe deep in thought. He remembered when he had sold his weapons to King Assad, with an agreement not to use those weapons against Americans. King Assad mocked Rowe but smiled anyway and accepted the deal with no intention of holding up his end of the bargain. Rowe made a fortune from selling those weapons. He had an acquaintance, a large manufacturer in Oshkosh, Wisconsin, willing to manufacture his ideas. It took them one and a half years to manufacture and test the prototype.

One day, King Assad provoked the United States into a bloody war. He taunted them that he would capture Kuwait and become the greatest oil exporter. He planned to use Rowe's weapons to carry out this plan and fight the American troops using weapons, scud missiles, and RPGs, which were part of Rowe's invention. The time came, and King Assad received an order from the United States President to withdraw his troops or he would face peril. King Assad was obstinate and stayed to pursue his wild dream of becoming the top oil exporter. Then King Assad saw the invasion he'd never forget in Iraq. He witnessed his men firing at the Americans, but no one was falling down. Not even a single troop went down. King Assad summoned his leaders about what was occurring; his face was red from screaming at his leaders to kill the Americans. The enemy in battle had finally realized that their weapons were not working and tried to run away, but the American troops caught up and arrested them for interrogation. However, one escaped and reported the strange news to Azeem, one of King Assad's fiercest Army leaders. Azeem took the same weapon and pointed it at one of his soldiers to prove to Assad that the weapon worked. The soldier fell dead, and they realized that such weapons worked on their own men but did not work against Americans or coalition forces. Azeem did not know that this was because the American Military had secret codes built into their uniforms connected to a chip in the weapons to prevent contact.

The coalition forces eventually found King Assad in a trench hole and took him to his people, who were supposed to judge their King. The people decided to hang him and throw his remains into the ocean to feed the sharks. They also knocked down his statutes which surrounded his whole kingdom in the desert. Most countries are jealous of America's freedom, powerful military, economy, technological innovation, robust education, and the people who are *indivisibly* resolved. Jealous evil forces have tried to control or destroy us by any means possible.

Rowe's thoughts were distracted when HG called his name twice through the headset.

"Rowe, Rowe, are you there?"

Rowe answered, "Roger that, I am here, HG."

HG continued, "I said you're clear to do whatever you need to do, full authority."

"Keep your faith," Antonette and Rowe said simultaneously.

Rowe boarded one of the aircraft with Antonette, pretending to be the Pilot and Co-Pilot the terrorists had demanded. Two CIA agents who were actually pilots dressed as flight attendants also boarded the plane.

"No extra people, one of the terrorists said.

"Don't you want to eat? It's a long ride to Cuba." Rowe said, calling the terrorists' bluff. The terrorists knew that if anyone suspected they were going for the twin towers, the entire plane would be shot down before they got there.

"Yes, bring the food," the leader said but tied them up in the back. As soon as they boarded, a couple of KAKO showed up and put a gun close to Antonette's head. Rowe did not have any choice but to obey and gear up the aircraft. Rowe knew they were headed to New York, to the twin towers. Rowe would not allow a second terrorist attack to strike New York City. There was another aircraft behind his plane, and Rowe figured that the terrorists had wanted to repeat 9/11 by taking out both towers. The terrorists now controlled Rowe and Antonette in the cockpit and commanded them to circle around New York and its neighboring states three times. Then they had planned to kill Rowe and Antonette, take the controls, and fly straight through the buildings. Their altitude went up to 29,000 feet and gradually descended. They were now two miles away from the south of the new twin towers, now called OWTC. Rowe glanced at Antonette, who was so calm amidst all the chaos. Antonette turned her head to Rowe's, and they read each other's minds. About two miles from the towers, Rowe nodded to Antonette, and he gradually turned the aircraft around despite the terrorist's threat. Antonette moved quickly and gave the terrorist a sharp punch to his throat; he gasped for air and gurgled a horrible sound. Antonette then swiped his knife with her left hand, deftly reversed her momentum, and finished him off with a swift right elbow to the jaw. Then she threw his limp body against the second terrorist before he could shoot with his AK-47, which would depressurize the cabin. She thought quickly and grabbed the AK-47, then turned it around and used the metal butt to knock the second terrorist out cold.

Meanwhile, Rowe successfully turned the aircraft around by 180 degrees. The terrorists had instructed the other plane's pilot on board to follow the first plane. Rowe communicated with the other pilot that there was a change of plans, and he also turned around his plane and followed Rowe's route. The terrorists on the other plane didn't know what was going on and asked to talk to their leaders aboard the first plane.

Rowe set the plane on autopilot. Antonette found the CIA agents dressed as flight attendants and cut the zip ties holding their wrists with the knife she had swiped from the terrorist. The captain and his co-pilot headed for the cockpit and called the tower so they could land the aircraft. They hovered twice over Manhattan then headed up to New York Harbor until the landing area was clear and landed safely. As they left the plane, they noticed that Rowe and Antonette had disappeared with the two terrorists and were nowhere to be found. The CIA agents said that their heroes were male and female, both wearing masks. They fought the terrorists and saved OWTC from getting hit. Their heroes turned the plane around and saved everyone.

Meanwhile, the passengers on the first flight were so excited that they saw the terrorists being dragged to the back of the plane. They then saw brilliant lights, bright like the sun and soaring in the sky, and they followed the lights until they disappeared from their very own eyes. The pilot from the second plane said he was following the first plane away from the city when they saw a brilliant light in the sky. Then there was a blinding light in the cockpit, and when they had recovered their eyesight, the plane was on autopilot, and the terrorists had disappeared. They were all aghast at what was happening but thankful the Guardian Angels were on their side.

"Of course. Guardian Angels protect all people with pure hearts and good intentions. Thank God they are on our side," the co-pilot said quietly to himself before pulling his rosary out of his pocket and kissing it.

The Commanding Officer from Camp Pendleton reported to the Pentagon that he believed the nation's two new Guardian Angels had saved America again. The news uplifted the President; he would never forget Lady Savior, who had rescued him from the disastrous attack at Camp David. And he would never forget the second Guardian Angel who saved so many people from getting killed by the magnetic IEDs by guiding the troops and anchoring terrorists to the ground. The Guardian Angels had liberated American hostages and delivered them to the U.S. troops for care. They had also saved troops from getting killed by the teenage insurgents who had attacked a Humvee.

Not only in the United States, but the media had been reporting that countries worldwide had seen the blazing lights with reports of insurgents disappearing and then the lights fading into nothing in the sky. The media reported that the troops on the ground saw the aircraft around, about 180 degrees, before seeing brilliant lights in the sky. There were many miracles in a matter of a few days; the people believed and hoped and lifted their hearts in gratitude. The lights inspired people to stay strong and resolve together amidst the mayhem. There are always more lights than darkness. The Guardian Angels had given them hope.

For example, one of the young captives interviewed by a TV host from ABC News was born a paraplegic. The insurgents broke in looking for refuge and entered their home, thinking they could avoid being captured or killed by holding the paraplegic hostage. Suddenly, they saw a bright diamond light. She felt an indescribable warmth in her heart when the light touched her and led her outside the building. She was gliding on air in her wheelchair and was found in the front yard able to move her legs slightly. The terrorists were nowhere to be found, and her parents were awed by the miracle and thanked the Heavens. She said that she was filled with a sense of overwhelming love, and maybe the world needed to come together, repent, and reunite. The media was moved and reported the young girl's story; it had gone viral all over the world that morning.

According to the President's daily briefing, the world was not free from the terrorists' control yet. There were more things to be done to fight the terrorists and protect American freedom. He admonished the people to stay home as the troops looked for those magnetic IEDs to detonate them. They had wounded many people, like the vice-president as he traveled from his residence on Connecticut Avenue. And the IED that had killed the CEO and brainchild of the counter IED equipment. It was a horrifying time of war in the nation that shocked America and the world, and many were still in disbelief.

The troops continued their barricade and searched the buildings of New York, Washington DC, New Jersey, Virginia, Texas, Nevada, and New Mexico. Everywhere, the insurgents were abundant in California, Atlanta, Chicago, Wisconsin, Michigan, Florida, North Carolina, and many more.

The President reiterated, "We are inspired by the two Superheroes of our time, these Guardian Angels, to hold onto our faith and hope that things will get better in the future.

CHAPTER 20

"For He satisfies the longing soul, and the hungry soul He fills with good things."

(Psalm 107:9)

Rowe and Antonette continued to switch work shifts; they monitored all of the CIA's areas for Intel and sent instructions to the troops when needed. They had both stayed in the spy bunker since the KAKO infiltrated the U.S. Rowe had enough experience on the battlefield to prepare for an attack. He had anchored explosives in hidden places to incapacitate intruders, particularly the enemy. He had told Antonette about the explosives to help her feel secure and safe in their home. He was very responsible and always Special Forces Operations-minded. He was all in, every day. Antonette placed her right hand over Rowe's chest and told him that she had stopped guessing about what she didn't know about her husband.

Rowe said, "And so are you. I adore you. You know I keep reminding you I can read your mind, right? I can hear the whispers of your soul. And how many times have you rescued me from getting hurt? Remember about the girl kidnapped by the insurgents? Of all the people, why was it Omar? I knew that he had been misguided by the KAKO, who threatened his wife and two daughters. He was even willing to kill himself and never believed me when I tried explaining it to him, so he fell into darkness. Antonette, my love, you saved me that day and the little girl's life by sensing those tangos and warning me right on time as they ascended the steps about to shoot me and perhaps the girl. Who knows what could have happened to me without your eyes and voice? Thank God for the signals; I heard you just in time. And oh, by the way, I haven't forgotten that you said I was a little arrogant," Rowe teased.

Antonette was about to defend herself, but Rowe deliberately hushed her by softly touching her mouth with his fingertips.

"What about if we change that word to 'confident'?" He asked, and Antonette smiled. "I learned it during my special forces operational training. Be confident and know what you're doing. Trust your instincts. Intuition doesn't lie. They are the messages of your soul, and your heart will never betray you. It helps you guard against enemies. I have always trusted my instincts. Just like when I first saw you, I knew there was something. Then we got separated, and we got separated again and again for the second time. I always had this instinct that we would find each other in time, and I would have the opportunity to be by your side and love you forever. The messages from my soul always said, *what is meant to be will never be taken from you.* Trust in Divine Timing." Rowe looked into Antonette's eyes, and the depth of his gaze went back centuries. Their souls had been separated for so long, and finally, being in unification was almost more than either could believe.

Antonette met his starry blue eyes with a loving gaze and was touched by his ability to express his heart. There were so many times when she felt that he had wanted to say these things to her, but he couldn't. He was married and not available to her that way, yet she felt it so strongly in her heart that he had loved her but couldn't express it. During their separation, she always lost herself to the fantasy of what they could be together. She had finally chosen over the fantasy and resigned it to a fairy tale; she moved on with her life and thought herself mad at times for silently loving this man that she shouldn't. But her inner knowing, her silent freedom, had kept an ember of hope alive in her heart. She held onto her faith and allowed her life to unfold as it was meant to be presented. At times, she still had difficulty believing that their soul journeys had reached a mutual destination. Being together at each other's side was like Heaven on Earth.

"Thank you for sharing your heart with me, Rowe. I felt the same way when we were separated. The last time we were together, I couldn't tell you how I really felt because you were married and it wasn't appropriate. I shouldn't have kissed you at the airport, but I worried that we might never see each other again," Antonette became slightly emotional.

"You will never lose me again, and I will keep you safe just as you keep me." Rowe hugged her tightly, and she quickly rebounded.

"Well, that's good to hear, my Rowe. I believe you're capable and know what you're doing. You are indeed capable of achieving miracles. But how can you maintain being a superhero if you are constantly working overtime, my love? You're now on my shift, and you ought to be in bed. Get some rest; tomorrow is another day and…"

Rowe kissed her lips while she was still talking and said, "Yes, ma'am. I was about to do that, but I'd like to get some overtime with you first. It is too bad you're on shift now. What about coming to bed with me, sweetheart, just for a little while? Antonette circled her arms around Rowe's neck and returned his kiss. Rowe scooped her up and was about to carry her to bed when HG startled them and came live on the monitor.

"Goodnight, heroes. My shift is done, and I'll see you in a few hours? My COS is here now. He can handle things for a bit; you guys take a breather and report back in 15 minutes." Rowe raised one eyebrow and Antonette smirked. It was as if she had read their minds.

"If you insist," Antonette said, "Good night, HG. See you soon."

Rowe carried Antonette to bed and whispered, "Just a quickie," and they both giggled.

It was Rowe's night shift. He woke up, took a shower, and found his coffee on the table. He loved Antonette for attending to his needs. She was a good wife, good nanna, and good cook and sensed his needs before he even said a word. He smiled when he thought about the last one; maybe she could read his mind too and wasn't telling him? Her eyes hypnotized him and made him submissive whenever Antonette looked at him. Her gaze always penetrated so deeply that it compelled him to tell her the truth. He thought of it like Wonder Woman's lasso and laughed to himself. There was something inexplicable in Antonette; he knew it the first day they had met. Just like he had seen something unique and special in Mark, his grandson who had the same blue eyes, he felt blessed that he and Antonette had the opportunity to watch Mark grow and help guide him on life's journey.

Antonette said, "I miss the grands and our children," as if reading his mind.

Rowe had assured her that Steve had picked them up with his private plane as soon as the chaos had started in the U.S. He thanked God that the KAKO was nowhere near Iceland, where they were staying at Steve's large villa on a remote island. It is such an innocent pasture and a land filled with happiness, a true paradise and far from the strife of the US. They both prayed for the family's safety and hoped that this disaster would soon pass so they could all reunite. Rowe missed Isabella the most and was sad to have missed the birth of their new granddaughter Parker. Rowe thought the name was a bit strange but didn't say a word because he would never impose himself. He missed his family terribly, but for now, he was just responsible for his country and Antonette, the love of his life.

CHAPTER 21

"Though I fall, I will rise again, the Lord will be my light."

(Micah 7:8)

The next day, people woke up to find another nightmare in their own backyard. The terrorists were seizing buildings in certain cities, taking hostages, brazenly beheading Americans, and displaying the traumatic murder on TV. People were frightened they were all going to be beheaded, just like they saw the Jihads. They asked how could this be happening here? How did they get here in the first place, and how could they invade our houses and territories and destroy our properties? Who had been funding their selfish, brutal, inhuman cause?

Boooooom! Boooooom! Another IED exploded! This time it didn't kill anyone. The troops detonated it before it could incapacitate anyone. The IED detonation campaign had been successful and demoralizing the terrorists. The troops had also been victorious in rescuing many hostages, especially children. They were being reconciled with their parents, and some parents had collaborated with vigilante groups to defend communities and find and kill the terrorists. The television news broadcasts had told them to stay home because that was the official word. But the military leaders were supplying them with ammunition and were grateful for any help to protect the children.

HG received some intel and relayed it to Rowe and Antonette. There was a plan to attack the buildings on Massachusetts Avenue in Washington DC that the terrorists were using as their main headquarters. They would rescue the hostages and send hellfire missiles confined to that particular building without harming the neighborhood.

Antonette and Rowe sat in front, focused, and were horrified at HG's intel report about the hostages. HG continued and said it should happen within 24 hours. Their dilemma was how to rescue the hostages out of the buildings safely. The dilemma was not about dropping the bombs onto the buildings. They planned to deploy all the troops, Regular,

Reserves, and National Guards in all branches of DOD. They agreed on a strategy to simultaneously ambush each building and would need a UAV to monitor all actions.

"They need miracles," Rowe said.

HG knew that Rowe and Antonette wanted to go and help.

"I heard you say that earlier, Rowe. This time we have to do our human part and prevent casualties as much as possible. Rowe, Antonette, we need your eyes and ears and your instincts. You will be our heroes' heroes. Each day brings a different job. Some days we need you to kick ass. Some days your only job is to pray, and other days it's to protect."

They both said in unison, "Aye, Aye, Captain." Evening fell as HG disappeared from TV.

"What's for dinner, love?" Rowe asked.

"Pizza nowadays, my Rowe, no gourmet dishes until the bad guys leave the country and we recover as a capitalist nation once again," Antonette said practically. Rowe grinned and looked at her with loving eyes. He cherished her love of Freedom, which matched his own.

"You're the jewel of my life. I am hungry and have a headache. What would I do without you, Antonette?"

"You might forget your survival skills since you don't have to fend for yourself in the kitchen," Antonette said with a smile as Rowe scooped her up and spun her around in a circle.

"Let's eat dinner and then get to work," Rowe said.

They heated a medium pepperoni pizza in the oven, ate it quickly, and drank some hot tea. Antonette said, "Aye, aye, Captain! In that order!"

Rowe said, "I miss my yogurt," and added a pout for emphasis.

"I could warm up some milk?" Antonette offered.

"I am okay Mi Amor. *Siediti accanto a me per favore.*" Just sit right next to me please.

Antonette ran her fingers through Rowe's hair and lovingly said, "*Certo amore mio.*" *Of course, my love.* "I will be here as long as you need me."

Rowe put his head on Antonette's lap like a child, and Antonette was concerned because he rarely had headaches. For a few minutes, Antonette put her hand on his forehead and closed her eyes, sending healing energy to Rowe.

Rowe opened his eyes and said, "My headache is gone! How did you do that? Of course, you can do that."

Rowe kept the rest of his thoughts to himself. He knew exactly what was going on with Antonette, just like he had seen signs in his grandson Mark who could always sense when someone was upset or not feeling well. They were empathic individuals and born to be healers. They both had an extraordinary charisma and gifts of healing that were supernatural enablements, given to a believer to minister different kinds of healing and restoration to individuals through the power of the Holy Spirit. This is not the first time he felt better after Antonette laid hands on him. Whenever he was sick, he always felt better instantly and empowered with renewed energy if she was near. He knew that her healing powers had not come without suffering and great cost. She had learned to heal herself through her own darkness during deployment and PTSD afterward. The power to heal her soul led to even more extraordinary healing powers that extended beyond herself. Rowe thought to himself, *"Healers are created through fire. Like the Phoenix, they rise from the ashes of strife and darkness by healing their shattered souls. They battle with fortitude until their light shines from within, like an eternal flame that can overcome any shadow of darkness. They understand that surrender and faith are at the heart of the journey. Through suffering, their souls are transformed and reawakened. Their purpose is to shine that powerful indestructible light so that others may follow the flame of hope through darkness and learn to heal themselves."*

CHAPTER 22

"O righteous God, who searches the minds and hearts, bring an end to the violence of the wicked and make the righteous secure."

(Psalm 7:9)

Antonette stared at Rowe and thought he was an angel of supreme power and the leader of God's army. He was the defender and protector of those in battle. They both knew that Christ was the center of the angelic world. She felt that they both belonged to Him because they were created through and for Him. They were His angels, sent to guard the world. Rowe read her mind, and as they looked at each other, they remembered when they wished to become superheroes, defend, protect, and heal the world.

It was clear to them now; they both remembered it instantaneously. That night of the terrible storm which had awakened them at 0333 hours, they suddenly remembered everything.

Rowe had said to Antonette, "I wish we could be superhuman to defeat evil in this world."

"I wish for it too; I wish we could work together to save humanity and uplift people for the greater good," Antonette replied.

That night they had felt the earth shake. At first, they thought it was just a bad thunderstorm. But the house became a sea of stars, and they saw a blazing light with thunder. They felt they were in another dimension and felt empowered. Then the dazzling light disappeared, and they remembered a Face shining like a diamond and the feet with a hole in each one. They were in a trance and heard, "Begin the Mission." The voice was like thunder and lightning, and they found themselves back on the couch as if nothing had happened. It was as if their memories had been deleted, but they both remembered it clearly now.

Since then, they have metamorphosed from mortal to immortal when they sense threats, with superhuman, angelic energy, durability, and very agile, with the ability to devour and defeat evil and deliver evil to the netherworld at the speed of light. It sounded impractical, but nothing is impossible to the Creator. Rowe and Antonette possessed the Ninth Sense. They could sense danger, and Spirit had been known to provide them with precognitive visions of incoming peril. They could travel at the speed of light and possessed the light of God to destroy evil instantly.

After Rowe and Antonette had recovered from their recognition of what had happened, they realized they were most needed on the scene. He flicked on the remote recorder of the monitoring devices and used one of his invented devices to monitor everything from a headset. Rowe could hear and see everything from the remote recorder even while he and Antonette were away. HG could slightly tell the difference or might not notice the difference at all if she called for a meeting. He held Antonette's hand and said, "Let's go," and they both transformed into superheroes together for the first time.

Meanwhile, Muzabar, the terrorist leader, had been on a mission to destroy American freedom and the world. He had slowly realized that his plan was failing but desperately grasped at the final effort to control the situation.

"Grab any American, children especially. They cannot touch you as long as you have these hostages. So, help yourself and grab anyone you can. Not long from now, we will rule this land. They would not harm your location if there were hostages present," he said in a prerecorded message.

Rowe's phone rang; it was HG.

"Rowe, make no mistake. These people are known killers and have no compassion at all. We are not like them. Guide the troops as they ascend and descend, saving these innocent lives."

Rowe answered, "HG, their leader's name is Muzabar, and he is hiding somewhere in Texas. He is communicating with his fellow terrorists, and they are executing it all simultaneously. They have been grabbing people, young and old, as baits for us to surrender. Like you said, they are known killers and will not hesitate to shoot their captives if we don't give them what they are asking for."

HG said, "We need the Superheroes. We need the Guardian Angels. We need miracles. We can't let them get away with this!"

Rowe answered, "You're finally with me, HG. This is a gigantic task that needs miraculous powers."

Rowe approached the first building; he had a vision of what had happened earlier and heard the cry of children as they were dragged from houses. He saw in his mind how the terrorists had beaten those children and women and mercilessly shot the men if they intervened. His resolve was fortified; he would not fail this mission.

A flash of light suddenly grabbed the innocent children, men, and women and dragged them out of the buildings as if floating on air. Then another flash of light grabbed the same on the other side, as KAKO covered their eyes until the blinding lights had disappeared, with their captives.

"La! Laaaa!" The KAKO screamed and were about to fire, when suddenly, Woooosh! A ball of light and fire grabbed them, and they found themselves circling in the air like a tornado.

"Aaah! Aaah!" They were screaming as they saw their distance from the ground. It was happening all simultaneously. The people saw and couldn't believe what was happening. There were lots of wailing and screaming from the buildings as the KAKO were lifted off the ground. The people were pointing at the KAKO forcefully coming out of each building, experiencing the strongest effects like ferromagnetism, the only form of magnetism strong enough to be felt by people. First in Washington, D.C., and then in New Jersey, New York, Pennsylvania, Virginia, Georgia, Texas, New Mexico, Nevada, Tennessee, and all over the United States. The media have covered the miracles happening simultaneously nationwide and worldwide. The KAKO have been disappearing one by one. The spectators could not see everything that transpired as it was happening at the speed of light; they could hear it. Wooosh! Wham! Woosh! All hostages also looked up as the KAKO disappeared from their sights. Children clinging to their parents and parents crying with joy for their liberation.

CHAPTER 23

"De Oppresso Liber"

That night Rowe and Antonette went to bed early. Antonette combed through his hair to help him feel better. Rowe had been deeply troubled by the terror occurring throughout the USA and the world. Antonette believed they could make a huge difference, especially with their combined power. She thought that *one plus one does not equal two, no. When Rowe and I are together, God joins in the middle, and we are three strong.*

Rowe posed an unexpected question to Antonette, "Do you love me?"

Antonette looked at Rowe, surprised, and asked, "What kind of question is that? Why do you ask? Have I not been good to you, and you don't feel my love every time I touch you?"

Instead of giving her an answer, Rowe posed her another question, "How much do you love me? What is it that you saw and liked in me?"

Antonette was wondering what was making him ask all these kinds of questions.

Rowe smiled and said, "You know I can read your mind, right?"

Antonette replied, "I think, my love, you need to shut off your innate readers for a while so I can give you my honest answers. I feel cheated if I start a litany of feelings for you knowing that I didn't have to speak because you can read my mind anyway."

Rowe agreed and said, "OK, fair enough," and he smiled at Antonette.

Antonette disclosed her sentiments to Rowe, feeling more comfortable that her thoughts could emerge truthfully from her heart without being intercepted before they could leave her lips. She spoke from her silent freedom

"I thought there was strong chemistry the first time I saw you because you were staring at me the same way I was. I didn't know who you were or where you were coming from, yet I loved you since I first saw you. There was something familiar in your voice. At first, I thought it must be the beard or the muscles beneath your dark shirt that showed a small, red heart in the middle with no text."

Rowe interrupted, "Wow… you remembered that all this time?"

Antonette ignored him and continued, "Olivia and David introduced me to you, and we both shook hands. I can't remember whose hand was colder, yours or mine. We formed that study group, and I appreciated it every time I saw you during the study group. I also admired your cadence while we were running during the training. I was running and smiling, feeling motivated, and made it through the four-mile run. It was what I needed. Your voice was my source of energy. You were a dynamite that empowered the core of my soul. The intensity I felt could have made me run 10 more miles without limping. You were magnetic and inspirational in every word. It felt so great running with you by my side while singing those cadences, and you seemed to be flirting with me. I wished at that time that we were both unmarried, and I probably would have said yes to you at that moment. I remember the sleepless nights during the training, which was about three months, just enough time for me to fall in love with you. I became jealous whenever I saw you talking to the other girls in the class. It was silly, I had no right, but I was. I had heard that you were married, but that didn't stop my freedom from loving you secretly. Besides, I was married at the time too and was surprised that I was falling in love with you. It was mysterious. I didn't understand those feelings, and the timing wasn't right, so I kept it to myself. Falling in love with you secretly was my motivation to finish the whole training. And I felt that you seemed lost in your newfound military occupational specialty, the AG. I realized that you came from the Special Forces Group first before you became one of us, so it made a lot of sense that you seemed to be uncomfortable with your new job. From SFG to AG, it must have been a difficult transition for you," Antonette paused.

"You didn't know how I felt after we all graduated from that training. I missed you, my heart ached, and I didn't understand, so I tried to forget it. You went back to your family, I went back to my family, and so did Olivia and Dave. Little did I know that you and I would see each other again. Then I saw you at Fort Benning, just briefly, while you were preparing to deploy. The embers still burned somewhere deep in my heart. Next, I saw you in Iraq, and we were lucky to share time together as friends before we were separated again. Do you know how your kisses at the airport made me crazy and melted my knees? My co-workers and duties helped distract me, but my heart ached to see you again, and I kept everything inside. I had hoped that wasn't the last time we would see each other; I thought about you every day. I am so glad that I found you in Richmond this time, which is a lot safer than seeing you in the combat zone. We couldn't focus on each other in Iraq because the enemy was lurking. So many of the troops were maimed and mentally incapacitated. I prayed you would stay safe. The stars finally aligned this last time, and we met again, both single and free to publicly love each other instead of silently and secretly. I thanked God when I saw you that day at the PX."

As Rowe added a trick question, Antonette shifted her position and stared at the ceiling.

"Do you still feel you love me for who I am after finding out what I have?" Antonette rolled to the side and shifted position back to face Rowe.

She flatly answered him, "No. I loved you when I found out you were a multi-billionaire!"

Rowe chuckled at the sarcasm in Antonette's tone. He believed that Antonette loved him for who he was and not for his wealth. He knew her well enough that he could read her mind and heart. Then Rowe asked, "What is it that you like in me the most?"

Antonette smiled and said, "I loved you more when I learned that you came from Special Forces. For some reason, I felt more physically and emotionally secure because I know the SFG's creed, and it is near and dear to my heart."

Rowe seemed to be delighted and asked her, "What is the special forces creed?"

Antonette scrolled her iPhone and read each line:

Special Forces Creed

- I am an American Special Forces Soldier!

- I will do all that my nation requires of me. I am a volunteer, knowing well the hazards of my profession.
- I serve with the memory of those who have gone before me. I pledge to uphold the honor and integrity of their legacy in all that I am - in all that I do.
- I am a warrior. I will teach and fight whenever and wherever my nation requires me. I will always strive to excel in every art and artifice of war.
- I know that I will be called upon to perform tasks in isolation, far from familiar faces and voices. With the help and guidance of my faith, I will conquer my fears and succeed.
- I will keep my mind and body clean, alert, and strong. I will maintain my arms and equipment in an immaculate state befitting a Special Forces Soldier, for this is my debt to those who depend upon me.
- I will not fail those with whom I serve. I will not bring shame upon myself or Special Forces.
- I will never leave a fallen comrade. I will never surrender though I am the last. If I am taken, I pray that I have the strength to defy my enemy.
- I am a member of my Nation's chosen soldiery; I serve quietly, not seeking recognition or accolades. My goal is to succeed in my mission - and live to succeed again.
- De Oppresso Liber

"De Oppresso Liber is a Latin phrase, meaning To Free the Oppressed," Antonette finished. Rowe was wondering, "How do you know what it means?"

"Because it's indelibly carved in my heart. Perhaps I should have become the first female Special Forces warrior?" Rowe exclaimed, "That would have been great!" Rowe rose from the bed and repeated his question, "So you love me the most because I was a Special Forces warrior, huh?" Antonette took his pillow and shifted her position, her face buried on the bed, and used the pillow to cover her head, and answered Rowe's question, "Yes!" But it came out muffled, and Rowe couldn't understand what she said. She was embarrassed and afraid it sounded shallow, but it was true.

Rowe reiterated his question, "Do you?" Rowe tried to pull the pillow from Antonette's head, but she held onto it tightly and would not let go. Rowe started pushing her shirt up and kissed her soft skin, her spine, slowly and lovingly, her shoulders and underneath her arm, and he did both shoulders and the small part of her breast showing under her arms. Antonette was still not letting go of the pillow. Rowe went down and repeatedly kissed her spine and continued going down until Rowe pushed her PJ down and kissed her buttocks, thighs, legs, and down to her feet, which tickled Antonette, and she finally yelped and let the pillow go! Rowe quickly grabbed the pillow and stared at Antonette, who shifted and met Rowe's eyes.

Rowe was now on top of her and said lovingly, "There is nothing wrong about loving a special forces warrior. It is angelic of you to love me for what I am; most people don't understand what it truly means. To be understood is the deepest form of intimacy." Rowe kissed the tears on both her cheeks, nose, forehead, and lips. Antonette found his touch irresistible but tried to suppress it. She started to wriggle away from Rowe's grip, but Rowe pinned her down, not letting her go, and kissed her passionately. Then suddenly, he felt a throbbing headache and laid down on his back. Antonette touched his face and ran her fingers through Rowe's hair again until he finally went to sleep.

Antonette kissed his forehead and said,

"You'll be fine. I promise."

As she watched Rowe, who looked sound asleep, Antonette ruminated on her answer. It was true; she loved him more because he was a special forces warrior. Rowe was her hero. He exemplified servant leadership. In her biblical readings, Jesus said that whoever wishes to be first among you will be the slave of all. For the Son of Man did not come to be served but to serve and to give his life as a ransom for many" (Mark 10:35-45). Rowe selflessly helped the oppressed and was willing to give his life as a ransom for many.

"God is good," she said quietly as she reminisced about all of his special forces operations and how Rowe had always been protected.

God kept him safe from harm and helped him to fight evil. She had been with Rowe on multiple missions with the CIA, and he had never shown fear. He was divinely protected. He did his part by planning and considering all possibilities and then entrusted everything to God. It was just the way he rolled. No one could execute orders like Rowe, and his faith was contagious. Antonette had learned a lot from his leadership, and HG Hawk had always trusted his capabilities.

Rowe admired Antonette's skills too. They had learned foreign languages when they separately went through the Linguist Academy in California. They both spoke multiple languages including Chinese, Russian, Pashto and Arabic, the languages used in Southwest Asia especially by Pakistanis and some people in India, Iraq, Afghanistan, and Libya. Rowe told Antonette many times that she had impressive linguistic skills, adding to her native language, Tagalog.

Antonette and Rowe grew up in this environment; their hearts were joined in patriotism. They were both extremely good at their jobs. Most of all, they both always endeavored to do whatever would result in the greatest good. They were *indivisible.*

CHAPTER 24

"God is our refuge and strength, an ever-present help in trouble."
(Psalm 46:1-3)

That night as Antonette slept, her dreams replayed in great detail one of their missions for the CIA before they had received their superpowers. Rowe had fired up the TV monitor one day and started observing a Special Forces Operation team as they invaded Sharqpur, Pakistan, to rescue a young SFG Captain Johns, his linguist, and a British Journalist. They were on a special mission in India, and the terrorists had caught up with them. A tipster informed the terrorists about the mission in India and the location of the American Force's hideout. Sadik was one of America's blacklisted individuals for supplying weapons to southern India's remote areas and in the southern Philippines to spread terrorism. Johns was on a mission with another unit with an embedded British journalist and a linguist. They were getting close to their destination when a truckload of terrorists fired on their tires, causing Johns' Humvee to stop. The terrorists circled the Americans before they could draw their weapons. In hopes of not having his throat slit, Johns raised his hands in surrender until he could find a way to escape. He advised the others to do the same, but the driver drew his weapon, was shot in the throat, and died quickly. Johns was infuriated and tried to fight, but one of the kidnappers hit him hard on the head, becoming unconscious.

HG called Rowe and said their passports could be picked up from Tango 11 at the Guardian's Airport, destination: Mt. Kahpur, New Delhi, India. A special operations rescue was being organized to save Johns and the other POWs.

Rowe and Antonette rushed to the airport and picked up their gear as instructed. They were both wearing sunglasses and a hat and acted like ordinary tourists bound for India. Rowe was wearing a sky-blue half-button kurta long sleeve cotton shirt, and Antonette wore the customary Indian tunic with palazzos. She was wearing a navy blue and off-white yoke design kurta with Shobna palazzos and a tiny red bindi on her forehead. They tried to dress inconspicuously as tourists on vacation. Rowe told Antonette that she would be noticed and stand out in a crowd because she was strikingly beautiful no matter what she wore. She was wearing long dark hair to her waistline, a silver necklace, an Indian bangle bracelet, and a matching pair of silver Juhmka earrings that looked striking with her navy-blue tunic. She epitomized an authentic lady from India. They were supposed to look like an average couple on vacation and planned to act like they were on their honeymoon. Antonette held Rowe's arm and pretended to be an authentic Indian lady who adored her husband from head to toe.

They had finally arrived in Chennai, India, and admired their hotel. They could see the Marina beach in Chennai along the Bay of Bengal, India's longest and the world's second-longest beach. It was predominantly sandy, and it extended approximately eight miles from Beasant Nagar in the south to Fort St. George in the north. From their hotel, they also could view the statue of Mahatma Gandhi in the Marina, which is centrally located, close to the lighthouse. They admired the beautiful sculpture of the Father of the Nation, behind which runs the shoreline of the Bay of Bengal. The Palace hotel was accessible to all modern amenities and state-of-the-art technologies. HG had reserved two separate hotels to deceive the two men that had been tailing them since they were waiting for their flights in Dubai. Rowe had called her about their strange shadows, and HG quickly decided to book two different hotels with a one-hour drive distance between the two hotels.

Rowe and Antonette first checked into the decoy hotel and saw that their shadows were still following them. They dropped their luggage off in the room and decided to visit the hotel's restaurant, then stepped out to breathe some fresh air and walk around the town to draw out the men stalking them. Rowe and Antonette had picked up their weapons with silencers planted in the room and were ready for the unknown attackers. Both knew it would be better to incapacitate the attackers and draw less attention than dead bodies and blood, but they were grateful to be armed. Rowe and Antonette started down the street, then ducked down an alley. Their attackers appeared and blocked their path. They both took a fighting stance, and Rowe took the lead. Rowe and his attacker traded blows, and Rowe used his martial arts training to break his attacker's left arm. His opponent then threw a punch with the right, but Rowe blocked it and then kicked the side of his attacker's knee hard, making a horrible snapping sound, and the assailant screamed in pain and crumpled to the ground. Rowe then kicked him in the chin, knocking him out cold.

Antonette observed the scene and determined the best move as her attacker approached. He lunged, and she deftly punched him in the throat before he knew what had happened, and he was sent to the ground gasping for air. She then finished him off with a backspin kick to the temple, and he was knocked out entirely.

"Those guys will regret taking this assignment when they wake up battered and bruised," Rowe said with a smirk as he watched Antonette straighten her outfit.

Rowe and Antonette returned to their room, gathered their luggage, hired a cab, and paid decent money to take them to their new hotel. They settled in and began to set up their cyber cameras to monitor Operation Vocifer in Sharqpur, Pakistan, to rescue Captain Johns, his linguist, and the journalist. The SFG found the shabby place well-guarded by the kidnappers as the monitor began.

Rowe told the SFG Platoon Sergeant, SFC Shamar, "Shamar, as you can see, four tangos are on the balcony. One in each corner. Four tangos are also on the watch ground, one in each corner. I see six people that seem to be playing cards on the kitchen table. I see three rooms and three figures inside the middle room who seem to be shackled. Wait… two guys went inside the middle room." Rowe adjusted his camera and saw one of the tangos waterboarding the immobile Johns. He poured water onto John's face over the breathing passages, causing an almost immediate gag reflex and creating a drowning sensation. It was their third day of captivity, prolonged torture for one of their own.

"Get in there now, go," Rowe said. Thug! Thug! Rowe heard two gunshots and saw that the two tangos on the balcony were down.

One of the tangos yelled, "'atlaq alnaar ealayhim! 'Atlaq alnaar! Atlaq alnaar! Atlaq alnaar ealayhim!"

SFC Shamar and his men understood what they were screaming.

Tangos were yelling, "Shoot! Shoot! Shoot!"

Thug! Thug! Two more tangos down. That left two tangos on the ground floor and six tangos inside, including the ones upstairs with Johns.

The SFGs heard someone yell "Ahdurhum!" meaning, 'get them!' "Atlaq alnaar!"

SFC Shamar thought that voice must be the Rooster's. Thug! Thug! Two more tangos went down.

"You woke up the rooster, and the chicks are coming out," Rowe said. "Four, four tangos are going to the front door!"

The tangos fired at the SFGs but missed their target; two SFGs moved closer to the gate.

Rowe saw tangos coming from behind the SFGs and yelled, "two, three tangos on your rear! Six o'clock!" One of the SFG warriors trailing their men fired at the three tangos about to shoot SFC Shamar's team.

"Thanks for the heads up Rowe. That was close. We always operate ready, and I have men behind my back," Shamar said.

"Roger that. I know you knew, but anything can happen at war," Rowe said.

"True that Rowe. True that, buddy. What is my status?"

"Move in now, before the Rooster beheads Johns and his comrades. And of course…"

"I know. Watch out for the fucking grenades," Shamar finished Rowe's sentence.

"Exactly, be careful buddy!"

SFC Shamar replied, "Roger that Rowe."

Shamar and his men donned their CM-7M full-face military gas mask respirators and rolled out a flash-bang smoke grenade. The SFGs heard coughs. Thug! Thug! Two tangos went down. The SFGs stealthily moved closer to the middle room.

Rowe exclaimed, "Now!"

Shamar tugged the door open and shot. Thug! Thug! One of the tangos was down. The Rooster's knife was on Johns' throat and threatened to kill him if the SFGs got closer.

"Sa'aqtulu. I will kill him if you get any closer. You must fulfill our demands, and I will hand him over to you alive."

"Easy, easy. I am going to lay my weapon down. Just let the man go," SFC Shamar said.

SFGs never negotiate, but Shamar thought he'd buy some time until his guys could get a good shot between the eyes.

Sadik, the Rooster, held up a grenade and replied, "Give me the money. I know you have it in your bag. Give me the money, and we will all go outside, or you will watch me kill one of your own."

One of the team members handed the bag to Shamar, "Ah, it's always about the money, of course. Yes, we have the bag for you. Here, catch!"

Sadik moved to catch the bag. Thug! One of the SFGs shot him between his eyes as they always delivered.

Sadik was down with his knife, as well as a grenade without a linchpin in his left hand. The grenade rolled, and Shamar grabbed two dead bodies and quickly covered the grenade. He then grabbed Johns and his comrades, still tied to the chairs and put his body on top of them. He only had six seconds. Wham! There was a silent explosion, and the dead bodies covering the grenade silenced the blast.

"Shamar! Shamar! Come in, come in! Shamar, what is your status, damn it!" Rowe shouted after hearing the blast.

No one answered. Rowe's hand was steady, but Antonette saw beads of sweat on his forehead, and he was running his fingers through his hair.

It reminded her of the gruesome grenade blast in Qatar. Rowe saved their lives by grabbing her and pulling her farther away from the grenade blast, and they were saved. Waiting to hear from their SFG team, she could imagine HG's worry while she watched the monitors and paced the floor.

Antonette knew there was nothing else she could do at that moment but hoped and prayed that the troops were free from harm. A few minutes passed, and they heard Shamar on the mic.

"Rowe, that was another close call, buddy. Rooster and the chicks are down, and we have untied Johns and the other men. They are free, and we're all unharmed from the blast. We need eyes for the Landing Zone (LZ) asap!"

Rowe and Antonette gave a big sigh of relief.

Rowe said, "The LZ is clear! Repeat, the LZ is clear!"

Shamar and his troops helped Johns and his men and got out of the building and then to the LZ.

Rowe came live again and yelled, "Shamar, I see two tangos running to the LZ. Hurry up!"

Shamar answered, "Roger that Rowe," and ordered the pilot. "Take it up! Go, go, go!" As he fired upon the two approaching tangos, who were firing on the helicopter. Thug! Thug! Two tangos were down. The Black Hawk took Shamar, his team, Johns, and his comrades back to the base and prepared for medevac.

"Rowe, prep for medevac." Rowe complied, "Roger," and he called HG. Another successful mission, although it was close.

CHAPTER 25

"Proclaim liberty to the captives and to let the oppressed go free."
(Luke 1:1-4; 4:14-21)

Rowe's loud snore snapped out Antonette of her dream. She was in a very awkward position and was trying to decide if she needed to remove Rowe's left arm that encircled her waist. He was sleeping on his right side, left arm around her waist, and left leg on top of her legs. She thought if she could just close her eyes and not move, maybe she wouldn't disturb Rowe, who was soundly asleep. She decided to stay in her position, a little sacrifice for her man. She drifted back to sleep, knowing that she would probably wake up later with a cramp in her neck. That night, Rowe dreamt that he and Antonette were shackled by their neck and feet with glowing golden ropes and were carried up to space. They were soaring, and when they looked down, they saw the universe beneath them, with all nine planets aligned in their orbits, other dark planets, and an infinite number of stars shining in space. They saw a clear blue firmament, unimaginably beautiful and serene when they looked up.

Then the movement stopped, and they were brought before a majestic throne. They saw pillars emblazoned with amazing jewels and angels ascending and descending with halos. A powerful voice put them in a trance, and they surrendered wholly with their hands stretched out above their heads, pressed together with fingers pointed up to praise and revere the powerful voice from the throne.

Suddenly, they were unshackled as the golden ropes fell, and they received instructions from the Voice that they vividly remembered. It was a wonderful, mellow voice that could heal any kind of disease and broken heartedness. They captured every word streaming from the loving and calming Voice and stored it somewhere deep in their souls. Rowe was taken back to his childhood and remembered his favorite song from the hymnal, The Solid Rock.

The Solid Rock
My hope is built on nothing less
Then Jesus' blood and righteousness.
I dare not trust the sweetest frame,
But wholly lean on Jesus' name.
On Christ, the solid Rock, I stand.
All other ground is sinking sand,
All other ground is sinking sand.
When darkness veils His lovely face,
I rest on His unchanging grace.
In every high and stormy gale,
My anchor holds within the veil.
His oath, His covenant, His blood
Support me in the whelming flood.
When all around my soul gives way,
He then is all my hope and stays.
When He shall come with trumpet sound,
Oh, may I then in Him be found.
Dressed in His righteousness alone,
Faultless to stand before the throne.

Rowe and Antonette stretched out on the ground with their faces downward and remained in that prostrated position praising the Voice, in awe of the grace and love filling their hearts. It was about four minutes before they felt a powerful hand on their shoulders, and the Voice told them to rise. Rowe recognized the edged sword and knew to whom it belonged. He marveled at the thought. As they rose, they saw the feet of the powerful One, the Alpha and the Omega, with a hole on each foot. They had mixed emotions and wanted to stay there forever. Rowe thought to himself, *are we in a place called Heaven? Are we dead and have finally seen our Maker?* It was a mystery they had longed for and been part of through the trials of war. The angels led them to a tall entrance door; they hesitated to leave, but the angels lifted them up, and they found themselves floating on the clouds. They both cried and begged to stay, but the angels led them by the hand, as they slowly descended to the earth. They passed the dark universe with infinite numbers of stars, the dark planets, and the nine planets. Rowe thought then that it was all a dream. He was becoming aware of his light consciousness in a half-dream state. He woke up with a jolt and was puffing as if he had just finished a marathon. He remembered himself pleading, "Please let us stay."

After regaining his senses, he looked around and exclaimed, "What a dream! It seemed so real!" He looked for Antonette, but she was not there. He got up wearing only boxers and grabbed his pants along with the black tee-shirt he had worn the day before. He was filled with anxiety that she was not there and silently screamed in his head while looking for Antonette. He glanced at the clock, and it showed 0333 hours. He rubbed his temples and slapped his face to wake himself up, still searching for Antonette. He went down to the situation room.

"Antonette! Antonette!" Yet no answer.

He stood still, did some tactical breathing, and calmed down, then began meditating. His thoughts were getting the worst of him; he grabbed his SIG Sauer Mosquito, a self-loading firearm that obtains energy from a chamber for the .22 LR cartridge, a semi-automatic pistol aesthetically based on the SIG Sauer P226 but 10% smaller in size. He quickly attached the SLX suppressor and tiptoed up the stairs. He peeked through the doorway to make sure the place was secure, and no terrorists were lurking around. It was a matter of habit, protecting himself and those he loved from an unknown enemy. He looked for Antonette all over the house and did not find her but was still calm. He entered the kitchen and saw food lying on top of the counter and two cups of coffee. He smiled, '*How did that woman always manage to make him hungry?*'

Suddenly, Antonette stepped out of the bathroom and was surprised to see Rowe up at this hour. He jumped as she caught him eating a piece of bacon off of her plate. Rowe smiled at her and said, "Good Morning, my love," and showed no sign of anxiety at all. Just a few minutes ago, he was worried and called her name anxiously when he couldn't find her.

She glanced at his SIG and said, "Jeez! If you wanted my bacon so badly, all you had to do was ask!"

"Ha!" Rowe smiled and revealed his strange dream last night and how he had woken up drenched. When he didn't find her in bed, he panicked, grabbed his SIG, and went to find her. Antonette revealed she had the same dream, and she had gotten up slowly so as not to wake him and decided to cook. She must have been in the bathroom when he was calling her name and missed his yelling.

Antonette, with all concern, asked if he was alright and had the headaches subsided? Rowe replied that he had never felt better. He felt stronger, energized like he could move mountains. He flexed his muscles, and Antonette laughed, then hugged him. She believed that Rowe was feeling much better and asked if he could help her carry the food and other things to the spy bunker. They had to endure going through this chapter of life until the terrorists were gone, and the world was safe. Rowe proudly obliged and followed Antonette to the basement. Antonette was surprised how Rowe hauled all the food in his hands and did not use the bags she gave him. They both felt empowered and energized as if they had just acquired more supernatural power. They looked at the clock, and it was 0343 hours. Antonette served coffee with light cream and warm banana bread. She then told Rowe she didn't think she could go back to bed and actually felt like working out after breakfast. Rowe agreed, they were synchronized, and he felt like flying over the horizon right now. They both finished their food, did a 20-minute HIIT workout, then decided to take a quick shower and got ready for the challenges of the day.

Rowe and Antonette vividly remember the Voice commanding them from the Throne of The Alpha and The Omega in their dreams the night prior. They pleaded to stay, but the Voice, with a sound of thunder and lightning, gave them this command that should not be broken.

Their mission: *"Proclaim liberty to the captives and to let the oppressed go free"* (Luke 1:1-4; 4:14-21).

CHAPTER 26

"For I know the plans I have for you," declares the Lord, plans to prosper you and not to harm you, plans to give you hope and a future"
(Jeremiah 29:11)

The terrorist leader spoke to his people through a recorded video message: "The Americans are known for their compassion. This is their weakness. They will not hurt you if you have hostages; we must use their compassion to our advantage until we have more cities under our control." Meanwhile, The think tanks in the Pentagon surrounded the sandbox and planned a successful execution of liberating the hostages before firing hellfire missiles on the buildings occupied by the KAKO. They had been using a virtual sandbox and found stark challenges in all aspects of the rescue. In one of their briefings with the President, the CIA director noted that an Intel investigation predicted that 10% of hostages might not survive the rescue mission. They were trying to figure out how to reduce the percentage. The rescue was to be coordinated nationwide for any known hostage situations but primarily concentrated in Washington DC, which was the terrorists' center of the organization.

Operation Sunrise was named after a consensus of belief that a new day would dawn, which would bring hope, inspiration, and trust that they would overcome the terrorists and regain their freedom.

It has now been a long week of fighting terrorists in their own land, and the President would not let it go any further. The catastrophic threat posed by the terrorists and their ideology must end now. But how? HG Hawk was on a three-way video conference with the President and the Pentagon. She suggested seeking the help of the superpowers. The President stood up and, with conviction, agreed wholeheartedly. He believed in the Guardian Angels after Lady Savior had saved his life.

The Pentagon General asked, "But how can we reach the Guardian Angels? I concur that we can decrease casualties during Operation Sunrise. This would also avoid moral injury, which occurs after the war. Moral injury refers to the lasting emotional, psychological, social, behavioral, and spiritual impacts of actions that violate an individual's core moral values and behavioral expectations of oneself." All eyes were on him as he continued with his speech, "Moral injury almost always pivots with the dimension of time, moral codes evolve alongside identities, and transitions informed perspectives that form new conclusions, and about old events. We all agree that the nation is in a state of disarray, but we also believe in Operation Sunrise. HG, where can we contact the Superpowers?"

Rowe heard the phone ring. HG Hawk repeated the consensus of the think tanks and how they had agreed to seek the Guardians' help in liberating hostages and eliminating the tangos.

"Rowe, we need to find them; it's a nationwide problem and also a world problem as they all go through the same disillusionment," HG said.

"Are you suggesting that we know the Guardians?" Rowe said earnestly.

HG Hawk answered, "You have all the answers, guys. I am just here to relay the President's message to contact the Guardians against terror. Please let them know we need immediate help as our freedom is in grave danger, and we must be successful in Operation Sunrise. We are being terrorized and sinking to the ground. I want our freedom back. Any questions?"

Antonette answered, "We'll find them HG, and we're in this together. We have your back. Maintain your faith and hope for a better future."

"You're always so sweet, Antonette. Thank you both. I am going to get a couple of hours of sleep as the Pentagon works out the details of securing the area once the hostages are clear. Let me know when you have reached the Guardians."

Antonette and Rowe replied, "Aye, aye, Captain!"

As soon as HG disappeared from the screen, Rowe and Antonette scanned the country and determined where the most important areas were where terrorists were holding hostages, especially children. The thought of it infuriated Rowe, but he had faith that they would be successful and divinely protected. Rowe turned on the autopilot switch in his spy bunker and paired his watch so he would not miss any calls, especially from HG Hawk.

Then he grabbed Antonette by her waistline, cupped her face, and whispered, "I love you with my heart and soul, you know. Thank you for taking care of me last night. I heard you when you said you loved me because I was a Special Forces warrior, but it came muffled. I read your mind, but I pretended not to understand because it was such a pleasure seeing you acting like a child. Your antics always crack me up, Antonette. I enjoyed kissing your soft skin, your back…"

"There's no time for that now," Antonette said.

Rowe smiled and interrupted her with a passionate kiss. Then she placed both her hands on Rowe's chest, touching the St. Michael pendant that dangled from a chain around his neck.

They kissed again before getting ready to save the world against terror. Neither was afraid. They knew that they were divinely protected as if St. Michael himself were going with them.

CHAPTER 27

"For we walk by faith, not by sight."

(2 Corinthians 5:7)

At the CIA headquarters in McLean, Virginia, HG brewed a new pot of coffee. She added some light cream to her cup before filling it and inhaled the aroma, then opened her single brioche pack and warmed up her bacon. She took the food to her desk, shoved a piece of bacon in her mouth then had a few hurried sips of her coffee before addressing her team.

"Good morning, ladies and gentlemen. What's new? I can always get the news on my phone, but there's nothing better than news coming from my capable men and women on the ground. Did anyone get a glimpse of our superheroes yet? What is the most recent status report on hostages?"

Gracie Kelly often teased as Grace Kelly, an American actress who became Princess of Monaco by marrying Prince Rainier III in April 1956, shared her screen with HG and said, "The President will be live soon. His press secretary announced that he's doing a press conference imploring the Lady Savior and the Saint of Warriors to help save the nation and the world."

HG said, "So, the President has another name for our second Guardian Angel now. There is only one Saint of Warriors, and I adore him. He will protect us as we fight terror and liberate the hostages. Let's keep the faith, ladies and gentlemen, and pray for our Guardian Angels. I have a conviction that the light will come in our time of need." She took the last piece of her bacon and ate two strawberries before the press conference began.

"Four, three, two, and one, Mr. President, the floor is yours."

The President of the United States delivered the message from his Oval Office wearing a dark suit and blue tie that matched his eyes.

"Good Morning, ladies and gentlemen. There has never been in the history of our nation an event that has shaken us beyond what we experienced during 9/11. But *we are one nation under God, indivisible, with liberty and justice for all.* We will prevail. If our enemy is listening to this message, this is your last chance to free your hostages who are innocent civilians, or you will suffer the consequences." The President was still talking when his COS approached and whispered what appeared to be some very important news.

"I've just learned some wonderful news about this impossible mission. Can we see the live footage?" The President asked.

The screens came live, showing a brilliant light sweeping across the nation. The light penetrated each building occupied by the terrorists and their hostages. They watched right before their naked eyes as hostages escaped from the buildings with small children. They were being liberated by the radiating light that continued to free hostages one by one. They ran out of the buildings and were received by the troops waiting in their Humvees.

"I knew they would come," the President whispered. Then to the American public, he said, "everyone, please hold steady and keep your faith, pray for our country. We are going to overcome the enemy." Then he ended the conference and ordered everyone to the situation room.

UH-60s revved up in the air and landed on secure landing zones, ready to receive some of the hostages. The gunners were well prepared for a potential ambush. The Pentagon think tanks had also ordered combat-ready pilots to execute the next phase, which was to hit the terrorist-occupied buildings. They were following the radiant lights and moving towards their targets. Suddenly, the pilots saw a blinding light and heard a reverberant female voice say, "Hold steady, abort air support. Target will soon be neutralized." The light was pushing them all away from the buildings and preventing them from executing their mission.

"It's like an invisible force field pushing us away," one of the pilots said.

Meanwhile, the other brilliant light force who have the jagged sword was retrieving more hostages. Some were running on the ground toward the Humvees, which were parked in front of the buildings. Humvees then moved to a tentative secure area built by the Army and the Marines and alternately went back to the buildings where more rescue operations continued.

HG was awestruck by all that had been happening as seen on her big screens. It seemed one of the radiant lights was pushing the Apaches away from the buildings. It appeared that the light indicated they should abort the mission.

The President, his advisory team, and the Pentagon think tanks were wondering what was happening. Everyone was confused, but the President said to remain calm because he trusted the Guardian Angels. It was a mission impossible for mortals, but not for the immortal superheroes as they *indivisibly* worked together. And reiterated to hold onto their faith. He believed in their superheroes. He believed in their Guardian Angels. The President was wondering who was pushing the Apaches away, "Is it Lady Savior?" He asked himself silently. He had seen such blinding light firsthand. There was a part of his memory that recalled a glimpse of Lady Savior right before he lost his sight. He had been trying hard to recollect her face, and the more he thought about it, the closer he was to remember the face. But then it'd disappear. The President got frustrated and eventually told himself that one day Lady Savior's face would come back to his memories. He thought to himself that if he was faithful, he might see Lady Savior and Jesus face to face after he died. The President snapped out of his wandering thoughts when the pilots came live.

"Delta, Delta, this is Charlie. We're hovering in the air; it's such a strong force pushing us away from the target. It appears the radiant force wants us to get out of sight now. Looks like they want to handle it themselves. Request to abort air support! Repeat, request to abort air support!"

"Charlie, this is Delta. I heard you loud and clear. Abort air support authorized! Repeat, abort air support!"

Everyone watched as the *indivisible superpowers* worked hand in hand with the rescue efforts on the ground. It was so fascinating to watch their lightning-fast movements as they entered buildings and liberated hostages. They were all watching and waiting to see what the superpowers would do with the terrorists.

HG thought she understood what was going on but also wondered what the Guardians were planning to do next. Why would they push off the attack meant to finish off the terrorists? She called Rowe and got the autopilot. Hawk won't be able to know the difference.

"Rowe, Alex, are you two seeing this?"

"Aye, aye, captain. We are watching."

HG answered, "Good!"

Based on previous experiences, nothing would be recorded for replay later. The Guardian Angels' paths were not traceable and were visible in the live feed, but nothing showed up when the footage was replayed.

The spectators were saying they had never seen anything like it. The technicians could not tape it, and cell phone recordings didn't show anything except the hostages running out of the buildings when the videos were played back.

HG murmured, "God still loves us. He sent us His miracles, and may God Bless America."

The Pentagon think tanks were still amazed by what they were witnessing. Some of them had believed the stories about Guardian Angels, and others were boldly skeptical. None could deny that this was truly happening. Some wondered, *are we all dead or hypnotized and seeing supernatural powers? Are they aliens*? The young technicians were awestruck by the blazing lights and the fact that all hostages nationwide were seemingly liberated at the same time. They saw how the diamond lights seemed to become the earth's orbit.

The President's crew in the situation room were also amazed, and they were all thinking it was surreal. All of the miracles happening had made them humble, and they watched in awe. After listening to the President's previous speech, they had come to believe that America was safe in the hands of Guardian Angels. Some people were crying tears of joy, and others were in apparent shock. They were all happy to see that the Guardian Angels had come in their time of need to preserve American freedom and help the world overcome this darkness.

The President requested for the Chaplain to come to the situation room and conduct an ecumenical service after the rescue to thank God for the Divine grace and protection. The Chaplain agreed and told the

President about a biblical story when Jesus saved a woman who had been suffering from hemorrhages for 12 years. And though she had spent all she had on physicians, no one could cure her. She came up behind Jesus and touched the fringe of his clothes, and immediately her hemorrhage stopped. Then Jesus asked who had touched him, and the woman came trembling and falling down before him, and she was healed immediately. Jesus said to her that her faith had saved her.

"There are many more graces like these, such as saving the blind, healing the Centurion's servant, raising Lazarus and a girl from the dead, and rebuking the unclean spirits. These are just some examples of how our faith can save us. We walk by faith and not by sight. For by grace, we have been saved through faith. And this is not our own doing. It is the gift of God. That our faith might not rest in the wisdom of men but instead the power of God. We are blessed because of our faith that God sent us our Guardian Angels, who are now working hard to save us and the world. We are saved by our Faith. As Jesus said, *Everything is possible to one who has faith.* Yes, Mr. President. We will conduct a service to praise God for these blessings." the Chaplain said.

The Chaplain was still talking when suddenly everybody yelled, "Look!"

The President and the Chaplain watched as the radiant forces took the terrorists up towards the sky in columns of light. The large screens showed the ubiquitous extraction of KAKO from all occupied buildings.

The Chaplain whispered, "It is omnipresence." It was happening nationwide and throughout the world, all simultaneously. This was more than just two superheroes and everyone who witnessed it was immediately a believer in Spirit. It happened quickly like thunder and lightning, and as soon as the radiance disappeared, their screens were enveloped with darkness. Everyone became silent, not knowing what was going to happen next.

HG now understood why the Apaches were pushed back by the Guardian Angels. They were trying to communicate that they would extract the terrorists out of the buildings and that there was no need for violence. They would take care of it, and God was with them, ensuring no collateral damage.

After the terrorists had disappeared and the screens went dark, the people were silent. Everyone wondered if the radiant lights would return and were curious about where the KAKO had gone.

CHAPTER 28

"And now these three remain: faith, hope, and love. But the greatest of these is love."

(Corinthians 13:13)

After everyone had recovered from what had taken place, one by one, the people came out of their houses and were happy to see the light of day once again. The troops set to work, making sure all of the IEDs had been cleared before the green light was given to be out and about.

It had been almost six weeks since the terrorists first tried to overthrow the government and rule the United States. People celebrated their freedom once again and enjoyed walking in the streets, knowing that the roads were safe. No more magnetic IEDs and RPGs. And they resonated Dr. Martin Luther King Jr.'s famous phrase, "Free at last! Free at last!" Every family hugged their own and shook hands with the people standing next to them. There was no division. No racism, no judgment, no hatred, as they all looked at their war-torn surroundings and cried.

The people were unified as One Nation Under God, and all wept the same tears and cherished the same Earth below their feet.

The buildings and bridges could be rebuilt; the most important thing was that they were alive and free. And they accepted that as long as they had faith and hope, they would survive with whatever they had and gradually build their towns again. After years of living in materialism, they would cope with and adjust to their new environment and simply be grateful for their most basic needs being met after living in a state of chaos. They embraced resiliency, and with faith, hope, and unity, and they would build a better future for themselves, for their children, grandchildren, and generations to come. They knew that the core to social resilience was acceptance and was now ready to promote cohesion and rebuild American freedom and American life.

They rekindled the principle they once believed in, One Nation under God, Indivisible, with Liberty and Justice for all.

Together, the people promised to be active and support a national security program, such as cyber intelligence or any other means that would stop terrorism. They also promised to fight against treason and respect, and the freedom that they had nearly lost.

They would protect women and children in foreign countries at all costs from an evil organization's social media propaganda and grass-roots recruitment aimed at vulnerable individuals. The instability posed a danger for the world because of the influx of foreign fighters in some regions that had expanded worldwide, like the state of chaos that everyone had just been through. Through synergy, they would all exterminate information used by the terrorists to spread their ideology.

They were grateful to the indivisible superpowers who had rescued the innocent people from the hands of the terrorists and removed the enemy. The people didn't know what had happened to the KAKO extracted by the indivisible superpowers. Everyone assumed that they had been taken to their maker to account for their sins.

CHAPTER 29

"And you will feel secure because there is hope; you will look around and take your rest in security."

(Job 11:18)

Thirty days later, Steve piloted his aircraft in Iceland and delivered Rowe's and Antonette's families to the United States. Steve and Rowe have communicated and determined it was safe for the family to return home. Rowe and Antonette saw pillaged buildings in Richmond as they drove to Dulles airport to pick up the family. They also saw the airport damaged by the terrorists, but two runways were still functioning.

"Everything can be rebuilt," Antonette said optimistically.

They drove a large bus so that everyone would be together for the drive home. The children had received word that their houses had been badly damaged in the chaos, so they agreed to stay with Rowe and Antonette until everything was rebuilt. The mansion was large enough to contain all of their families, and Antonette was thrilled to have a full house. Rowe and Antonette were lucky and smart to have secured the perimeter, which had prevented the terrorists from attempting to invade their territory.

The next day they visited the Appomattox River and found that the boats were ravaged. Antonette hugged Rowe and was tearful after seeing their boat broken into pieces. The terrorists had, out of jealousy, destroyed anything that represented the American way of life and the freedom to succeed. Everyone cried at the memory of the wonderful ceremony that had taken place not so long ago, and now the harbor was in ruins. Everyone agreed they were lucky to be alive and safe through all of the turmoil. Material things held little emotional value, and their happy memories would remain intact.

The next day, they heard the news that 12 terrorists had been found bound together in ropes at Kabul International Airport. They were left there with bottled water in front of each individual. The Taliban's leader Ali asked where the others from that group were, and the bound men were crying and screaming that their unit had separated, and the rest 'went to hell in a ball of fire.' The radiant lights had spared them and returned them to Kabul because they never had anything to do with the attacks and had never hurt anyone. The violent section of their group had chosen to hold innocent people hostage and paid the consequences. They didn't want to partake in the war crimes of killing innocent civilians. They refused to harm women and children, were pure of heart, and deserved mercy. The KAKO had threatened to murder their families if they refused to join the Jihadists, so they had been coerced to join the team and propagate evil on United States soil.

Ali told his men to untie the 12 and give each one a bottle of water. Amar was the first to speak and told Ali that they wanted to disengage themselves from Jihad and start helping to build their country and promote love, not hatred. War would neither bring them any good nor help improve their living standards. War only destroys and creates nothing.

"War has to stop now. Love Allah before anything else, and love thy neighbor as thyself," Amar said as he knelt on both knees. He grabbed Ali's right hand and kissed it repeatedly, pleading and asking to help rebuild Kakogryztan, the neighboring country of Iraq, Pakistan, and Afghanistan, to improve people's lives.

"I am tired of war. I am tired of hating. I am tired of jealousy and envy," Amar said.

Ali's reaction was the opposite initially, but when the others also begged him to live in harmony and unity, Ali began to consider his age. Then he thought about the lives of his children and grandchildren. Suddenly, he was shown a vision of his youngest grandchild and only grandson as a grown young man, dying on the battleground in a foreign war and crying out to Ali, *"Why didn't you stop it?"*

Ali agreed to stop fighting for the sake of his lineage and to focus on rebuilding the country for the people's sake. He agreed to work towards living in unity and acceptance of others and in respect towards all human life.

"We are one, don't you see?" Amar said. "We must propagate love and stop fighting. After all, we look at the same sky, stand on the same Earth and breathe the same air. Our children will prosper if we start building now."

They all hugged each other and promised to carry out the change for the highest good of their people.

CHAPTER 30

*"Fear not, for I am with you; be not dismayed, for I am your God;
I will strengthen you, I will help you, I will uphold you with my
righteous hand."*

(Isaiah 41:10)

One night, a few months after the KAKO had been driven out of America, Rowe had a large family meeting in the living room about Operation Homebuilding. Rowe had been discussing a large-scale project with some local businessmen and had decided to lead a home building project to construct 982 houses in and around their neighborhood. He welcomed anyone in the family who wanted to help, and the finished vision was to be like a resort with shopping plazas and restaurants. They would rebuild the community and bring in jobs and new industries. Many of the old housing areas were pillaged by the terrorists, but not the people's indivisibility. Local builders, plumbers, and construction teams had already expressed interest in joining the project. Everyone in the family agreed all at once, there was no hesitation, and they all wanted to offer their special skills. Their own homes had been destroyed, and they looked forward to building something amazing that would bring the community back together.

All finances would be coordinated with John and Zed, who nodded their heads and said they would handle it. Emy and Armand would head Contracting and Real Estate planning. William and Rosgil would handle maintenance after contract closeout. All of Rowe's children said they understood, were on board with the plans, and looked forward to working together.

Antonette's family agreed, since they did not have homes to go back to either, they would all relocate here and live close to Rowe and Antonette. Patrick was a mechanical engineer, but he mentioned that he had done a civil engineering job while he was an officer in the U.S. Regular Army. He and Rowe had something in common, both were mechanical engineers and civil engineers by trade, and they laughed as they talked about the challenges each had seen. Rowe was satisfied with everyone's input and helped Antonette as she set up the dining table for everybody.

"We have lumpia shanghai, longanisa, tocino, noodles, fried rice, rice cakes, pork bellies, chicken wings, and pizzas for everyone. I found a Filipino restaurant that just opened at Langley on Newport News and Fort Eustis and Mama Sita pizza nearby." Antonette said. New businesses were already cropping up to replace ones that had been destroyed.

"They said they would deliver, so I ordered, and the food is still warm. We are very fortunate! Drinks are in the cooler in the corner," Antonette said.

Zed said graciously, "This looks great, and I am famished for dinner."

Antonette and Rowe blessed the food, and everyone said, "Amen."

Mark grabbed a plate and said, "Let's eat!" And everyone laughed.

Over dinner, they all talked excitedly about the future neighborhood. It would be diverse in culture and offer a resource for the arts. They would encourage many different types of food and services. This was the first time in a long time that they all truly felt hope for a better future.

CHAPTER 31

"Finally, all of you, have unity of mind, sympathy, brotherly love,
a tender heart, and a humble mind."

(1 Peter 3:8)

After two years, the housing community was finally completed. Rowe and Antonette were proud of their family for building something that would positively impact the future. They were grateful to the others who had also helped, and they both accepted an invitation to attend Saturday's town hall meeting with their big family.

LeBron was there at the town hall meeting. He was a retired Command Sergeant Major in Personnel Services, I Corps, Fort Lewis, Washington. His late wife was from Richmond, and they had decided to make it their retirement place. He was also a pastor and a high school football referee at Joint Base Langley high school on Ft. Eustis. He had dedicated his time to coaching the youth into champions and didn't mind the long commute from Richmond to Langley. LeBron was a widower, and his two kids were both grown and lived in New York. He was a strong advocate of spirituality during his time in the Regular Army and continued to do so. His mission at his church was interrupted by the arrival of the terrorists. He had known Rowe since he moved to Richmond, and they had become close after learning that they both served in the same Army. They became very close when LeBron read Rowe's bio about his best weapon inventions in the magazines. One day, he met Rowe when they were out walking, and LeBron was humbled at how modest Rowe was, and they became quick friends. LeBron kept telling his neighbors he was proud to live in the neighborhood. After the chaos had settled down, seeing all furniture thrown all over the place, broken windows, loose ceiling tiles, and feces all over the place, they were both sick. Rowe felt that LeBron's calming presence and leadership could make a big difference during the rebuild and afterward. Rowe had trusted him to oversee various aspects of progress in the new neighborhood, including constructing a non-denominational church.

"There's nothing I wouldn't do for 'ya Rowe. After seeing what the terrorists did to our community, you can count on me to help."

LeBron had volunteered to be the emcee at the town hall, and everyone applauded. LeBron had superb PR skills and got along well with everyone before the chaos had started. He and Rowe had discussed several weeks ago that they would need to elect Board Members and make plans for the near future. They organized an election, and this was the first town hall meeting under their care.

At the town hall meeting, the newly elected Board Members asked, "What do the people want to name their new community?"

Eric raised his hand and said, what about "The New Richmond?"

"Nah. It does not have a gist to it. No history. We need something new and different," Larry said.

Eileen stood up and suggested that it should be named after the heroes who helped drive out the terrorists. "We owe the guardian angels our lives, our freedom, and our survival. If not for them, who knows what would have happened to us?"

Larry quipped, "Eileen is right. We should name our community after the heroes who saved us."

LeBron stood up and, without hesitation, went on the stage and said, "Look, as we have heard in the news, there were two guardians who drove out the KAKO. The KAKO, whose purpose was not the conversion of non-Muslims to Islam by force but rather the expansion and defense of the Islamic state. That is why they were here, to expand their Islamic territory. But two patriots saved our asses and our American Freedom. Look at the reason why we are here. They gave us back our land when the enemy destroyed our homes. How could we forget? I think it would be fitting that we build them a statue and name this community, '2 Patriots, Guardians of the World Villas'."

Oscar raised his hand.

"Yes, Oscar. What is your proposal?"

Oscar said, "That sounds a bit like 'Guardians of Galaxy.' What about '2 Patriots, Saviors of American Freedom and the World'?"

Connie stood up and suggested that it was really too long. "Look, what did we observe from the state of chaos? Did we renew our resolve? Were we united in fighting the terrorists? Did we feel closer together? Yes, I think we can all agree on that," she said with emotion.

LeBron pondered and nodded, "Connie, what you just said holds a lot of common sense. What I felt from the state of chaos we have been through and how we pulled together to rebuild afterward is togetherness, *indivisibility*. We've never been closer as a community. I feel that we are reunited, and actually, it led to reshaping our lives and rebuilding our community together. Our faith kept us united and it rekindled our hope that the future would be better. The future will be better!"

Everyone said in unison, "Yes, we are *indivisible* and united as one! We will have a better future!"

LeBron continued, "Then, as Connie's statement alludes, we are inseparable. *One Nation under God, indivisible, with liberty and justice for all!* How about we call our community '*Indivisible?*' Can I get Amen to that?"

Connie was the first one to scream, "Amen!" Then added, "Actually, maybe we should name it *Indivisible* Villas."

LeBron's eyes widened, "Connie, that's perfect. It has a ring to it. What do you think, everyone? *Indivisible* Villas!"

Everyone applauded and voted for *Indivisible* Villas.

"That's great that we finally concluded, and I like it. We have the short wall at the entrance going up next week. I'll talk to the vendor and have him add a sign that says, *Indivisible* Villas, along with a huge American Flag. I can envision the wall, which will tell everyone that our community holds together during times of crisis."

"LeBron, why don't you run for Governor?" Eric suggested, "I will vote for you!"

Connie said, "I second the motion, dammit! LeBron for Governor!"

Two strong men came forward, carried LeBron, and the crowd chanted, "Go, Lebron. Go, Lebron. Go, LeBron! LeBron for Governor, yeah!"

Even Jacky tried to stand up from his wheelchair and cheered for LeBron.

Ming, Lucy, and Bill said, "We love this new community, we are so lucky to have wonderful neighbors, and we feel safe here."

Just then, Rowe, Antonette, and their families arrived. Everybody applauded and said, *"There they are!"*

The community was very proud of Rowe and Antonette and their family. They generously gave their time, efforts, and Rowe's money to rebuild the community. It was a quick turnaround to rebuild their community through their benevolence. Rowe had personally donated a great deal of money to the beautiful new Catholic church that had been constructed using a few of the stained-glass windows that remained from the original church, along with new pieces donated by Rowe and Antonette.

The community was unaware, though, that the couple were the guardian angels who had saved their great nation and the world from terror. It was an impossible mission, but because of their steadfast faith and hope, they became *indivisible* superheroes. Rowe was glad to have Antonette by his side; they were *indivisible* and free to love each other and show love and light to others who had nearly given up on their lives. They worked together to raise building funds for Operation Innovation. This endeavor would make Richmond the home of innovation with some of Rowe's great ideas. The project would build industries and offer much-needed employment and help Richmond rebuild its economy.

One thing would remain top secret: Rowe and Antonette could never tell their children and grandchildren about the secret spy bunker in the basement. It would remain a secret that they were the superpowers, and they cherished the secret held between their two hearts.

At the end of the town hall meeting, a group of people was talking with Rowe and Antonette about having a huge party for the grand opening of the Villas after the wall was finished. LeBron, who had been listening to the conversation, said he wanted to take charge of the food and music at the grand celebration. The family liked his idea, and everyone agreed it would be the best party. Then he invited everybody to the front of the Town Hall and made a general announcement about the grand celebration.

Rowe invited HG Hawk to the ribbon-cutting ceremony of *Indivisible* Villas. It was like a big reunion celebrating their freedom and life. There was a good reason for victory dances; they hadn't danced in so long. Moving their bodies rhythmically to the lively music promoted confidence, expressed joy, and energized the people. They had patriotic songs intermixed with the most current pop and R&B songs.

They struck a powerful family pose, and Antonette's youngest son Chris filmed everything, so they could always look back on the happy times and the grand opening of *Indivisible* Villas. Chris later became popular as a filmmaker and cinematographer after producing a documentary about the rebuilding of the now thriving community resort in Richmond. The documentary attracted tourism to the Villas, but no one knew it was the home of the superpowers.

JR, Antonette's oldest son, joined Zed and John to manage Rowe's financial assets. After all, he was a seasoned, popular certified public accountant. His wife, Jodie, a real estate attorney, had joined Emy and Armand's real estate team. The four of them were all gathered in a group and congratulated each other on a job well done.

LeBron, the community leader, suggested they should build a statue for Rowe and Antonette to recognize their great service. Rowe had always played a low profile, being a Special Forces warrior. Antonette behaved the same way, they were both raised the same, and she wanted to follow the Special Forces Creed. Since she had married Rowe, they had become *indivisible* and were a true couple, equal in the relationship. They were loyal to each other and always supportive of each other. They both felt it would be too much to have statues and politely declined. Rowe smiled as Antonette entwined her arm in his right elbow. She had finally changed her last name to Rowe's name. It marked her being part of Rowe's rib, and it was simply fitting to follow his name. Rowe did not coerce her and gave Antonette the freedom to choose what she wanted to do. Antonette cherished her freedom and cherished Rowe for not smothering it.

Rowe carried Isabella to the area where the family was gathered and said, "You've grown up, Princess. You're almost as tall as Grand!"

Isabella giggled and grabbed Rowe's face with both hands. "I miss you, Gran and Nanna. But I like the green stars in Iceland, and I will go back there. Uncle Steve says I am always welcome to visit."

Rowe laughed and said, "Is that so? That sounds great, and who are you going to take with you when you visit Iceland and see Aurora Borealis?"

"You!" Isabella said emphatically, Rowe hugged her, and everyone laughed. Then Isabella said she missed Nanna too, after which Antonette scooped her from Rowe's arms. Rowe kissed Isabella on the forehead and brushed his lips against Antonette's.

"Ewwwwwww," Isabella said and made everybody laugh.

Rowe then moved over to William and Rosgil and started playing with Parker, who was now a toddler. They had waited to have Parker baptized until the Catholic church was completed, and everyone was looking forward to the ceremony.

Rowe's phone vibrated, and he noticed on his watch that it was HG calling. If it was an emergency, she would call back right away. He didn't answer the phone and decided to call her back later after the awesome reunion.

When everyone had almost finished eating, Antonette held onto Rowe's hand and led him to the stage. Antonette used the mic, and the music started for her favorite song, "God Bless the USA." by Lee Greenwood. She surprised everyone, especially Rowe, who read her mind that they were both going to sing this one together. He didn't know that he had married not only a hero but a singer too! Antonette let Rowe sing the first few lines and chimed in the middle of the song. They had perfect harmony and made their audience cry, except for Isabella and her brothers and cousins, who were all playing with balloons. They were running around after the balloons and cheering for their 'grand heroes' on the stage. The audience chimed in at the end to finish the song together, *indivisible* at that moment in time. Everyone was in union with God and with Rowe and Antonette.

After they had finished, LeBron stood by the newly erected 50' flagpole at the entrance to the Indivisible Villas. As he raised the 10' x 15' American flag, the people were silent. When it reached the top, everyone let out a unified cheer; then Rowe and Antonette led the crowd in honoring the flag and the country…

PLEDGE OF ALLEGIANCE

"I Pledge Allegiance

To The Flag Of The

United States of America,

And To The Republic

For Which It Stands,

One Nation Under God,

Indivisible, With Liberty,

And Justice For All."

AFTERWORD

Aurea retired from the 101st Airborne Division, Air Assault (AASLT), and deployed to Iraq in support of Operation Iraqi Freedom for four years: two tours with the 101st and two years as a civilian contractor.

She received numerous medals and awards for leading her troops, including two Bronze Star Medals for meritorious service in a combat zone.

The first Bronze Star was received while she was with Bravo Company, 101st Soldier Support Battalion, serving as a Casualty Liaison Team Leader in support of Operation Iraqi Freedom in Mosul, Iraq (2003-2004).

The second Bronze Star was received for outstanding performance as Human Resources NCOIC, 101st Combat Aviation Brigade, COB Speicher in Tikrit, Iraq (2005-2006).

She holds three master's degrees: two Masters of Business Administration and one Master of Public Administration.

She works in Washington, D.C., and continues to support various veterans programs.

She is proud to be a lifetime member of the Federal Asian Pacific American Council (FAPAC), previously serving as chairwoman of FAPAC's Mentoring Program.

She is currently serving as FAPAC Committee Advisor. To her, it is one way of giving back to the community: providing mentorship, strength, hope, transformation, and inspiring those who seek to improve themselves, thus, improving the world we're living in.

Aurea's favorite charity is the Women Veterans Giving. Their website is womenveteransgiving.org.

She is an active member of Veterans of Foreign Wars (VFW), and The American Legion. She published her first book in September 2021, Silent Freedom: A Memoir of Service with the 101st Airborne Division Air Assault in Iraq.

Aurea always remembers the proverb: *"The Lord does not see as mortals see; they look on the outward appearance, but the Lord looks on the heart"* (1 Samuel 16:1-13).